Manifesting Shadow

Church K. Calvert

Manifesting Shadow

© Church Calvert 2017

Acknowledgments

This book was written over several years, and through many life changes, challenges and evolutions of my mind. It was because of certain people that inspired me, challenged me, and encouraged me to finish the book, that I am finally able to share it with the world. I'd like to thank my friend and original confidant, Angel, and daughter, Miracle, for being my first fans, and being so excited after reading my first copy, although it was atrocious and incomplete. I'd like to thank my best friend, Jake Luria, he was able to encourage my vulnerability and I was able to share the book with him. He lit the fire in me to move forward. I couldn't be more grateful to have met Jake, and he has taught me so much that will make not only this book but the entire series complete and important.

I want to thank all my test readers, particularly the first ones who had to endure the story before spell check. So thank you to Anne Vires, Isaiah Rubio, Susan Cadena, Edith, and Lauren Thomas. I want to thank my editor, Anne Pottinger, for her meticulous work on making my story a work of art. Lastly, a special thank you to Lauren Thomas, my partner. You have inspired me to push this story to the finish line. I have done more in this year to prepare for the release of this book than I could have ever imagined. You gave me that final push, and now I get to see my dream come true. Thank you for your patience and inspiration, and I promise I will try to finish the second book in less than two years. Thank you to everyone named and unnamed for your contributions.

Prologue

I had been there for three years. Every day was the same. When I first arrived, I knew that I was not insane, but as the days went on, I became less sure of myself. Everything that I knew to be a reality began to fade, almost as if it never happened. "It never happened." This is what they kept telling me, that I have some disorder and I imagined these things. It was beginning to feel just like that. There has always been this darkness invading my life and consuming me. The world outside no longer seemed real, just a collection of memories playing like a movie in my mind. I could watch them and relive the things I had done, but in so many instances I felt as if I were in the audience instead of the one performing. At some point, I just watched the terrible things unfold, and I knew there was nothing I could do about it, and I accepted this darkness inside me. As the movies faded, so did my connection to this world.

"Danielle?" the doctor interrupted my thoughts. I turned in her direction. "Are you going to involve yourself in this session or is it going to be like the rest?"

The expression in her eyes was of exhaustion, not only from life but from her work as well. She was my thirteenth doctor, and this was our first visit. My doctors were always so hopeful when first meeting me. Doctors; they love a challenge but like any human, hate failure. Doctors think their solutions can fix everything. They are drawn to me because I appear to be a puzzle, easy to solve. If, however, you don't believe my story, then you will never solve this enigma. This is why they give up. They never take the chance to see if the story is true. This new doctor . . . Dr. Joy . . . was pleasant, attractive, early forties, dark hair, relatively thin. She had an aura of compassion and exhaustion at the same time. It was almost pathetic as if she were desperate for something. I've seen this characteristic before in many variations.

I sat on the opposite side of her big wooden desk, in a wooden chair with no cushion, as she sat in a seemingly comfortable office chair, swiveling back and forth slightly. I glanced down at my wrist wraps. They were slightly tighter than usual, binding my two hands together in my lap. I fidgeted with them in an attempt to achieve a more comfortable position, to no avail. She had a couple of framed photos on her desk facing away from me, patient files, a cup of coffee, a phone, and stationery. The room had one big window behind the doctor. It was covered with sheer curtains; the light penetrated through them and dispersed throughout the room providing light, but no image of what lay beyond. Part of me desired to get up from my seat and move the curtains aside to glimpse the outside world, another part of me wished there was no window at all in this room.

"Well, I've spent a lot of time reviewing your file. Twelve doctors in three years. That's quite an accomplishment,"

I contrive a sarcastic smile and raise my eyebrows.

"I see you have hallucinations, a history of violence, aggression, memory problems, you had an almost deadly encounter with another patient, and the list goes on and on. Oh and let's not exclude the . . . 'murder.'"

I twist my neck at the way she nonchalantly threw the word out there.

"Does that phrase make you uncomfortable?"

I smiled and gave a slight shake of the head implying it made no difference. I really wanted to kill time as fast as possible. I began to make myself space out so that I couldn't hear any more of the words coming out of this woman's mouth when something caught my attention mid-sentence.

" . . . see I've done my research and unlike the other doctors, I contacted your family and came across this while rummaging through your stuff." She tossed down a book onto the table. My head began to spin with this one sentence. She saw my family? Are they alive, are they okay? Do they hate me? Did they actually keep my stuff? And how could she, of all people, have my most personal possession sitting on her desk? If my arms weren't bound, I'd leap for the book and attempt to destroy as much as possible before being quickly sedated. Instead, I sat there. My journal, from the beginning, every secret of mine, had been read by this woman. She sat across from me with a hidden smile and a sense of such accomplishment. Although so much frustration was pulsing through my body right then, one other thing was coursing through me: hope. If I could read it, just one more time, I would know once again whether what I believed actually happened, or if these quickly fading memories were just a figment of my imagination.

"Let me see it," I said. The first words I had spoken to a doctor in a very long time.

"Why?" she scrutinized my obvious desperation.

I sat quietly without response. I had spoken so little over the years; the sound of my voice was almost foreign to me.

"Danielle if I let you see it, will I get the truth?" She observed me questioningly.

"If you let me see it?" I asked.

"Yes."

"If you allow me access to something that belongs to me?" I replied, attempting to use my tone to emphasize how absurd this agreement sounded.

"One entry, a day; you talk to me for at least ten minutes a day, and I will let you read one entry. Sound fair?" she asked raising an eyebrow, waiting for a response. I hated this woman already.

3

How dare she treat my secrets like her personal property. I swear my doctors became more and more twisted, every year. What did they teach in modern medicine, because I think their ethics were lacking.

"Fair?" I faked a sarcastic laugh to myself, "No, but I'll give you what you want." I saw an expression of relief and excitement, as she began flipping through pages and pages of notes, she seemed to have been compiling for months.

"Okay, so let's talk about this particular incident. It seems like a pivotal point to everything, like everything begins to become . . . unhinged . . . you're at the hospital visiting your aunt . . ."

"Wait . . . What?"

"Is there a problem?"

"Yes, I'm not talking about that."

"Perhaps you didn't understand the deal we just made, you talk for ten minutes, and you get to read an entry. What part of that did you not understand?"

"Wow . . . you are one funny lady," I replied scanning her with my eyes questioningly, "How did you get this job?"

"Miss Blake, I received this job because no one else wanted it, so you're stuck with me," she said with a hard blink and a forced smile.

"Oh, so it's a quite prestigious position," I replied sarcastically, "I'm just saying if you want me to talk, you should start at the beginning of the story, not the middle. I want answers as much as you, but that memory is not something I have visited for a very long time. It will take a while, and some refreshing before I can divulge things like that. I think if I read an entry at the beginning of each session, it would refresh my memory enough to try to explain what exactly happened."

Check. The doctor folded her fingers, and moved her chair slightly back and forth, obviously wondering if I was bluffing, and if so, was it still worth a try at getting to the truth. She exhaled.

"Fine, one entry, and no touching the journal, I will hold it open, and you read it."

I smiled, knowing the more information she wanted, the more she would have to let me read. She sensed my victory in this part of the game and returned a quick fake smile. She walked around to my side of the desk and pulled the journal toward me.

As I looked at the cover, memories immediately began to flood back. I became nauseous with anxiety and excitement. There were so many phenomena between the covers of that journal that I wanted to remember and so many episodes I wished to forget. She flipped open to the first page. I looked at the opening line which read: "Something is wrong with me."

"So how did this story start?" the doctor asked, excited and impatient.

Chapter One:
The Favorite

I remembered sitting in the back seat of our old SUV looking out the window, watching the trees, sky, and miles of the road pass us by. My brother was sitting next to me, asleep; my parents together in the front chatting, already drained from hours of driving. I looked down at my brother sleeping so peacefully, all curled up with his light brown hair covering half his face. I found it impossible to sleep in the car, I don't know how he managed to make it appear so easy.

That day was an extraordinary day, and not in a positive way. My parents had received a call that morning from my grandmother, saying that my great-grandmother was dying and she requested our family come immediately. It was also unusual because it happened to be my thirteenth birthday, and that was definitely not the way I'd envisioned spending it. Why of all days would she feel the need to die today? I didn't mean to appear selfish, I just thought that day should have some significance for me. I had become a teenager, yet she was all anyone was talking about.

You see, my great-grandmother was not your average person. She was ninety-five and looked more like sixty. No one in our family particularly liked her. She distanced herself from everyone. Another reason I didn't understand why she would want us there. I knew she was present at the birth of every child, grandchild, and great-grandchild ever born into the family. I knew that because apparently out of all of them, I was the only one who made her smile, when I was born thirteen years ago to the day. My parents said she refused to hold me the day I was born; something she did with every child in our family. Then the next day she never left my side. I knew I was what people would call the 'favorite,' but out of an abundance of children, grandchildren, and great-grandchildren, I couldn't give you a reason why. I was nothing exceptional, especially then. I looked at the lackluster reflection of myself in the window. I saw dark eyes, long dark hair, light skin, and an overall impression of insignificance that no one should endure. I felt guilty, the way she only inquired about me and my life and ignored everyone else's. I just wished she would treat me like everyone else.

"The doctors say there is physically nothing wrong with her, that maybe she just needs some attention from her family," I overheard my mom whisper to my father. "Yeah, right, I said, she doesn't want anything to do with us." My mother scoffed at the doctor's suggestion.

"Well, come on, honey, you never know, this could be it. Not to mention she's held on to that fortune long enough, haha." They both laughed together. They must have believed I was sleeping. By now you would think they know me well enough to remember that I never sleep in cars, or hardly at all for that matter. It wasn't a secret that my great-grandmother had plenty of money at her disposal, all of which the family wanted a piece of.

"Is Christian going to be there?" my father asked.

"Yes, you know he wouldn't miss a chance to cash in on something, I told him he should have just ridden with us. He said he was getting there early to see if it was a false alarm."

"Yeah right, more like trying to grab as much as he can and get out of there before anyone else gets there."

"Alex! That's my brother you're talking about," she said with laughter in her voice, "You know he's going to push her down the stairs and make it look like an accident, then get the stuff and leave."

They both laughed together. Everyone knew my mother's brother was a dirt bag, but that's a different story. I just wished they didn't make jokes at my great-grandmother's expense. I couldn't imagine dying and wondering if everyone's just waiting for you to draw your last breath so they can divvy up everything you've worked for. Was she also wondering if one of us is just concerned about their birthday when she won't celebrate anymore herself? This thought made me feel guilty and sick to my stomach. I decided to pretend that it wasn't my birthday, not that anyone else seemed to notice.

"Shhh. Don't get so loud, you'll wake up Grandma Elizabeth's favorite."

"Ha, ha. Well, at least we hit the jackpot there. I wouldn't be surprised if she left everything to Danielle. I swear it's so creepy the way she asks questions about her. Like 'Does she sleep well at night? Does she have many friends? How old is she now'?"

It became quiet. I recognized from the tension in the air they had both just realized my birthday was today; they had forgotten. I quickly pretended to be fast asleep and felt them look back to make sure.

"Shit. We totally forgot," I heard my dad say.

"We? I told you to buy her that damn computer weeks ago."

"She doesn't like that stuff. She's into weird things like . . . I don't know. Stuff." I nearly laughed, listening to their whispered argument.

"We'll figure something out and make it seem like we didn't want to celebrate on such a tragic day. I mean, who wants to hear, "Your great-grandmother is dying . . . happy birthday?""

"Yeah, yeah, that's good. It's true too. No one wants that," They both seemed convinced that their idea was good. We hit a sizable bump in the road, and I used this as an excuse to wake up.

"Oh man, where are we?" I asked pretending to sound groggy.

"Oh sweetie, we're just about twenty minutes away," mom said in the most loving tone possible. "How did you sleep?"

" Uhhhh . . . great."

"Hey, what's going on?" My brother must have been awoken too by the jolt. I jokingly pushed him back down.

"Go back to sleep. We're not there yet." He fell back then shot back up again.

"Yes, we are. Mom said twenty minutes," he laughed, trying to disengage my hand from his face, as I kept trying to propel him back down.

"You're five, do you even know how long twenty minutes is?"

"Uhhh, yeah. One, two, three, four –" I knew where this was heading and quickly dragged his pillow over his head to drown out his annoying counting. When eventually I remove it, he said, "Twenty!"

"Oh, wow, look, we're still not there . . . geez guess you were wrong," I teased.

"Maybe you guys should just go back to sleep for a while longer," my dad suggested hopefully.

"Nah," we both responded.

Not long afterward we pulled up to my great-grandmother's house, or as my mother called her, Grandma Elizabeth. I guess it made her feel less old. I saw only three cars parked out front of her substantial house. Actually, the house wasn't that big, considering the amount of money she had, but compared to our little house it was a mansion. Two stories high, quite old, but still elegant, and clean. She had most of it remodeled years ago, so it has less of a lived-in smell to it. She even had a few butlers and a cook. But to a great extent, my grandma took care of her. This was unusual because my grandma seemed much older than my great-grandma. All her siblings had already passed away. She was the only child remaining. My great-grandfather died decades ago; he was actually still young when my great-grandma became a widow. Even with her young appearance and money, she never wanted to share her life with anyone again. My great-grandfather was a lot like my Uncle Christian, so nobody really missed him when he was gone, except Grandma Elizabeth, I guess.

As we walked toward the door, it opened, revealing my grandma. The first impression was how old and exhausted she appeared. These days she stood a little over five feet with a slight hunch. She had a full head of gray hair, and wrinkles covered her face. We called her Grandma Ivy. She hugged all of us, with an expression of despair on her face, as though the entire family had been killed.

"Oh, sweetie, I'm so glad you guys made it. It's . . . it's not looking good," she said, close to tears. My Grandma Ivy had a knack for dramatization and exaggeration. Not that we didn't think it was important, it was just that Grandma Elizabeth had lived so long. What more could anyone want?

"Hi, sweetie. Your great-grandma has been asking for you every day," she said, choking back more tears as she half knelt next to me. I didn't welcome the amount of pressure being put on me to be this dying woman's last wish.

"Oh," is all I could say as I tried to rush inside before my grandma actually started crying. I just wanted to go somewhere and hide, but as soon as I walked in, I was greeted by my uncle. He stood almost six feet tall, with a muscular build and light brown hair, cut in a rugged but appealing style. His face was almost clean shaven. He undoubtedly was a handsome man. He seemed to still be sober, and he dispensed one of his phony welcomes.

"Hey, girl. How's my favorite niece?" I was getting so sick of hearing the word 'favorite' associated with a reference to me.

"Hi, Uncle Christian . . ." I muttered. He gave me a big hug, lifting me slightly off the ground.

"Happy birthday, baby girl. How old are you now, thirteen?" he laughed then cast his eyes around, knowing he'd said the wrong thing. My parents just flashed fake smiles and attempted their own rescue.

"That's right, we were just talking about how we wanted to make it so special, once you know, all of this has passed," my mother said, moving her hand in a circular motion. "It's just so dark right now."

"Yeah, only the best for our baby girl," my dad chimed in, giving me a hug.

"I see, well, I got you a little something," my uncle said, handing me a rectangular wrapped package that I hastily placed under my arm.

"Thank you, Uncle Christian. I'll open it later," I responded, noticing the embarrassment on my parents' faces.

I expeditiously used this as an excuse to escape; sparing them further awkwardness, and sneaked off into one of the living areas, while they remained chatting in the entryway. I realized my brother had found my uncle, who was giving him the "hey, sport" speech. Christian was boasting he had a surprise for my little brother, Nathan, as well. I rolled my eyes in frustration. Of course, my brother got a gift on my birthday. I was glad to be away from the clamor and falsity of everyone.

I glanced around the room I'd stumbled into. It was beautiful. Oak furniture was everywhere, projecting a feeling of richness and hominess. I sank into an unbelievably soft couch. One of the walls across the room was covered from top to bottom with photographs of the family. There were hundreds of pictures.

So many people, so many stories behind each photo. They all portrayed a family or children; everyone was smiling. This was true of them all except those including my Grandma Elizabeth. Hers seemed so dark and depressing. Then, in the crowd, I spotted the legendary photo of her holding me, with a smile on her face. I arose from the couch and crept toward it to get a closer look.

The photograph drowned out all the darkness of the other pictures. It was like seeing a different person. It was an expression of happiness that I knew I had yet to experience. I moved closer to the photo; perhaps there was some other reason she was so happy. It was hard to tell. I knew before my great-grandpa died she smiled and was happy at times. I just didn't understand why if he was such a jerk. I'd heard my mother say he was a drunk, even abusive at times. All I thought of when I tried to picture him was Uncle Christian, and I failed to understand how he could make anyone happy.

"You know, that picture is a legend," my grandma said from behind me. Startled, I direct my gaze away from it.

"Not even the day her own children were born did she smile like that. She was happy of course. I guess it had been so long since anyone had seen her smile, that we were just so taken off guard, and you of all people . . ." my grandma's words trail off. I sensed a lot of jealousy, "It's amazing they got it on camera."

"Yeah, amazing." I wished they hadn't gotten a picture, that way it would still be unbelievable.

"They've already started going in to see her. Your turn should be in a short while."

My grandma seemed quite spaced out. I grasped that as a chance to slip in to see Grandma Elizabeth while I could still just stand in the background, hoping she wouldn't even notice I was there. I didn't want to be alone with her. I wasn't ready to watch someone die.

I made my way up the stairs as slowly as possible and crept along the hallways, pretending I didn't know which room she was in. A butler quickly approached and directed me saying, "Down this hallway," while pointing in the direction I was already heading. I nodded and moved just a tad quicker.

The hallway contained artwork and a fancy rug that ran its length, covering the wooden floorboards. Elegant windows were every few feet. I walked on the outside of the rug thinking my shoes would somehow taint its elegance. Then I thought about my great-grandma's impending death and decided to place my feet on it instead.

The door to her room was wide open, with everyone talking, Uncle Christian the loudest of course.

"Grandma Elizabeth, I will make sure all of your last wishes are carried out exactly the way you want them." His voice dripped with sincerity; he is a convincing liar.

"It's okay, Christian, I have someone to take care of it, you won't have to do a thing," I heard her voice for the first time. It sounded neither old nor sick. I wondered how anyone could actually believe that this woman was dying.

"No, grandma, I want to."

"No, Alex, you will be my executor," she said, referring to my father.

"Oh, wow. Grandma Elizabeth, are you sure? Someone in the family perhaps?" My dad attempted to wriggle out of it.

"No, my family is after my money. I cannot trust my family. I'm old, dying, but I'm not stupid," she said matter-of-factly. I could tell my uncle was put out by this, and I heard him begin pacing the room.

"He'll take care of it, Grandma Elizabeth," my mother said quickly, sealing the deal for my dad. "We know where all of your documents are."

"What's an executor?" my brother asked.

"Nothing, sweetie. Go say hi to Grandma Elizabeth," my mother told him.

I peeped around the door and watched him reluctantly walk over and give her a half hug in the bed where she lay. He pretended

14

to tend to my great-grandma, as he ran a toy car over her leg as if it was driving down a road.

"Honey, why don't you put Uncle Christian's gift down a minute," my mother urged him. He pretended not to hear and continued driving the car up and down the blankets on the bed.

I retreated to listen to their ongoing banal conversation from the seclusion of the hallway, crouched out of sight against the wall, grateful no one noticed my absence. They talked about the will, the house, the family.

The conversation seems to drag on for hours, then my uncle, apparently still frustrated, declared: "You don't even look sick!" The silence was palpable. Eventually, he continued, "I mean, I know that you're getting older . . . much older, but the doctor says there's nothing wrong with you. Why are we deciding all these major things unless you're dying? No, I think we should let you rest and then revisit all these important things-"

"Christian, you may convince yourself and everyone else, but have never convinced me that you can be trusted with a single thing. Your judgment is clouded by your habits and your greed. You're a damaged individual and capable of the most atrocious acts. So if you came here looking for a handout from me, then you came to the wrong place. I don't care if I had all the money in the world, you would be the last person I would want to see."

This caught everyone off guard, including my uncle. It became so quiet I could hear my grandmother downstairs weeping in the kitchen. I was scared of what my uncle might say or do next. He is known for his short fuse. I wished more than anything I wasn't sitting outside the room. I probably looked as though I was eavesdropping.

Suddenly he just left, storming out of the room so violently I felt the floorboards shake beneath me. I thought he hadn't noticed me and allowed a small sigh to escape; he quickly jerked his head back and walked up to me.

"The favorite . . ." he laughed under his breath. The expression in his eyes reflected both hatred and jealousy, "The Fucking Favorite!" he shouted before storming out of the house while slamming into everything humanly possible.

I hoped more than anything that somehow nobody heard his last outburst. Everyone remained silent.

"Grandma– " my mother ventured.

"Don't! Don't talk to me about him. He is a vile creature . . . a parasite!" she said with disgust.

"He's not Grandma. He just—"

"Don't make excuses for him Bridget. I can't hear it from you." Grandma Elizabeth retorted.

"I should probably go make sure he's okay," my dad said heading out the door. I was attempting to press myself against the wall and become invisible when I heard the words I've been dreading.

"Where's Danielle?"

My father looked down at me, his expression apologetic, but despite my obvious reluctance, I knew he had no choice.

"She's here," he replied, nodding his head in my direction.

"Tell her to come in. It's time."

* * *

I sat in a chair across from her bed. Everyone's aura reflected shock from the interaction moments earlier. My brother appeared confused, my mother stared out the window, and my father was still trying to escape the room, with any excuse he could muster.

16

"Please leave us alone," Grandma Elizabeth requested, looking only at me. She appeared so young, so healthy, so full of energy. I was convinced that if she wanted to she could get up out of that bed and run a few laps around the house. However, I tried not to stare for too long. I felt her eyes boring into me. My father took her up on her request as quickly as possible. My mother more reluctantly crossed the room to gather up my brother.

"We'll be right outside," my mother began.

"No, please we would like some privacy, close the door, will you?" She had reverted to a sweet tone. They slowly exited and closed the door. The awkward atmosphere increased in the room as she scrutinized me. She inspected every inch of me while I made a pretense of examining the room in minute detail. It was clearly not her room. It had the appearance of a makeshift guest room, appropriated for the purpose of dying I supposed. There were no decorations on the walls. It was much like a hotel room, with the bare minimum of furniture: a bed, nightstand, a few chairs for guests, and dresser.

"Come sit closer," she said, waving her hand to indicate next to the bed. I moved the chair over, and sat once more, half-heartedly reaching for her hand which she seemed to pull away or perhaps not to notice my attempt.

"You," she said, still looking at me. I responded with a halfhearted smile.

"Me . . ."

"I've waited so long for this day, my dear. At one point I thought it would never come that I'd be stuck here forever. Then here you come, after I had given up all hope. You came into this world, and you were so perfect . . . Not a thing wrong with you, not an ounce of pain in your heart. You didn't even cry when you were born. It was as if you knew why you were here, and you had already accepted it." In these words I found nothing but confusion, perhaps her mind was much further gone than anyone had realized. I just sat there staring, trying to think of something to say. Realizing my confusion, she suddenly appeared confused herself.

"You know what I speak of, of course?" she asked. I shake my head.

"Yes, you are still young. Thirteen to the day." I respond with a smile, happy that she remembered, then questioning what I had assumed about her mental state.

"I remember at your age I was so lost. That's when it started and I didn't know what any of it meant, or if it was even real. I thought I was going crazy," she laughed. The same thought occurred to me.

"We are special Danielle, but not in the way anyone would wish. Our curse disguises itself as a gift. It is powerful, it is remarkable, and most of all, dangerous. You must never underestimate what you can do, the pain you can cause. We hurt everyone we love," her eyes drifted off with an impression of regret.

"Grandma Elizabeth, I'm sorry but I don't know what you're talking about. I have no gift." I stopped short, realizing how stupid it sounded.

"Child, I wish you were right, and I wish I could tell you what is coming next, and how to prepare yourself, and that it's not as bad as it seems, and that it will get better, but I can't. This burden will haunt you every day of your life, it will steal away every chance of happiness, belonging, and optimism a person can have, and do not mistake pleasure for happiness. True happiness will never be yours. It will feel close . . . like it's right around the corner, or that you think you just about have it, and then just as quickly it will be taken from you. Do not subject anyone you love, or think you love, to that sort of torture. You can't help anyone, not really. Sure, when you're young and have the whole world ahead of you, you get your Mortal Nights, but they come and then they will go. You will wish you had lived more those days, or died more."

I sat beside her, growing more confused and impatient. This was not the conversation I had expected. I almost wished she had just started talking about how much I was her favorite, or how she would give me all her money; this was overwhelming and depressing. If she wasn't really dying, this conversation wasn't worth the pain.

"Tell me about your brother. He's just the cutest thing," she changed course with a little smile.

"Nathan? Well, he's a great kid. You want me to get him?" I asked, pleased at the prospect of more company.

"No! No, tell me about him. What does he like, what does he want to be when he grows up? What's his favorite thing to do? Is he a trouble maker?"

"Ha, ha, yeah, he's a little bit of a trouble maker. He does it in a sweet way though. Like just the other day he about destroyed my entire wardrobe. My clothes were all cut up, colored with marker. I was so mad at him. I was yelling and yelling at him." Remembering the story made me feel guilty for making him feel so bad. "He told me that he heard I had wanted new clothes and that Dad had said we didn't have money for new clothes, so he decided to change my clothes for me. Make them better, I guess."

"Ha ha! Aw, that's just the sweetest thing," she said with a smile.

The knowledge of how he really did want to help made me ashamed. I had just been so mad. I remembered not being able to control myself and shoving him aside, not paying attention to what I was doing. He had stumbled and smacked his head on the end table in my room. At that point, all the anger had disappeared from me and I'd grabbed him quickly to see if he was okay. He'd closed his eyes, and I'd thought he was about to cry. My heart had sunk into my stomach knowing I had caused him that pain. Instead, he had opened his eyes, smiled, and ran out of the room laughing.

I just remembered sitting on the floor, my heart racing and thanking God that I didn't hurt him. All throughout dinner that night I kept glancing at him in the light making sure there wasn't a mark, black eye, or anything my parents would notice. I promised myself that day to never lose my temper with him again. Not like that. No matter what he did.

I realized that the room had grown very quiet as I had drifted away into my thoughts. I could see my great-grandmother was trying to figure out what was going through my mind as if it was familiar to her. Then something hit me.

"I don't understand. How come you have never asked about the other children, grandchildren, or great-grandchildren before? How come it's always me? I'm the only one you visit, the only one you talk to. Am I the only one you care about? 'Cause if I am, then I'd rather be ignored like the rest. It's not enough for anyone to only be loved on the day they were born and the day they die."

She studied me but didn't seem at all angered at my harsh words.

"But I do care for them and love each and every single one of them. In some ways, I even love Christian, or at least a part of him that I'm not sure still exists,"

"What is it about Christian that you don't like? I don't understand. He's a drunk and a jerk, but from what I hear he's a lot like the man you married," I had become emboldened with my words, trying to get to the bottom of this riddle. She remained unruffled by my remarks but had an air of curiosity as to why I would know so much.

"You're right, Christian, in many ways is a lot like your great-grandfather, which would be his grandfather. Like his grandfather, Christian has an uncontrollable drinking habit, a short temper, and a knack for hurting the people he claims to love. With Christian, I know things that would turn your stomach inside out. I cannot believe that he still has the audacity to show his face around me. Does he think I'm so old I wouldn't remember?" As she spoke, she gestured with her hands. "Things like that, a person never forgets. I know he blames me for the person he has become. I did everything I could . . . but he still turned out . . . well, we all know the person he is."

At that point, I felt defeated. I didn't care to know what horrible things she spoke of, so I returned to my original point. "Then why don't you visit anyone else, Christian, I guess I could understand, but the others? What about them?"

She seemed to be collecting her thoughts.

"You remember when I said earlier that we hurt everyone we love?" I nodded, thinking about my brother again, then tried to push that memory from my mind. "We can't help it. To the ones we love, we are like a disease. The closer we get to them, the more dangerous we are to them. That's one of the reasons I was with your great-grandfather. Part of me hated him so much, it's like I thought I could never love him enough to hurt him, but you're with blood, it's as if it's already written on the wall, you don't choose or decide who, or how you love them, it comes naturally.

"I've lost count of how many people I've loved that I've had to watch leave or be buried six feet under. Then I got to a point where I realized I couldn't do that to anyone anymore, so I let them be. I miss them. God do I miss them. You think a day goes by where I don't want to see my only remaining child? My grandchildren? My great-grandchildren? I have one child left, and the others have been in the ground for years. I've watched three grandchildren and two great-grandchildren go to their graves before the age of ten! I have not seen my own child since she arrived at this house four weeks ago. I won't even let her come into the room. I don't know what I am capable of at this point, and I don't want to find out."

She was clearly getting upset. I felt I had definitely overstayed my welcome and pried into her business more than I should, but there was just one more thing I needed to know.

"Then why am I different?"

21

"Because I can't hurt you."

As I try to compute this information, she starts talking as if time were of the essence.

"Listen to me, I have left you something in my will. Journals. You must find them, read them. I hope that it will give insight to what is coming. I keep them in a trunk in the attic, there're tons of books in that trunk so they will blend in. There will be a red one. That will be the one with the rules. Read everything. Protect them, Danielle," she says with the sternest tone.

"Okay," I said, not knowing how else to respond.

"There's just one more thing I need you to do," she said.

Grateful that this conversation was coming to an end I perked up, receptive to her last request. "Yes, Grandma Elizabeth, anything," I say. She reached out her hand and I placed mine in hers.

"Don't forget to control your emotions, they can manifest into the most dangerous things, and cause unspeakable damage," she said, looking directly into my eyes.

I didn't know how to respond, so I gave a slight nod. I attempted to extract my hand, but she tightened her grip. I was startled, but she continued staring at me. I started to panic for a second, then something extraordinary happened.

I felt something I had never experienced before; like a current coursing through my veins. It resembled a black hole of energy opening up inside me. All that passed through was pure energy. I began to feel elated, and a sense of relaxation flooded through me, a sense of pure joy. It was the best sensation I'd ever felt in my life. It was like every drug meant to make you feel good pulsing through every blood cell in my body. Nothing but pure euphoria. I was so lost in this feeling, I had forgotten to open my eyes. When I did, I saw my great-grandmother staring at me with an expression of contentment and hidden worry.

"Thank you," she said and released my hand.

I remained sitting there. The sensation I'd had moments before, now seemed so far away. I studied Grandma Elizabeth. Years had caught up to her in moments. Wrinkles and scars she never had, all now clearly in evidence. She no longer looked at me. I pulled my hand from hers and rapidly stepped back. I looked back at her again, but there was nothing to see, nothing to hear or feel. She was dead.

* * *

"So you had a traumatic experience, watching your great-grandmother pass away. This was some sort of trigger." Dr. Joy said, taking notes and nodding her head. I contemplated if she had been asleep the whole time I was talking.

"I'm sorry?" I asked.

"You watching you great-grandmother die, caused a chain reaction of unusual behavior and symptoms. It's like from that day everything was downhill according to your file," she replied, glancing at her notes as if she were reading them all at once.

"Uh, no, that's not at all what happened. I mean, everything from that day was downhill, and perhaps the beginning, but I was not . . . you know what, I don't feel like trying to explain this to you." I said, stopping suddenly. I knew the more I tried to explain the crazier I would sound.

"Is it because the theory makes sense? Is that why you don't wish to continue? It's understandable that a thirteen-year-old, on their birthday at that, having to witness a family argument, the nonsensical last words of a close relative, and the death of that person, would result in permanent psychological damage."

"Damage?" I laughed at her diagnosis.

"Yes, I would describe it as PTSD. You see when someone is subject to—" she began.

"I'm not stupid. I know what it means. I'm not saying your theory doesn't make sense or is illogical, but sometimes in life, you have to abandon logic. If you brought me in here to label me with this or that for whatever bullshit to make yourself feel smarter, or that you've figured something out, guess what? You can go fuck yourself," I countered, rising from my chair.

"Oh yeah, Dani? Guess I'd better just take this home then," she shot back, patting my journal that lay on her desk, "It's a quite entertaining work of fiction," she lifted her eyebrows in a questioning fashion. I responded with a mild laugh.

By that point, I was emotionally drained, irritated, and had plenty of anger to project. So I did just that. Despite both hands being shackled together I stretched halfway across her desk and shoved everything I could reach onto the floor. Papers from various files floated in the air, the framed pictures crashed into the wall, glass shattered and scattered in shards across the floor.

"Backup now, Dr. Joy's Office," she said quickly into her phone. A mild tremor was evident in her voice. I didn't know who or what the pictures were of; I didn't care. I just hoped they were of something important. Two staff members rushed through the door to aid the doctor. They immediately subdued me. I offered no resistance; this didn't stop them from drugging me.

"How would you feel if someone tried to convince you that everything you know is a lie?" I asked. The staff paused momentarily, maybe to offer the doctor an opportunity to respond. She refused to look at me. I saw a glimpse of pain behind her eyes.

"The patient might have sustained a mild injury, be sure she is treated before returning her to her quarters," She said, attempting to appear in control.

"Doctor, are you all right? Should we call the supervisor? He could file a report, and— mm" one of them suggested.

"No. I'm fine. Give her another shot. I don't think the first one did the trick."

Chapter Two:
Hard Times and White Lies

After the passing of my great-grandmother, nothing unusual happened. I was so scared they would surge into the room pointing fingers and asking what I had done. No, everyone seemed just fine with her death; well, all except her daughter, but what would you expect? Weeks turned into months, and the memory of the event began to recede into a dark hole in my mind. It was like everything that someone would never forget quickly becomes hidden in the deepest crevices of my mind and seems almost to never have happened. It's as if my mind knows what I do not wish to think about and quickly goes to work trying to erase it from my memory. My uncle was talking to the family again, and everyone was getting along just fine. In fact, tonight he was coming over to talk to my dad about something important. It must be, because my family has tried to distract me and my brother from being around when he arrives.

I was worried about my family. My dad had a really good job, but he was laid off shortly after my great-grandmother died. He was stressed out and short-tempered for weeks and I didn't understand why he hadn't gotten another job yet; I didn't know why anyone wouldn't want to hire him. I just watched him becoming more depressed every day. My dad and mom had been fighting a lot, and normally they never fight. The food we were eating; the clothes we had been wearing; everything was starting to feel different. My Uncle said he could help us out. I was just worried about what he meant by that.

He arrived at our small, three-bedroom, wooden home in the evening, saying friendly hellos to everyone, including me. It's amazing how not only him but my entire family can make believe that nothing is wrong. I took my brother into his room and sat with him till he fell asleep then cracked the door open to hear if there really is something good coming our way. Since my last eavesdropping incident, I had learned to be a bit more careful. From my brother's room, I could hear them clearly, chatting away in our kitchen. It sounds as if Uncle Christian started drinking hours ago. Finally, when I was on the verge of dozing off, they broached the real substance of their conversation.

"Still haven't found work, Alex?" Christian asked.

"Uh . . . no, nothing yet. I actually have an interview next week. It's part time work but—" my dad starts to explain.

"Part time? You're too good for that Alex. No, you need real money," he said.

"Yeah, you're telling me, but the jobs just aren't there, ha ha, it's ridiculous," Dad replied with despair in his voice.

"How far behind are you?"

"We have two months before we can't afford to stay here anymore," my dad said. I felt my stomach lurch; I had no idea things were so bad. We wouldn't have our house? Where would we live?

"We're going to figure it out," my mom asserted, but she couldn't disguise the doubt in her voice.

"And the will?" Christian asked. "I'm guessing we didn't get the payout we were expecting."

"No, I haven't even looked at it for a month. She split everything evenly per family. I was really depending on something from it. We're set up to get about $10,000. Besides that, there's some sort of trust with over half of her money, which no one knows anything about, and no one can access."

"Ten thousand? Are you fucking kidding me? You spend all the time raising the favorite, and all she can come up with is ten thousand. Ha ha, that woman sure was a crazy old bitch. How far will the ten thousand get you?"

"My original estimate included that ten thousand. We're just so far out of our means, going from what I used to make to making nothing," my dad replied. The room fell quiet. I leaned closer to the door to hear what they might say next.

"What if we could change that?" Christian's voice extinguished the silence. "Would you be interested?"

"Short of breaking the law, I'd do just about anything," my dad said with a mild laugh.

"What if you had to bend the law, but you wouldn't have anything to worry about for a very long time?"

"Christian, we're not going to do anything illegal, just to get caught up with our bills, what if we go to jail?" my mother said hopelessly. "We have kids." There may have been a tinge of curiosity in her tone, but clearly, my parents were angered by what Christian was inferring.

"I'm trying to help you. You want this kind of life for your kids?"

"What do you expect from us, Christian?"

"Are you even feeding your kids three meals a day, 'cause if I'm not mistaken, they sure are losing some weight," Christian shot back, with false concern.

"How dare you . . ." my mother said, the disgust in her voice was something I'd never heard before when she spoke to her brother.

"What's your plan?" my dad asked, his voice completely calm. Silence returned.

"Alex . . . you're not serious," my mother challenged, dumbfounded.

"We've tried everything. I am not going to lose my house and my family because I can't find a job! I'm one step away from robbing a bank to put food on the table, and if there's an easier way, then I want to at least know about it."

"Here's the deal," Christian ventured. "Grandmother Elizabeth's available worth is over two-and-a-half million dollars. Now I'm not suggesting we go rob a bank. I'm just saying we take what is rightfully ours. You said she split up the money evenly right? All we have to do is change it to say she left half for you, and the other half to the rest of the family."

"How could we possibly do that? We're four months into probate, and nothing's been done," my father pointed out.

"Exactly, no one has seen the will," said Christian.

Dad laughed. "Ha ha, yeah, except her lawyer."

"I know," Christian replied.

"Wait, what is it you're not telling me?" my father began.

"Her lawyer has a copy of the will I'm proposing, and he is willing to verify and enforce it. All we need is your cooperation."

"What's in it for him?" my father asked.

"Seventy-five thousand dollars," Christian replied. My father laughed with surprise.

"And the big question is," my father continued, "what's in it for you?"

The silence was palpable. In my mind's eye, I could see them glaring at each other.

"Five hundred thousand dollars and I want the deed to the house," he answered eventually.

"The only person left out of the will getting the most. How ironic," my mother said under her breath.

"Listen, we don't have any other choice!" Christian's voice rose.

"Any option is better than that!" My mother shouted back.

"When have I not taken care of you?! I've always been the one you turn to. Why are you acting like you can't trust me?" my uncle responded in an injured tone. "You're starting to sound like Grandma Elizabeth. I knew one day she'd turn you against me. You used to be on my side."

My mother made no further comment.

"Stop. Stop yelling at each other. The way I see it is, either we do this or we're out on the streets. Even if I got a job today, we wouldn't get our life back for a very long time. I can't live like that, and I won't let my family live through that either. I'm in," my father affirmed.

"Alex . . ." my mother whispered hopelessly.

"We need the money, and we need it now." Everyone could hear the desperation in my father's voice.

Lost in my thoughts, I missed the conclusion of the conversation. The words exchanged and decisions reached that night would change our lives forever.

* * *

Surprisingly enough, Christian's plan worked perfectly. There were no setbacks, no questions, no one even second guessed Grandma Elizabeth's new will. The family was amazed that I didn't get everything, and it seemed no one even noticed that we gave Christian 50% of what we had as well as the house. He sold the house quickly and indulged in many things that money could buy. It definitely financed his drinking habit.

Our lives also changed. Things got better, my dad found a job, food was back on the table, and we even moved into a different house. It was closer to Christian's new house. Everything was looking up for my family. I had been so furious that they would consider not fulfilling my great-grandmother's wishes, but we reached a point when I breathed a sigh of relief because they didn't.

Chapter Three: Fragile

I stared at the clock on the wall, waiting for the minute hand to reach the twelve so that I would be taken for my counseling session. I found this unusual. Something I'd ignored or dreaded for so long was now the thing I'd become increasingly impatient to start. I'd been dressed and rehearsed what I would say a dozen times already. I'd even dedicated a little extra time to getting ready. My escort arrived before it was even time and I was relieved to leave a couple of minutes early. A couple of minutes out of my room was a couple more minutes with the doctor and a couple more minutes with my journal.

I was shackled hands and feet, this time metal not cloth, and was walked to her office by the staff. The doctor hadn't yet arrived, so I sat in the room, fidgeting impatiently, waiting for her. When she finally appeared, she had the same confident yet exhausted air about her. She didn't greet me right away, pausing to shuffle her papers. I knew she was only pretending to find her place in our notes. I had no doubt that she anticipated our visits as much as I did. However, she showed considerably more restraint than I.

"So, where were we?" she said, at last breaking the silence.

"I think you were just about to tell me about your weekend," I replied in a tone of sarcasm. This resulted in a brief expression of worry, which she erased after noticing the smirk on my face. She examined me closely; I could sense her analyzing me. Her demeanor returned to something more businesslike, and she seemed to have a multitude of questions.

"No, we were talking about the will, and your special talent, remember?" She said impassively.

"Oh, of course. Sorry, I'm just so crazy I forget things sometimes, remember?"

She glanced up at me with a face that said, 'I wish I could sedate you right now.' I laughed a little, wondering if she could really think things of that sort in her profession.

"Now," she walked around to my side of the desk, "what can you tell me about this passage here?" She pointed at words that I had compelled myself to forget forever. I didn't even remember writing them. I immediately become reclusive in my thoughts, thinking but unable to voice. I knew she had read this passage already and became aware we had reached our first impasse; there was no way I could share something like this, with someone like her. She was so perfect, so precise. And judgmental.

"No, not that one. It's irrelevant, we can just skip it. The really interesting part—"

"I want to know about this," she said assertively. She paused as if faced with a brick wall. I knew there was no way around this portion of the story, yet I'd have done anything to avoid it. She knelt next to me and stared into my eyes while I did everything possible to avoid direct eye contact. It was bizarre having her in such a position next to me. I didn't understand why this would mean anything to her.

"I can't. Not to you," I told her the truth.

"Me," she asked, "why not?"

It was something that could not be explained by mere words. It was the first expression of self-doubt I had perceived from her. Suddenly, I didn't want to talk at all, despite having looked forward to this meeting for days. Now, I just wanted to be back in my room. With frustration evident in her voice, the doctor began resorting to reason and logic, and anything else she considered useful, as I began to tune her out while steadying my mind.

"This is a waste of my time," she began to climb to her feet. In the process, she grasped the arm of my chair, and her hand brushed against my arm. She returned to her side of the desk, but her touch lingered. Everything in the room faded away as I looked down at my arm and experienced the sickening pain of guilt as it coursed through my body. It was her pain. It was so concentrated, so loud, so raw, it caught me off guard. The emotions of this woman, who moments earlier seemed almost robotic, were so strong. It reminded me of my pain. It was pure shame, regret, guilt, and loss. Trying to regain some sort of composure, I bent over in my chair and closed my eyes to stop the room from spinning out of control, but her pain was disgusting and revolting. I began to feel nauseous and opened my eyes just in time to see the doctor hastening back to my side of the desk.

"Dani! What's wrong?" She reached for me, and I jerked away, hoping that not even a finger would get close enough. "What is it?"

She reached again, "Don't touch me!" I shouted. She appeared scared and embarrassed and took a step backward. I regained my consciousness slowly and things began to clear. My chest rose and fell as I tried to catch my breath.

I watched her watching me. Her eyes asked almost as many questions as did mine.

Still breathing heavily, I had to know, "What did you do?"

The look on her face changed from concern to disbelief.

"Don't act like you don't know what I'm talking about," our eyes locked, and she was now the one trying to look anywhere else. She tried desperately to change the subject.

"You know what, Danielle, if our sessions are going to turn into dramatic scenes every time we meet, then maybe I'm not the doctor you should be seeing," she said firmly. It's evident she wanted to keep her story hidden.

"There's a reason you want to know about my journal, and I think it has more to do with you than me," my voice was surprisingly calm. "I'll tell you my story; in exchange, you tell me yours."

She waited for a long time before responding.

"These compromises are quickly becoming a pattern for us. An unhealthy one I think. You'll get your answers when I get mine."

* * *

My story was one that makes me sick to this day. I didn't know where or what I did wrong. I just remembered feeling emotions I knew I was too young to feel. It was after the death of my grandmother, after the will, after all the changes. Things were looking up. It was always at these points in my life when things should be best that everything came crashing down around me. It was summer, and I was playing some video games with my brother, in the spacious living room of our relatively new, beautiful two story home. The phone rang from the wall in the adjoining kitchen. Neither my brother nor I thought twice about picking it up and instead carried on with the game.

"I've got it, thank you for not answering, so I can handle this possible pending tragedy myself," my mother remarked sarcastically. She answered and began speaking quickly. I half listened while continuing to dominate in the racing game against my brother. He, on the other hand, was concentrating on the television.

"What? Really? Oh my gosh, it's so much sooner than we expected . . . Yes . . . I'll call Alex right now, we'll be there in an hour! Tell her to wait till we get there!" My mother gave a little shriek, while hanging up the phone, and turned to us smiling. "Hurry, get your shoes on. We have to go. You're Aunt Sara is having her baby!"

Not especially thrilled at the prospect of seeing a baby born, we gathered our shoes. My Aunt Sara was my dad's younger sister. She had got married just a few months earlier, probably because she was pregnant. She and her husband were a great couple. They did everything together, and they were excited at the prospect of being parents. If I remembered correctly, the baby was a boy, and she was going to name him Alexander, after my father.

"Do we have to see them cut the baby out of her stomach?" My brother asked, looking at me wide-eyed, with disgust and excitement.

"Well, of course, that's why the family has to be there, and you're the youngest so it's tradition that you cut the cord!"

"Wow!" He said and ran to my mother, "Mom, I'm going to help get the baby out!"

My mother glanced at me disapprovingly, "Really?"

"Well, he did ask," I laughed as my mother pushed me out the door. We all jumped into the car and headed to the hospital. Fortunately, Aunt Sara was my father's only sibling living in the same state as us, so we didn't have to travel, and no other family would be there. It wasn't that I didn't like my dad's family; they were ten times better than my mother's, well at least they were a little more normal. It's just I hated getting together with family, and not knowing who to shake hands with, who to hug, what I'm supposed to remember about them, and what I should or should not say. Everyone had to interpret glances that said 'stop talking about that,' or 'they asked you a question.' It was all very uncomfortable.

By the time we reached the hospital, my father was already waiting out front for us, impatient to escort us to the birthing center located on the second floor. As we rounded corners trying to find her room, we passed a window with all the new babies on display. I looked through it, fascinated; I had no idea hospitals in real life had these viewing windows. What if the babies didn't want to be seen, or what if their parents didn't want them to be seen?

We all slowed down momentarily to check them out. It was like a car accident; you just can't pass by without ogling the scene, even briefly. There were only a few, but each one was unique and beautiful. I guess that explained why they were on display. I realized there's nothing more beautiful, and precious than a newborn; nothing more pure or fragile.

We made our way to Aunt Sara's room. It was just her, Peter, and I guessed, Alexander. She lay in bed with the baby resting against her. She was quite small, and I wondered how she could carry a baby. Her skin was pale with blue eyes, and short brown hair. Normally, she was quite pretty but now appeared drained and exhausted. Peter was good looking and a little scruffy. He had short, dark-blond hair and a big build. His humor made him a fun person to be around. Peter rose to his feet and shook hands with my father, hugged my mother, brother, and me.

"Congratulations, Peter," my dad said.

"Thanks, oh man, I wish you would have told me how nerve-wracking it is to have a kid. Apparently, he couldn't wait, he came out a month early! Can you believe that?" we all nodded in agreement. "But he's perfect! They said everything is working the way it should, he's breathing right, and should develop fine."

"That's so great," my mother said with relief in her voice. Peter had apparently answered the questions she had.

"You want to hold him?" Peter asked proudly, "I know Sara is exhausted, so maybe Alexander should get to know the rest of his family. Alex, you should do the honors."

"Oh, of course," my father said.

"Be careful," Aunt Sara warned as Peter lifted the baby from her arms as gently as possible, and placed him in my dad's arms.

"Oh yeah, he's definitely good looking. He deserves a name like Alex," my dad laughed.

"Here let me hold him," my mother extended her arms. My father carefully transferred the baby to her. I try to peer over her arm. He was adorable. Then I start to get nervous, hoping they didn't want me to hold him. He was so small, and fragile. What if I didn't hold the head right? Would it fall off? I began to edge toward the far side of the room hoping to avoid the invitation.

"Can I hold him?" My brother asked. Of course, a five-year-old is braver than me.

"No honey, he's too small, you can look at him if you want," my mother told him.

"Not fair, why did I come if I can't even do anything?" My brother complained, crossing his arms and planting himself on a seat nearby. I stared inflexibly out the window, hoping to fixate on something worthwhile.

"Danielle, you want to hold him?" Peter asked. My stomach turned a somersault.

"Oh, no, thank you," I contrived a smile.

"Come on, your newborn cousin wants to say hello," he persisted lifting him out of my mother's arms. She flashed a questioning glance at my father, which he returned while including me. The manner in which Peter hurried across the room with little Alexander made him seem less fragile than I had imagined.

"Peter cover him up so he doesn't get cold," Aunt Sara said, holding out a blanket. Peter wrapped it loosely around his little body.

"Here," he said and deposited the baby into my uncertain arms. I looked down at him, into his eyes for the first time. I saw him, but he didn't see me. He was perfect.

"See, just like holding a football," Peter laughed. I responded with a laugh, wondering why I was so nervous in the first place.

His little arm waved back and forth under the blanket till it was free from the wraps. His arm was so small. His fingers, so little and cute. I rubbed my thumb across the soft skin of his little arm and smiled. I realized why people loved to see newborn babies. It's such a rush, such a great feeling. Yet, a familiar sensation. I looked up, still smiling, expecting to see smiling faces looking back at me.

Instead, I saw stares of horror. The blood had drained from all their faces. Sara tried to sit up as best she could to interpret the expressions on their faces. They all rose to their feet at once.

Abruptly, the room became very loud. everything merged into a blur. Peter ran up to me and practically yanked Alexander out of my arms. My mother ran out of the room, screaming for a doctor. My dad crowded around Peter as he held little Alexander. In my confusion, I saw little Alexander's face again, but It wasn't the same, he was blue in the face, and looked lifeless.

"I NEED A DOCTOR!" Peter shouted with dread in his voice. Medical staff appeared in a rush and engulfed the room. Everyone was shouting, and crying, and questioning.

"What happened? What did you do?" A doctor asked with disgust in his voice. Some glanced over at me questioningly.

As the room faded out into darkness, the last thing I saw was the horrified expression on my brother's face as he held his hands over his ears. I fell back into an enveloping darkness, crashed into a food cart and dropped to the floor unconscious.

* * *

In my unconscious state, I drifted into what I can only describe as the most peaceful place in the world. However, I know that a place like this does not exist in reality. When you are awake you feel everything, the floor, the walls, the pain it's all very hard, concrete, unchangeable. In this special place, everything was soft, and light. White covered everything, it was pure, with light emitting from every direction. I laid on a bed of the softest fabrics. For a moment I wondered if conceivably I had, in fact, died, then I remembered the fall I took wasn't that bad. In truth, I was dreaming.

This place was different; peace enveloped me. It was a resting place for my soul after a long day. Pain flowed out of my heart here and I wished I could stay forever. As I finally began to relax, I looked around, assuming I was alone. It was then I felt a hand on my arm.

"Wake up, Danielle," all I remembered were green eyes observing me closely.

I felt consciousness returning and not wanting to open my eyes, not wanting to lose my grip on the dream. There's always that fleeting moment of peace when you wake up before you remember the horrors of the past. The opposite of awakening from a nightmare. That moment where everything is still pleasing. Then, just as you start to breathe a sigh of relief you realize that all those terrible things really did take place. You don't want to move, you don't want to wake up, and you would give anything to return to that time where none of it happened, but the body can only sleep so long.

"She's fine, and I must say I'm surprised. With a fall like that, I suspected a concussion. She might be a little sore, but everything checks out." I didn't open my eyes, but I knew this must be my doctor speaking.

I heard my mother: "Thank you, doctor."

"If you need anything, just ask one of the nurses and they'll be able to help you," he said and I heard him walking away. Silence ensued, and I wasn't sure if just my mother was in the room, or both my parents were there.

"Alex," my mother whispered. Just the sound of that name was painful to my ears.

"Alex, look at me," my mother said again, "what did the doctors say?"

I felt my heart beating so loud, I thought they must surely hear it too. I tried desperately to quiet it so I could hear. But the pounding in my ears was almost deafening. I had to know if baby Alex was okay. Did I do something wrong?

"We need to leave as soon as we can," my father says, despair evident in his voice. Tears begin to run out of my eyes, and I felt like I couldn't breathe. I wished I could pass out again. I just wanted to get out of there.

* * *

I remember finally leaving the hospital. No one said anything, not even my brother, not the whole way home. The thing I remember most about our departure was once again we passed the window with a view of all the newborn babies.

This time, I didn't look.

Aunt Sara's baby was revived after four minutes. The doctors said his organs had begun to shut down. They attributed this to his early birth. He spent the next three months in the NICU. Aunt Sara, Peter, and my parents were questioned relentlessly. Their concern was not how suddenly his life had drained out of him, but that the bones in his little arm appeared to have multiple fractures, which rendered the bottom half of his left arm practically useless for the rest of his life. They could not explain what would cause something so traumatic to manifest itself. The family shared their bewilderment, but I could tell they blamed me.

After that day, we hardly saw Aunt Sara again; she and my father had an intense falling out. She had more children, but we were never again invited to their births. My parents never questioned me about the event, never blamed me. For that, I couldn't be more grateful. Although the birth certificate had already been filed, Alexander was never addressed by that name again. His middle name was Gabriel, and from that day forward, that's what he was called.

Silence filled the room for a long time. The look on the doctor's face made me question whether she knew the story was finished.

"Well, that's all the time we have for today."

"Are you serious?" I asked.

"Of course I am. Why do you ask?"

"I told you my story. You said you would tell me yours."

"You misunderstood me, Danielle. This is not a game, I'm trying to help you get better. Do you want to be in this place forever?"

"You've got to be kidding me."

I was extremely irritated by this mind game but intrigued, nevertheless.

"This is bullshit . . . ," I said slowly.

"What was that?" the doctor asked, raising an eyebrow.

"Nothing, can I just go back to my room now?"

"Of course," She replied, buzzing her phone, "Patient is ready for escort."

Chapter Four:
Walking in the Dark

After the day at the hospital, I wanted answers; anything to tell me about who I was and what was wrong with me. All I could think of was my great-grandmother, and the day she died. She was trying to help me, and she said there was no way to prepare me for what was ahead. I remembered that she never held any children or grandchildren when they were born. Now I knew why. She was obviously the only one who would get me closer to resolving this dilemma, and it behooved finding her journals and learning her secrets. The only problem was, in the old will I was supposed to get her journals, but in the new will Christian inherited all of her possessions. I waited months for my opportunity to get my hands on those books. In the meantime, I was preoccupied with my suspicions and killed time with investigations of my own.

First, I searched in the most obvious place, the internet. But it proved confusing. At first, some really good information came to light, then I realized it was all superstition, dreams, and movies that I was reading about; really good movies, I might add. It was entertaining but frustrating. Was it really possible that the only person in the world who was like me was already dead?

I reached a point where I was afraid to be around anyone. I was fearful I would hurt everyone I got close to. I started covering up as much as possible to avoid contact with people. I didn't think this had any effect at all. It just caused me to be really hot all the time, and my parents worried.

The first time anything useful occurred, I was in my room, lying on my bed, contemplating all the thoughts that constantly invaded my mind those days. A loud thud on my window startled me. My heart racing from this unexpected sound, I got up and cautiously crossed to the window. It was already daylight, so a potential robbery didn't concern me. The view from the window revealed nothing, and I was about to return to my bed when the bright sunlight revealed a faint imprint on the glass. When I leaned closer and looked down, right under the window I saw a bird. It seemed it had sustained major injury from its collision with my window.

I carefully crept out of my bedroom. Everyone was still asleep, so I tried to be as quiet as possible. I opened the back door and rounded the house to the side overlooked by my bedroom. There on the ground lay the small bird. I knelt down to get a closer look. It was only about the size of a baseball, brown with little hints of white feathers in its wings. Its neck was twisted at an unnatural angle and it lay motionless with its eyes wide open, looking at me. It was as if it was asking for my help, staring into my soul, pleading that I had the decency to put it out of its misery. I reached for it but pulled my hand back quickly.

Disgusted by the prospect of hurting something, I stood up. As I did so, the bird made a small noise that sounded so pathetic. Its wing twitched a little. I stood there for several minutes as my mind became frozen in time and refused to contemplate my next move. I took a deep breath and knelt back down.

My hands shook as I reached for the bird, thinking that at least on this occasion, my curse would actually do some good. Gently, I scooped it up in my hands. It lay very still. For a long time, I just held it, wanting to help it find peace, but not knowing what to do or say. I discovered a place deep inside of me that held pity for this creature and covered it with both my hands. An affliction coursed through my veins, like an electric shock. I saw a faint tint of blue gloss over my vision. I exhaled and knew what needed to be done; had to be done. Sitting on the ground with my hands still closed, a lump built in my throat. I hoped that when I opened my hands again, the bird's eyes would be closed. I knew its death was my fault. Why did I keep my window blinds open? How was it to know that it wasn't an open window? I slowly opened my hands.

The bird's eyes remained open. It was still staring at me. Its dark eyes seemed to look through me completely. It startled me by blinking; then it began to move. It struggled to stand up, and perched, using my hands as a platform, and began bouncing around, examining its surroundings. It chirped once then took off in flight. As it departed, I heard a voice behind me.

"Another bird flew into the window?" Once again I jumped. By now, I was really tired of getting startled. I wished people would announce their presence. This time it was my father.

"Yeah," I said, quickly getting to my feet, wondering if he had seen what had happened.

"Sometimes they hit the window and go into shock. You almost think they're dead, then they just get up and fly away like nothing happened." My dad gave a little laugh. I was not so thrilled to hear this but pretended to be.

"Yeah . . . that must be what happened," I began to walk back into the house. My dad grabbed me by the arm gently.

"Danielle, you alright?"

"I'm fine," I said, definitely not wanting to discuss my encounter with the bird.

"You sure? You've been acting a little different lately. I'm concerned," he said with sincerity. My dad was always genuine in his conversations with me. It was difficult to lie to him.

"I'm fine, Dad," I gave him a small smile to reassure him. He gave me a hug, and I began to head in.

"Oh, Danielle," he said quickly.

"Yeah, Dad?"

"You're going to your uncle's this evening, both you and your brother," I was excited by this news and gave a quick smile that obviously took my father off guard by the expression on his face. He knew Christian, and I didn't get along and wasn't expecting his news to please me. He quickly changed the subject, "and wash your hands if you touched that bird."

* * *

Apparently, my parents had arranged some sort of date night. A concert, or play, maybe. It's hard to remember the details. Clearly, they were reluctant to leave us with Christian; it was something they never did, at least not alone. I assumed we wouldn't exactly be alone with him. Ostensibly, he was seeing some girl; they had been going together for a couple of months. This must have put my parents at ease; maybe Christian was settling down, perhaps even drinking less.

When we arrived at Christian's home, he stepped outside onto his porch with his fists on his hips in a sort of Superman pose. It seemed he wanted us to be impressed by his new house. It was beautiful — new and huge. You could still smell the fresh wood and paint on the walls. His much younger girlfriend joined him and put an arm around his waist. This was the first time we were meeting her, she was perhaps in her late-twenties, compared to Christian's late-forties. Everyone was obviously thinking the same thing: money.

She was gorgeous with blonde hair, tanned skin, hazel eyes, and a perfect smile. She dressed like a college student going out for the night. It made me question if we had some unknown plans. I couldn't stop myself from staring at her. She made me feel distinctly uncomfortable, and I quickly pretended not to notice her.

"Hey guys, great to see you. Hey, Alex what do you think? Eh?" he said waving his arms and presenting the house.

"It looks great, Christian, not the low-key investment we had discussed, but it's lovely," my dad said in a somewhat nervous tone.

"Right? It is badass! I know. Oh! I want you to meet Cindy," he said displaying his girlfriend from head to toe," she stepped forward politely and shook their hands. My mother seemed baffled.

"Nice to meet you, Cindy . . . You're . . . you're so beautiful," my mom said, clearly meaning it.

"Nice to meet you," my dad said in a carefully neutral tone. I was sure he could feel my mother watching him from the corner of her eye to see if he was ogling Cindy. In fact, my mother was stunning that night as well. She'd really gone to a great deal of trouble to impress my dad I suppose, or possibly to impress herself. I could tell she was a little embarrassed that someone could look so attractive with so little effort while she had tried so hard that night. Cindy took care of her insecurities quickly.

"Thank you, Bridget, you as well, I love your hair, where do you get it done?" This put a smile on my mother's face because she'd had her hair done that day, for a pretty penny, but it gave her something to talk about and to be proud of. They launched into a discussion about hairstylists and salons. So far, I think I liked this girl, Cindy. Maybe things aren't always what meet the eye although the eyes couldn't be more satisfied.

"Well, we gotta go if we're going to be on-time," my dad said.

"Yeah, go have a great night, you can pick up the kids tomorrow if you want some sexy-time alone."

"Christian . . ." My mom said with a 'shut-the-hell-up,' look.

"What? I'm just saying. Alex. Think about it," he said pointing his finger at him. My dad just shook his head, and they were off.

"Come inside guys, we got food, games, a pool!"

"A pool?" my brother said.

"That's right, you want to do some swimming?"

"Yeah!"

"Alright then, let's go!"

We all trooped into his house, which was quite spectacular. Colorful, modern, electronics were everywhere. Big screens, gaming consoles, art. Why art, I have no idea because Christian knows and cares nothing for it. I assumed he had someone decorate for him. This was confirmed later, although Christian still took credit for its beauty.

"We're getting in the pool," Christian said. "You want to join us, Dani?"

"No, I'm good, I don't have a swimsuit and —"

"Oh come with me, we've got extras, I'm sure I can help you find something," Cindy said, grabbing my hand and escorting me to a room filled with clothes. She rummaged through the garments looking for swimsuits and found at least ten.

"I'm going to wear this one," she said grabbing a purple top and bottom. "Why don't you look and see if you see anything you like. I'm going to get changed." She stepped into the adjoining bathroom, only halfway closing the door. I wished she had tried a little harder to close it. I sorted through some clothes, knowing there was no way I would wear anything there. Then, I found my eyes wandering. The way Cindy undressed, she was obviously proud of her body. I didn't blame her. I averted my eyes, feeling guilty, and focused my attention on the walls.

"Dani, could you help me a sec?" I heard her call. I paused for a moment, not knowing what to say. Not wanting to be rude, I went into the bathroom, trying not to stare right at her body. She gave a helpless face, as though there was a problem she just couldn't resolve, as she dangled the back ties to her bikini top in her hands and asked, "Can you tie this for me?"

"Uh . . . sure," I said walking toward her.

"It's okay. We're both girls, right?" she laughed. She obviously sensed that I was not used to being around girls revealing so much. I took my time tying the knot around her back.

"So, how old are you, Dani?" she asked

"Uh, just recently turned fourteen," I said, not sure if I had stated a complete sentence. She smelled so amazing.

"Wow, fourteen, you're closer to my age than Christian," she laughed, "I'm not with him for the money, you know, I really do like him. Well . . . most of the time, anyway. He's funny and does whatever he wants. It's just nice being around a guy that knows his own mind."

"Yeah, I guess," I said, stepping away. She leans back on the bathroom counter, facing me.

"What about you? Any boyfriends?" She inquired with an eyebrow raised. I got the impression she had further implication with her words.

"Nope," I said simply.

"That's good, you're young. Enjoy it, be free."

"You are like, really pretty," I blurt without thinking. She smiles, knowing my embarrassment.

"It's all real too girl," she said giving a quick spin.

I was feeling extremely confused and awkward. Christian came to my rescue.

"Damn, are you girls coming or not?" he yelled from downstairs.

"Be right there!" Cindy returned and winked at me.

We went downstairs. I had made up my mind not to go swimming and just sat and watched them have fun. It disgusted me to see Cindy all over Christian. I didn't know if it was because I hated him, or I was jealous of him. I banished the thought from my mind but watched them in the pool for a long time. Nathan seemed to be having a great time. I knew a big part of me did hate Christian, but I could understand why my grandma said she loved part of

49

Christian; a part she didn't think existed anymore. Maybe this was that part. He looked happy.

The night progressed; we ate and settled in to watch a movie and fall asleep. Unfortunately, the only one with sleep on his mind was Nathan. He went out like a light after so much swimming. I went upstairs to a guest room and tried to fall asleep, but could only think of finding those journals my great-grandmother spoke of. They were probably in the garage. He must have lots of junk stored in there because all his cars were parked outside.

I thought, they must surely have fallen asleep by now, so I made my way tentatively down the stairs. Christian and Cindy were still awake, but without-a-doubt preoccupied. I saw Cindy sitting on Christian's lap, facing him. His back was to me. They were kissing . . . a lot, and I grimaced at the sight. Cindy noticed me, but she said nothing to Christian; in fact, she kept him preoccupied. It was as if she knew I was trying to find something. She gave me a questioning glance like, "what's up?" Trusting her, I pointed to myself, then to the garage, enforced with a desperate expression. She seemed to understand and turned his head away from me as much as she could, pulling him down onto the couch so that he was on top of her, and then motioned with her hand for me to head that way. When I had turned the corner, I heard her say, "Why don't we go upstairs to the bedroom so we don't wake up the kids?"

I assume Christian agreed. Fortunately, his room was at the furthest place from the garage. I sneaked in quickly and quietly. With a new house, you don't really have to worry about floor boards or doors creaking.

I was right about him storing my great-grandmother's things in the garage after I turned on the light, I saw it was packed from the floor to the ceiling. All uniform, unmarked boxes. Who doesn't mark boxes? How are you ever going to find anything? I felt overwhelmed but had to start somewhere, so I grabbed the boxes furthest from the door so that they might conceal me in case he walked in. There were so many things, knick-knacks, decorations, some quite expensive. However, I was looking for the box with, seemingly, the most worthless items. I was worried that Christian had probably disposed of the journals because of their ostensible lack of value. Eventually, I located some boxes actually containing books. This gave me hope. Perhaps he hadn't had time to go through her items yet. I dug through three boxes full of books before I knew I had found the one I was looking for. Dozens of journals, all black, all tattered from being carried and written in and discarded. I hesitated to know what these books could tell me. I saw one very small volume that looked like a schedule book and quickly grabbed it and put in my pocket; knowing I wouldn't be leaving empty handed. I seized others, flipping through them quickly, seeking anything important. Nothing jumped out immediately. Then, slowly words became familiar: Euphoria, anger, pain, confusion. One passage stood out clearly, the first word I caught said: Christian

It felt wrong to read the words that I knew no one else ever had, even though my great-grandmother had insisted I should, I still felt ashamed. It wasn't only her secrets in here, but the whole family's secrets. I stopped myself. Whatever was in Christian's past could wait for another day. As I was packing everything away, I noticed a glint of red protruding from under the pile of journals overflowing inside the box. I reached for it and tried to read it quickly and soak up information. What was in this book that I was meant to read? What hidden message?

I heard footsteps approaching and began to try to rip out pages that might be of importance, anything to guide me, but every page I tried to tear either ripped upward or across the middle. I don't know why I assumed they would have any sort of perforation; they were decades old. I slowed myself down to be more careful, and at least save one page. Just as it was detaching from the journal ninety-five percent intact, Christian opened the garage door. I jumped knowing I had been caught red-handed. He looked suspicious at first, but not the least bit angry.

"I thought I'd find you down here at some point," he said, with a shake of his head.

"Sorry . . ." I said in a low tone, hoping to appear sincere.

"Listen, I know you probably miss her a lot," he said kneeling down next to me.

"Yeah," I lied, and adopted a sad expression to confirm his inaccurate suspicion.

"I miss her too," I think he lied as well, then he became very serious and contemplated me, "I am so sorry for how I acted that day."

The words felt real. I knew Christian was the best actor, but nothing seemed to slip through the cracks this time. I search his expression and found no sense of falseness.

"You are a lot like her you know, I mean both stubborn, stoic, passionate, and loyal. I don't blame her for hating me, you know? I deserved that. I've done the worst things that you probably can't even imagine at your age," his gaze shifted as he tried to repress the memories he spoke of, "I'm not that person anymore, Dani, I promise you that. I don't drink, and I don't hurt the people I love. I'm not perfect, but I think I'm getting better. Cindy might have a little to do with that."

I smiled, thinking that he was right. He had changed, there was no denying that. For how long, was the real question.

"I forgive you," I said, and meant it. He smiled in acceptance.

"Now let's get outta here, it smells like old people in this garage. I've been meaning to get rid of this shit."

"Get rid of?" I ask.

"Well, the unimportant stuff, not everything. Don't worry if it's important in any way I intend to keep it, and I'll let you go through anything before I get rid of it, promise," he wrapped one arm around my shoulder and lead me back inside. I relaxed, knowing I might have another chance to retrieve what I needed.

* * *

"Danielle, if I may interject," Dr. Joy said, holding up one finger and looking at me over her glasses.

"Yes, doctor, who suddenly wears glasses that I don't think you even need. What is it?"

"Uh-huh," she said disdainfully. "What is the significance of the story?"

"I don't know, the part about the journals, and Christian . . . it will eventually be important," I stated blandly.

"Well, what did the pages say? It's not in here."

"At the time it didn't make sense to me . . . like it just seemed like a riddle or casual advice. It talked about disciplining your emotions and not investing too much into one thing. If your emotions became too concentrated, they would be like a ticking time-bomb, but in saying that, it works both ways. It could be good or very bad. But that's true for everyone, right? Letting our emotions get the best of us can be all too dangerous. The little book I kept was nothing more than an address book, irrelevant for the time being."

The room grew quiet, and I fidgeted a little in my restraints, for the most part, they're relatively comfortable.

"I don't understand you, Danielle. If what you're saying is true, then why can't you prove any of it, why can't you just accept the fact that maybe none of this ever happened, at least not the way you think it did? A ninety-something-year-old woman dying, a journal that says nothing supernatural, a bird only half-dead, a premature baby in critical condition. These are things that happen every single day."

"It's real . . ." I replied, offended, but I could hear the slight doubt in my voice.

53

"Then, why not prove it right here right now?" she said insistently, but in a tone that implied she didn't think it was impossible. Apparently, she really wanted to know.

"I can't."

"Why not?" she asked.

"I don't feel the way I did then. It's still there, but it's not the same; I'm blocked out. It's inside, and it can be felt, but not accessed," I spoke rapidly to convey my point convincingly while at the same time not destroying my fading credibility.

It was true since the second week of my confinement to this hell-hole, things had begun to change. I felt no connection to other people, other than my encounter with Dr. Joy; I could not help nor hinder anyone. It was as though it was all part of my imagination, but as I read the pages of the journals, I could not help but believe that at one point it was real; that all these unbelievable acts really did happen, and that people lived because of me, and more importantly, people died because of me.

"I've read your journal, I've listened to what you've said, I've talked to your family. It seems you are under the impression that you have the power to inflict and heal pain telepathically . . . but it's not true," she said as if she was imparting the worst news ever.

"I'm done for the day," I said, sensing that the doctor was giving up on me.

"Very well," she said, disappointed, and pressed a button on her phone. "Escort for room 7."

After I was returned to my room, I spent hours replaying what the doctor had said, over and over in my head. On an average day, I loved my tiny room. Because of events upon my arrival here, I was segregated from other patients, and I had a room to myself; it's small but quiet. White-painted brick walls, a creaky metal bed, a relatively small window, sealed-with-wire mesh to prevent escape. The floor was the cheap linoleum tile you might see in a school cafeteria. I liked it because my room was bright, all the time. There was even a lamppost outside the window that made it bright at night.

Today, however, it was much too quiet. Perhaps there was too much room for my mind to wander. I'd rather be in a place reverberating with a million voices so that I couldn't hear my own thoughts. I wouldn't mind so much if my thoughts were productive in the slightest way, but they were on a loop of unproductivity, replaying the same ideas and doubts over and over again, making them more frustrating every time they crossed my mind. I was becoming angered by my frustrations when I heard a knock at the door.

"Danielle Blake, it's time for your medication," the voice preceded a face at the door.

"Umm, come in?" I said. It was a weird introduction for a medication dispenser. Normally, they just walked in.

A girl nervously pushed the cart in and fumbled with a cup as well as the pills. She was surprisingly small, with long dark hair, and light blue eyes. They projected a somewhat vacant expression. She handed me a cup with water.

"Please, take your medication, Miss Blake," she said in a falsely authoritative inflection, giving the impression she was acting out a part in a play, and not very successfully.

"I'm not taking this," I replied. She appeared confused; clearly, she didn't know what to do or say next.

"Miss Blake, it is important that you take your medication on a daily basis; if you need assistance in taking your medication, I can have alternate staff come in to help you," she said.

"No, I didn't mean it like that," I said with a mild laugh, "This is for Daniel Black, I'm Danielle Blake . . ."

She looked down at all the medication again, searching for mine. I laughed out loud at this.

"Ya know, that's a good way to get fired around here," I said continuing to laugh.

She finally located the right medication. "Here," she said, shoving it toward me with the water.

"Thank you," I said, raising my glass in a 'cheers' fashion. I looked down at my cup before swallowing the pills.

"What are these?" I asked, not really that curious.

"The usual," she replied after examining her chart, "at least that's what it says on here."

"They look different," I shifted my head to the side, as though they might actually change size or color.

"Well, you know what it most likely is, they're giving you generic now. It's the same pill, technically. Let's see . . . yes, you've been taking the new version for almost two weeks now."

"Weird, I guess I never noticed. I mean I have been feeling different; I feel like I'm on fewer meds, but I can't complain about that, I suppose. My mind is just on overdrive."

"Well I'm sure the doctor has something to help that," she said.

"Dr. Joy, do you know anything about her?"

"Dr. Joy?" she asked hesitantly.

"Yeah, I'm curious, where does she come from? Is she new? Family? Married?"

"I'm sorry, Miss Blake, I don't know Dr. Joy," she said, tapping her hand on the cart, "I just started, and I mostly stick to dispensing."

"Right," I said.

She nodded and exited the room.

Chapter Five:
Peyton

I sat waiting for my next session with Dr. Joy to begin. She did her usual scanning of pages and scribbling of notes for five minutes or so, then looked up. After two-and-a-half weeks of our sessions together, she suggested an interesting topic to explore.

"Let's fast-forward a bit. Let's talk about when you met Peyton,"

I looked up and sat silent.

"Peyton . . ." I hadn't spoken her name for a long time. I tried not to even think about her. The doctor must have done her research because as important as Peyton was, I did everything in my power not to talk about her. She was my best-kept secret within those walls. I had barely written about her in my journal for that very reason, fearing someone else might get ahold of it. I always wanted her to be only mine, my secret.

If there was one person in my life who had a completely pure heart, it was Peyton. The day she came into my life was the day I found hope, not only for me but for humanity as a whole.

I was seventeen at that point; barely a senior in high school and school had been uneventful up until then. You would imagine that with my unwelcoming disposition and avoidance of any activity, I would be a target for other students, fortunately, that wasn't the case. By choice, I ostracized myself from them, and they never bothered me. I liked it that way; I was quite the loner, not wanting to cling to or get involved with anyone or anything.

"Hey, mom, where are you? I'm waiting outside," I had just gotten out of school and normally she was there to pick me up, but today this wasn't the case and I'd phoned her.

"I'm so sorry. I had to take care of some things. Is there any way you could walk home?" she asked.

I would normally say yes, but not today.

"I can't walk home; it's about to rain," I said, taking in the overcast sky. I wasn't sure it was going to rain but didn't care to get caught in the middle of a storm on the way home. Plus, walking would take almost an hour.

"Well then, take the bus," she suggested.

"The bus? I don't even know what bus I ride."

"Danielle, it's bus 50. Hurry, and don't miss it on purpose, because I can't pick you up. Okay? Love you." She hung up, not allowing me an opportunity to argue.

I walked toward where all the buses gathered and reluctantly approached bus number 50. It was bad enough riding the bus, but the worst part involved trying to find an open seat next to someone who seemed receptive to someone else sitting with them. Usually, this was never. I climbed the steps and thankfully there weren't too many people already on the bus, and I found a seat toward the back that was completely unoccupied. It was over the wheel, and my feet sat awkwardly, but I didn't mind at all, provided I didn't have to ask, "Is this seat taken?"

Everyone else piled aboard, mostly underclassmen: freshmen and sophomores. It was embarrassing being a senior. I looked out the window, waiting to get going. A group of girls was conversing outside. People around me had their windows down, and these girls talked so loudly, it wasn't hard to eavesdrop on their discussion.

"Peyton, come on, we're riding home with the boys," a tall brown-haired girl said to another girl.

"Yeah, come on," a short blonde-haired girl echoed.

"No thanks; I think I'm just going to take the bus," a girl with light brown hair, green eyes, and a perfect tan replied. She was exceptionally attractive, and I recognized her from around school. She was in track, so her body was strong and tight, but still very feminine. Her appearance was perfect, at least in my opinion. She turned toward the bus as I was observing at her, and I thought she might have noticed me staring, so I shifted to face forward in my seat but still listened.

"You always ride the bus, why don't you just bring your car?" asked another girl with dark flawless skin, and long dark hair tied back, although she only seemed half interested.

"I like the bus . . . I'll see you guys later," she said while climbing aboard the bus.

I peered over the seat to see if she had had the same problem trying to find a seat. Of course, she did not.

"Hey Peyton, you can sit here," I heard a boy's voice from behind me.

"No, sit here!" came another guy's voice.

She waved to them. As she drew level with me, she glanced down, seeming to recognize me, although we hadn't met before. I half smiled, and she shook her head slightly as if realizing her error, but she still pointed to the seat next to me.

"Is this seat taken?" she asked with a nervous smile.

I was so surprised she even asked, I didn't give a verbal response, I just shook my head.

"Great," she said with a sigh of relief and plopped down next to me.

I thought this could be an exceptionally awkward trip since the seating arrangement positioned my leg close to hers. I felt my leg twitch out of nervousness and hoped she didn't notice.

"So, what's your name?" she asked, turning to me.

"Dani," I answered.

"Dani? Is that short for Danielle?"

"Yeah," I said shaking my head.

"I like Danielle better," she said with a smile, "I'm Peyton."

She extended her hand, and I shook it. I always thought it was weird that people meet and still shake hands, but did it anyway.

"Nice to meet you," I said.

"So, you going to the football game tonight?" she asked.

"Uh, no, are you?"

"Maybe . . . Do you ever go?"

"I used to . . . with my family, but haven't been this year."

"That's cool," she said, pushing her hair back with her left hand. As she raised her hand, I noticed scars lined her wrist. It was hard to detect with her tan, but still visible.

"What happened?" I asked pointing at her wrist, then immediately regretted my impulsive question.

"I think that's more of a personal question than you intended to ask," she said with a smile.

"Oh, I didn't know –"

"Do you want the truth or the lie I tell everyone else?" she asked.

"Both."

"I have a very vicious cat, at home," she said, and laughed, casting her eyes downward.

"And the truth?" I prompted.

"The truth . . ." she said looking at me, squinting her eyes as if she was searching for something. I held her stare as she searched, trying to convey that it was safe to tell me. She bit her bottom lip and explained, "The truth is, I did it to myself."

I was caught off guard by her blatant honesty.

"You tried to kill yourself?" I asked in a non-judgmental tone.

"No, not at all," she said.

"I don't understand," I confessed.

"Well . . . do you ever get so mad or frustrated or upset that you feel like you're just going to lose your mind?"

"No," I said wanting to be able to understand what she was talking about, "I don't think so."

"Well, I hope you never do."

"But why did you do it?"

"When I get all of these emotions, they are overwhelming. I start to lose control of myself, so I cut just a little. It's like letting the air out of a balloon slowly rather than just popping it. It makes it so I can actually get to the next point in my life."

"Doesn't it hurt?"

"No."

"Does it make you feel better?"

"For a moment . . ." she said, looking at me and giving me a smile. I sat quietly for a second. I hadn't had a serious conversation with another person in a long time, much less a virtual stranger.

"I know what you're thinking: she's beautiful, athletic, smart, rich; what does she have to be sad or angry about, right?"

"No . . . not at all." I tried to hide that that was exactly what I was thinking.

"Do you know how many people hate you when you're popular and your family has money? Almost everyone does, including the people who claim to be your friends. I just wish I could tell them that they don't know what I've been through; what I go through. Everyone has a story that no one knows."

"I believe that," I said, definitely being able to relate to her last comment, "I wish you didn't feel like you had to do that."

Peyton just gave me a small smile back.

The bus began to empty out to the point where we were two of the few people remaining. Peyton began to glance around nervously.

"Do you want me to move to another seat?" she asked.

"Uh . . . I mean if you want, that's okay, but you can stay," I said, not wanting her to leave but at the same time, not wanting to seem weird.

"I do want to stay," she said, "So, how come I've never seen you on the bus before?"

"If I was on the bus before, do you think you would have actually noticed?" I asked in a joking manner.

"Of course, I wouldn't have ridden the bus today if you weren't on it," she said with a wink. I enjoyed her sense of humor.

"So, you're on track, right?" I asked hoping it didn't give the impression I was stalking aspects of her life.

"That's right, how did you know?" she asked suspiciously.

"Oh . . . um, I've seen you around . . . in uniform."

"Oh, yeah?" she laughed.

"Yep, so how's that?"

"I love it," she said, "I just feel I've been caged up for so much of my life, when I'm running, I'm free, I could go anywhere, and do anything. Plus . . ."

I was watching her eyes intently as she explained hoping to pick up the emotion behind every word she spoke. I suddenly saw an unexpected discomposure cross her eyes as her pupils expanded. It was an embodiment of terror. I tried to register why she would have this reaction. Then I heard the sound of thick tires screeching against the road attempting to stop in their tracks but to no avail. I knew it was heading straight for us. Peyton stared over my shoulder, then locked her eyes on me. Everything stopped. It was as if the world was trying to stand still so I could process what was about to happen.

Everything faded into a purple almost lilac tint and fixated in time. Everything except me.

I had my back to my window and twisted to see. Only feet from the bus was a semi-truck. The driver wore an expression of complete despair, as he gripped the steering wheel, slammed on the brakes, and simultaneously braced himself for impact. He knew what was about to happen. I turned back toward Peyton, her eyes fixed on mine. Time slowly came back into play, millimeter by millimeter, the truck initiated its collision with the bus. First, the glass gave way sending shards like droplets of water across the bus, then the metal began to cave in under pressure. It was a direct hit with where we were seated.

With chaos ensuing around us, I could not be distracted from the penetrating eyes of Peyton; my heart feared for her. I felt an obligation inside me to protect her. Instinctively I reached out and wrapped my arms around her and pulled her close to me. I immediately felt her arms wrap around me as the time returned to full speed. The truck ripped through the bus like an explosion.

* * *

I awoke, or so I thought, in the same place I remembered from when I was previously in the hospital. It was pure white on a bed, soft as silk, comforting against my skin. I rolled onto my back and put my arms behind my head. I thought I could definitely get used to the feeling I had in this place. I only wondered why I was here. This time I had surely died.

"Danielle," said a voice.

I noticed a person standing beside my bed. She was tall, thin, with very dark skin, exceptionally short dark hair not even an inch in length. Most intriguing were her green eyes, my only memory of the last time I was here.

"Yeah?" I said as if I knew her. She sat on the side of my bed and smiled.

"Do you know what brings you here?" she asked

"Something bad happened, so I decided to take a peaceful nap?"

"Do you know what this place is?" she chose not to provide an answer to her previous question.

"A dream," I countered definitively.

"Close," she held her hand just above my body, in the middle of my chest "This is the place where your soul comes to heal when it is damaged, confused, or hurt. A dream in a sense that your mind creates the environment you see around you. It is your rationale of a place that would provide healing, and safety."

She removed her hand from above me, "It seems as though your soul is quite damaged."

"I feel fine. I'll probably wake up soon," I countered.

"You can wake up whenever you feel the need to do so; I suggest you wait for the healing process to complete. You wouldn't want to enter the world with a piece of your soul missing. That would be quite foolish."

"How will I know when I'm ready?"

"Your body will awaken itself, and you will find yourself in the present time, sorting through the pieces of what time has elapsed since you left."

I absorbed these words. It was unusual because, although I knew nothing of this place or this person, it was dream-like because it all made sense. I knew I had to be here, I felt parts of me growing stronger the longer I lay in the peaceful oasis.

"And, who are you?" I asked, already comprehending the answer.

"I am what your mind created to explain to you what you do not know, and there are things I know that you do not."

"Do you know of my great-grandmother?"

"Yes."

"Did she ever come here?"

"All too often I'm afraid, but she was much older than you the first time I saw her. Her imagination created a glorious place of healing, yours depicts a very basic, simple definition of tranquility. Hers was breathtaking, and it transformed over the years to become more glorious. She had a lot of reasons to be here."

"So this place moves?"

"Not exactly, it transforms, based on how your mind defines it, based on your life, and your experiences."

"Are there ever other people here?" She looked away from me.

"Sometimes the mind will create . . . illusions of other people in this place, but be careful about inviting them in, and letting them stay. In order to heal, their presence must be extracted, and once they leave, the mind loses them. They can only hinder the healing process."

"I see," I said, then I remembered her first question, "So, why am I here today?"

All at once, she appeared to be addressing someone else.

"It's the most unusual situation. To the common observer, it would appear that she was in an unconscious state, in a coma if you would. However, our tests indicate an unusual state of REM sleep, something I've never seen before, as is the other victim. It's like a double phenomenon if you exclude the situation from the other day."

Then I heard my mother's frantic voice.

"I don't understand, Doctor, when is she going to wake up? What's wrong with her?"

The person from my dreams spoke again, but as my dream state faded and reality sets in, she appeared standing in front of me, in a white coat, clipboard in hand, her expression perplexed.

"Mrs. Blake, I promise you as soon as we know anything, we will let you know as well."

"How soon can we start getting answers? We've been here for days," my mother asked again, frustration evident in her voice.

"I don't know."

I could hear monitors and machines, beeping and buzzing around me. I couldn't help wondering how many times in my life I would wake up in the hospital. Knowing how this charade would play out, I struggled to sit up in an attempt to make a break for the adjacent restroom.

"Dani!"

"Danielle!"

"Miss Blake!"

"Yup," is all I could muster as I undertook the task of getting up out of the bed.

"Don't get up!" my mother said.

"Get my team in here," the doctor half-shouted with urgency from the doorway. I raised my hands to silence everyone, then renewed my efforts to extract myself from the bed. I tore an IV from my arm and a similar device attached down by my thigh received similar treatment. That one hurt.

"Stop!" they ordered, but I feigned not to hear. Despite their attempts to stop me, I managed to squeeze into the bathroom, shutting the door quickly behind me and locking it.

I heard about ten voices from behind the door, all talking at once.

"What's going on?"

"Don't lock the door."

"How do you feel?"

"Do you remember what happened?"

I looked into the mirror. Everything appeared the way I remembered it should. I laid my head against the mirror and closed my eyes, preparing myself for the insanity on the other side of the door. I began to decipher the many voices outside.

"The other patient is coming to, Doctor,"

I heard a number of the staff retreat from my room and decided it might be safe to open the door.

All eyes were on me, replete with shock.

"Sorry . . . I just needed a moment to myself," I said, bypassing them and reaching for my clothes.

"Miss Blake, please sit down," the doctor ordered. I sighed, abandoned my efforts and obediently sat on the side of the bed. My parents were standing to one side of the bed, the doctor was seated on the other.

"Miss Blake, do you remember what happened the other day?"

"Other day?"

"Friday," she said.

"What's today?"

"Tuesday."

"Tuesday?" I repeated.

"You don't seem too surprised," said the doctor.

"Well, I just feel really well rested," I said matter-of-factly.

"What is the last thing you remember?"

"The accident."

"So you remember what happened?" she seemed confused.

"Yeah, of course, I was right there, wasn't I? Speaking of the accident, what happened to Peyton? Is she okay?" I had a sick feeling in my stomach.

"Miss Blake," my focus begins to waiver with the doctor's inordinate dramatization of my condition and turned instead to my parents, whose eyes were fixed on the doctor. I realized she must be about to reveal something important so I reverted my attention to her and picked up what she was saying with

" . . . this might be hard to grasp, but according to eyewitnesses, there were only four people involved in the accident. Those four people were the bus driver, the driver of the other vehicle, you, and Miss Deason. Both of you were found lying in the road."

I fell silent. The question etched on my face. She was completely wrong. I crossed my arms and fixed her with a stare. It was obvious everyone was waiting for my response, but I didn't know what to say.

"Peyton? Is she hurt, or . . . ?" I asked, knowing I probably didn't want to hear the answer.

"Her condition is identical to yours."

"Which is what? I don't understand."

"You two were the only passengers on the bus, you were hit by a semi-truck, at which point you were ejected from the bus onto the road, and you both sustained no injuries."

"What?"

"It's a miracle the both of you are even alive, it's impossible that you are both unharmed."

I felt unusual emotions coursing through my body: fear, anxiety, disbelief. It was cold and rigid. I sat unmoving for several seconds, staring down the doctor. Angered by her implication that I was unaware of what happened, and apprehensive that something had happened that I didn't understand.

"Can we leave now?" I demanded, raising an eyebrow at the doctor.

She was clearly at a loss and scrambled through her paperwork and charts, trying to find a reason that justified me staying.

"I believe you need further observation —" she began.

"Can I leave? That's all I want to know. I don't care what your charts say. I don't care what people think they saw. You said I'm not hurt. So, can I leave?"

The doctor paused for a second.

"I'd recommend that you did not, but I have no definitive reason to keep you here."

"Wonderful," I said getting up again and rushing to put on my clothes before anything catastrophic could prevent my departure.

"Dani, are you sure you —" my mother began.

I rudely raised my hand to stop her. I felt bad making such a gesture but was too overwhelmed to explain myself. I was mostly dressed and began to walk out through the door.

"Danielle, you need to fill out your paperwork," my father interrupted my departure firmly.

"Can you guys please take care of it? I can't take another minute in this place," I appealed. "I'll meet you at the front."

I slipped out of the room, and just around the corner heard a commotion, similar to what had ensued moments before in my room.

"I'm fine, what's the big deal?" It was Peyton's voice. I smiled understanding how she felt and knowing I wasn't the only one who thought the situation was ridiculous. I poked my head into her room. She turned my way, relieved to see a familiar face.

"Want to get out of here?" I asked.

"You have no idea," she said and began throwing on her clothes as well.

"You need a parent to discharge you. Unfortunately, we have been unable to make contact with either one of your parents since your arrival. So, until they get here, we cannot allow you to leave," a male nurse told her in an overly authoritative manner.

"I turned eighteen last week. I don't need anyone to do anything for me," she responded, firmly. She gathered up her belongings and headed toward me. I grinned and followed her out the door.

I wanted to get out of that hospital as fast as possible. As we walked, it became very quiet in the main area of the ICU. People stood up to see us better. People came out of their rooms to catch a glance. They looked at us as if they were seeing ghosts. It was a completely captive audience as we passed by. People grabbed the sleeves of the people next to them and pointed our way; people whispered to one another. I tried walking a little faster, becoming more uncomfortable by the second. I felt a tug on my shirt and came to a reluctant halt and turned around.

"Can you help my grandson?" asked a small Hispanic woman from behind me. She was perhaps five feet tall, just starting to age, with an expression of pure innocence on her face. I glanced around assuming she couldn't be talking to me.

"Me?" I said, indicating myself; she nodded her head.

"My grandson, he's very sick," she said pointing to a room, that I had no desire to enter. "I heard what happened to you was a miracle."

She looked at me with hope and so much pain behind her eyes.

"No . . . I can't help him . . . I'm nobody," I said.

I turned around and walked away.

As we walked in silence down the hallway, I heard the woman begin to cry. It killed me inside.

* * *

"What is it about this girl, Peyton, that struck you so hard?" Dr. Joy asked, right after the conclusion of the story. I was surprised by her order of questioning.

"I felt sorry for her."

"You felt sorry for her?"

"Of course I did. You see, I had the luxury when I woke up to be in an unknown, unexpected place, not knowing what happened, but having my family at my side. I can't even begin to imagine, having been in the hospital for several days, and wake up, and no one is there waiting for you. What kind of parent . . . No, what kind of person would allow that?"

"As you said, there was nothing wrong with either of you two, perhaps she wouldn't have even wanted her parents there," the doctor suggested.

"No . . . I'd like to give them the benefit of the doubt, but I saw the look on her face that day. I saw the pain, and I felt it. She appeared so bulletproof to the world like nothing could touch her, but as I got to know her, I saw how fragile she truly was."

"What happened to you after that?"

"Several things happened. My parents were extremely concerned about me. They thought I had some sort of disorder and considered my behavior unusual. I don't blame them. A couple of weeks later I started seeing a psychiatrist who put me on wonderful drugs, and I'm not going to lie, it helped. It helped me feel stable; it helped me feel real. I felt normal for the first time in a long time."

"And how did you feel about what happened with the woman at the hospital?"

* * *

After leaving the hospital, I spent the next day locked away in my room, trying to quiet my mind. Nothing helped. It was in overdrive and spinning out of control. I paced back and forth, unable to get that woman out of my head. The idea of returning to the hospital did not sit well with me at all. I'd developed a great distaste for that place. Not to mention, I had no desire to see any of those people's faces again, but something was drawing me back.

After much contemplation, I went into the bathroom in my house and examined myself in the mirror. The person looking back was not the person I expected to see. I had grown older. That wasn't it though. I just didn't look the way I thought I did. The longer I stared, the more foreign the reflection seemed to become.

If I returned to the hospital, I didn't want anyone to recognize me.

I took some scissors from a drawer and went to work, shearing inches off my hair, cutting away the familiarity; cutting away the confusion that clung to my reflection. It was kindred to ridding myself of a part of myself I had outgrown. My hair was short, a mess. In the mirror, I now saw a hardened heart, distrust, coldness. The amazing thing was, I stared into the mirror and for the first time, I recognized the person staring back at me. I grinned at my reflection and returned to my room to grab a jacket from inside my closet and throw it on.

Everyone was asleep as I quietly exited the house.

The hospital wasn't far from my house, however, it did take almost an hour to walk there. Considering it wasn't fall weather yet, I grew uncomfortably hot in my clothing. It was nice, however, to have less hair. I felt the wind blow against my neck, and it was comforting to me.

I reached the hospital very late, almost one o'clock in the morning. When I arrived, I started to wonder what I was doing. What did I expect to find? I proceeded upstairs to where I had been the day before.

Some people glanced at me, wanting to question my presence, but for some reason thought better of it. I made my way to the room the woman had pointed to and checked inside to see if it was occupied. Hearing and seeing no one, I crept inside and stood at the end of the bed. It was a difficult sight.

He was a very young boy, younger than my brother, with short, dark hair, his eyes closed. There was a tube down his throat, IVs, and machines hooked up to him at every possible location. Somehow, I sensed he was strong and had endured much already. I could tell his time was running out and knew if I was going to see something I had come on the right night.

I slipped behind the curtain in the room. It was dark so it would provide concealment should someone unexpectedly come in. I stood silently for several minutes, listening to the beeping of the machines, trying to breathe quietly. I don't know how long I stood there, waiting. Maybe five minutes, then I felt I had to leave. I slipped out the door and headed back down the hall. As I did so, I heard the all-too-familiar commotion coming from his room. Nurses and doctors sprang into action. People with carts and equipment rushed into the room. I pressed myself against the wall and tried not to listen. I knew what was coming.

"What happened? I was only gone ten minutes. That's my grandson, please help him!" The woman from before went running in behind them. She was crying between her pleadings to the doctors. They told her to stand back and leave the room, but she wouldn't.

The distance between each beep became less far apart. The doctors raised their voices and shouted multiple commands at a time.

"His heart's failing," I heard in a low but distinct voice.

I headed down the hallway, but feeling a tug on my arm, turned, expecting to see the woman, but saw no one. I closed my eyes, trying to drown out the noise, scared. I had my back against the wall and slid to the floor.

My eyes were shut tight and when I opened them, something intrinsic had changed. Everything around me appeared in a green tint, almost dreamy and dark. I watched myself get up, leaving my physical body behind and walked right into that little boy's room. The ongoing commotion was nothing more than a blur of conversation; no words were audible, and everything seemed slower. I approached his bed and observed them as they worked on him. No one noticed my presence. The doctors' frustration was palpable as the boy's life-force began to fade. I watched them glance discreetly at the grandmother as they worked. She stood with her eyes to the ceiling praying. Eventually, each doctor slowed down and stepped back as they realized one by one that their efforts were futile. They all stood back and glanced at the grandmother who still had her head toward the ceiling praying. They averted their gaze.

"Call it."

Suddenly I sensed someone observing me. I glanced across the bed and saw the little boy standing next to it. He was like a ghost. He had his hand on the rail and was leaned over to contemplate his own lifeless body on the bed. He raised his head to meet my gaze, smiled, and gave me a small wave. I was taken aback by his recognition. He then crossed to his grandmother, seemingly passing right through the doctors, as they attempted to console her. He put his hand on her shoulder and leaned in to whisper something in her ear at the same time pointing at me as if the woman could hear him. She gave a slight nod of her head.

I glanced down at the bed where his body lay and reached out my hand, I needed to touch him. I needed to know if he was really there, or if I was trapped in some sort of dream. As my hand was inches from his chest, an explosion of energy rushed through my body to my hand. It was a bright green light that created a shock wave in the room and knocked everyone backward.

I blinked. I was no longer in the room, but back in the hallway, sitting on the floor exactly as before. There was no longer a green tint to the world. It had resumed to its former appearance. My head was spinning, there was an immense amount of pain leaving my body. It felt as if poisonous blood was being drained from my heart. It took several moments for the feeling to pass, and when it was gone, it was gone.

I looked down the hall toward the room, hearing nothing at first; then a commotion, but not like the earlier commotion. People were rushing to the room from all parts of the hospital wing. Some left again cheering, crying, and hugging each other. I heard many of them say:

"It's a miracle!"

I stood up, glanced back one final time. I then ran out of that hospital. I ran down the stairs, ran out the door, ran all the way home.

I finished my story, and the doctor sat quietly. She didn't look at me. She twirled her pen in circular motion. I began to wonder if she knew that part of the story was over.

"You mentioned it felt like a dream," she said.

"Yes."

"Can you be sure that it really happened? You mentioned watching yourself, a kind of dissociation, in which you questioned the reality of the situation. This memory . . . is it real?"

I sat back for a moment contemplating her question.

"I can't be sure."

"I think that's enough for today," she said, still not looking at me. She summoned my escorts to take me back to my room without another word.

As they ushered me out, I kept my eyes on the doctor. She glanced at me for just a second. I couldn't discern the expression on her face. It was one I had never seen before. I think part of her wanted to believe me, but I think she, like me, was also filled with doubt.

The days passed slowly that week, in my small cell. The doctor canceled our other appointment, causing me to become nervous. I felt over-exposed to her. I had told her things I had never told anyone else. I feared she would use those things against me; how I was unsure. I became extremely irritated. That afternoon, I was once again greeted by the medication dispenser.

She was always quiet. She came to my room multiple times a week and never said much. She just checked on me, more than any other dispenser had before. Every time she entered, I gave her the 'I'm still here' expression. She would smile slightly and bow her head.

At the end of the week, she appeared to have something on her mind. Something she wanted to tell me.

"You alright?" I asked, assuming she wanted me to ask.

She moved her hair behind her ear. She had an expression of innocence about her that was unnerving to me.

"Nothing."

"Nothing?"

"I just heard . . ."

"Heard what?" I asked.

"Heard things about you," she said, not looking at me.

"And . . ."

"I just find it hard to believe. You don't seem like that kind of person; you seem different."

"Hmm," was all I could think to say, wondering what she could have possibly heard that was unbelievable. I had my suspicions.

"What's different about me?" I asked.

"I don't know. I'm just pretty good at reading people, and I don't get a violent or malicious energy from you," she said.

"Is that right?" I asked and stood up. I was much taller than her; she took a step back.

"You say that you don't believe what they say, yet you back away," I said, observing every nuance of her movement and expression.

"Habit," she said.

"Huh," I said and took several steps toward her, this time she held her ground, but appeared nervous.

"How do you read people?"

"I don't know I'm just sensitive to the energy they give off. Around here it can be very intrusive," there was a look of stress on her face.

"Maybe you're just not looking close enough," I grabbed her hand quickly before she could pull away.

She tugged back and glanced toward the door debating whether to call out. I grasped her wrist and moved her hand to the middle of my chest. Her palm flat against where my heart would be.

"Nothing beats between these walls anymore. Everything you heard. Guess what?" I let go of her wrist, giving a sarcastic laugh, "It's all true."

She stepped back quickly and began rubbing her wrist. I turned my back toward her and moved toward my bed, pleased with myself.

"You're wrong," she said, taking a deep breath. "Something is there."

I turned to face her. She continued to rub her wrist.

"It's painful . . . it's powerful . . . like it's caged up, but when it escapes . . ."

"I'd be scared to see that day," I said with a mild laugh.

"You'd be crazy not to be scared of what's inside you," she said and walked away.

Chapter Six: Magnets

My doctor eventually returned to our regular sessions as if nothing unusual had happened. She insisted on picking up right where we had left off. I appreciated getting back to where we were, it seemed I was finally starting to understand some things. Things I didn't even realize the first time I lived my own story. These few years had given me a different perspective on so much. Things that seemed normal, or exciting at the time, made me realize I should have known all along what was going on. The evidence was right there in front of my face, and I was blinded by my naivety. To relive some events and realize what they really were also brought a sick feeling to my stomach, and sometimes it made me wish I was never able to remember anything. However, there are still pieces missing that I need. Till I can collect all the parts, I must keep going.

"So, how did you and Peyton become so close?"

"It was the weirdest thing, like some sort of cosmic connection. We were just obsessively drawn to each other, like magnets. We were more than friends, more than lovers –"

"Were you two lovers?" she asked in a parental, questioning tone.

"Aha no, we were not," I said to be very clear.

"So, you had no attraction to her?"

"Of course I did. I won't deny that. But I had no intention of approaching her in that manner. I cared too much for her, and I knew she deserved better. I loved her. I did. I gave her everything I could without going to that place. It was like I felt a line between us, and if I ever got too close to the other side, I felt that it was unsafe for her."

"You two spent a lot of time together?"

"Every possible minute, at least at first. I figured after the accident we would go our separate ways. I didn't expect anything from her. She had her life she lived with the world, and I had my life I lived with myself, but she went looking for me."

"She went looking for you?" the doctor was surprised.

"Yeah, I know. I was surprised myself. She was right though. No one really knew her. She wasn't just the attractive, popular girl who everyone wanted to be or be with. In fact, compared to what she really was, none of that stuff even mattered."

"What do you mean?"

* * *

I sat in my living room watching TV as everyone else got ready for the night. My brother waited on the stairs impatiently, shoes tied and ready to go. The carnival was in town and tonight they were all heading out. My mom, dad, and little brother were going, but not me.

It's not that I didn't enjoy their company or even the carnival for that matter. Something in me just didn't fancy a family night tonight. Everyone had heard the story about the accident, and I had done rather well flying under the radar and avoided drawing attention to myself, and it seemed to be working. I told them I wanted to stay in; they fought me a little, but gave in eventually. Everyone in the town went every year. It was a big thing. My parents were heading down the stairs, doing their final checks before leaving.

"Let's gooooo," my brother pleaded in his most impatient and whiny voice. For a ten-year-old, at times he still behaved like a very young child.

"We're leaving," My mother said, as she continued to gather her things.

"Ughhhhh," he sighed as loud as humanly possible.

There was a knock at the door. I continued sitting on the couch watching TV.

"Are we expecting someone?" my mom said looking toward the door.

My dad said, "I got it."

I half listened in, wondering who it could possibly be.

"Hello?" my dad says almost as if he was answering a phone. I couldn't hear what the other person was saying.

"Dani? Yeah uh . . . let me go get her," my dad said. I found this confusing because I never had people looking for me. My dad walked into the living room with his thumb pointing toward the door.

"That girl we gave a ride home from the hospital is here for you . . . Peyton, right?"

Without thinking, I sprang up off the couch so fast I got a major head rush.

"What? Here? Why?" I was confused.

"Well, I don't know. Why don't you go ask her?" he suggested.

"Yeah," I said standing there nodding my head at my dad, "yeah I should."

I still stood there.

"What are you waiting for, a written invitation?" my dad asked perplexed.

"She didn't —" I started.

"Just go get the door," my dad said, suppressing a laugh.

I went slowly, thinking he had maybe confused her with someone else. I checked myself to see if I was wearing anything ridiculous. Nothing bad: hooded jacket, jeans, eh the usual, nothing crazy. I opened the door, and indeed, it was Peyton. I stared for a second. She looked amazing, casual, but very nice. She too, wore a jacket, and jeans, but made them look much better than I did.

"Uh, hi," she said.

I then realized I hadn't said anything when I opened the door.

"Hi, are you feeling alright?" I said, immediately thinking that was dumb.

"Uh yeah, I'm good. You?"

"I'm good, just really good. Were you looking for me or —" I asked still somewhat confused.

"I was. I was just thinking about, you know, what happened and, well not really, but I was . . ." She trailed off. "Do you want to go to the carnival with me and some friends?"

"The carnival?" I said, almost laughing. She sighed and smiled.

"Don't tell me you're too old for it?"

"Dani isn't going to the carnival, cause she said there are too many people there and —" my brother began shouting loudly from behind me, I quickly closed the door.

"He was dropped as a child a lot," I said. This made Peyton laugh.

"I wasn't planning on going. My family is about to go," I said wanting to be honest.

"Oh, that's totally cool, I just didn't know. I mean I hear people go every year. I heard it's kind of a tradition around here, but of course, you know that. Why am I still talking?" she began to look embarrassed.

"You know what? Let's go. I'll grab some money and I'll be right out," I said. She gave a look of relief.

"Okay."

I ran upstairs grabbed, my stuff, and bolted down again.

"Hey, I'm going with Peyton to the carnival," I called to my parents.

"She gets to go before we go?" my brother said in disbelief.

"I thought you weren't going?" My mom asked in a sarcastic tone. She observed my expression of impatience, "Be back by midnight."

I almost ran out the door, slowing before I got there. I was excited. I seldom went out with friends. Not that I didn't have any friends. I just wasn't very social. Most of my free time I spent doing nothing, rather than hanging out. This was perhaps why I didn't have any close friends. This was even more unusual because Peyton was well known throughout the school.

That last thought coursed through my head. Why would she want to hang out with me? Was this some sort of prank? Or maybe she felt she owed me something for my parents giving her a ride home. Maybe her parents put her up to it. These thoughts made me uneasy, but it was all I could think of. Something didn't add up.

"Ready?" she said as I opened the door.

"Ready."

The carnival was a good thirty-minute walk from my house. For the first several minutes, nothing was said between us. I was so trapped in my head about why she was there; thinking of every possible explanation.

"I like your new hair style. It suits you," she said sincerely.

"Thanks."

"Why do you look so worried Danielle? Don't tell me you're scared of rides," she said with a small laugh.

"Huh? No, not really. I mean some," I said.

"Oh, good, cause I'm deathly scared of rides."

"What? Really?"

"Yes, quite scared, but I'm willing to take the risk," she said with determination. "Your family, they seem really nice."

"They are, they're good people," I said.

"You're lucky."

"Yeah . . ." I didn't know how else to reply. "Why did you come to my house?"

"What do you mean?" she almost seemed as if she wanted to avoid the question.

"Like, I don't know. Why did you come over tonight?"

"I just felt like it, I wanted to see you. I mean, we did have a near-death experience together, remember?"

"How could I forget, I think normally those come with a few scars."

"Ha ha, yeah, so I thought as well," she was quiet for a second. " That stuff that I told you. You didn't tell anyone, did you?"

"About you? No, of course not. Is that why you came?" I asked, thinking I had made a breakthrough.

"Oh my gosh, Danielle, no. Is it so hard to believe that I just want to hang out with you?"

"Well, kind of," I said, honestly.

"It's just, what happened to us, and the stuff I told you, I've never had that kind of conversation with anyone, and definitely not that experience. I just can't think of anyone else I can be completely honest with and expect them to keep it between just us. For some strange reason, I have that feeling with you. I don't even know why

I told you what I did, I just felt like I didn't have to hold anything back; like I knew that you would never betray me."

I walked quietly for a second thinking about her words.

"You're right," I said, stopping. She stopped too, and looked straight into my eyes, "I would never do that. Plus, I don't have any friends to tell, so you're lucky." My words lightened the mood. She laughed and gave me a slight slap on the arm.

We eventually arrived at the carnival; it remained all it had been for years, smaller, but the same. We paid for our tickets and headed in. It was packed with hundreds of people. Pretty much the entire town made it out for this significant occasion. You could smell the funnel cakes being made, and the various animal aromas, and see the dirt kick up and move in the breeze as crowds trekked through. The rides lit up the area with a multitude of colors that danced in the darkness. We zig-zagged in and out of people heading nowhere specific. Then, we ran into Peyton's friends from school. It was the three girls from outside at the bus.

"Peyton!" they screamed in unison.

"Hey guys," she responded.

"Oh my God, where have you been?" Bailey asked.

I'd figured out from school, the dark one with green eyes was Alicia. The one with brown hair was Bailey, and the short blonde was Patricia.

"Yeah, we haven't seen you since the accident," said Patricia.

"Trish, you can't just say shit like that, she might be traumatized," said Bailey, "But really, where've you been?"

"Just laying low, recovering and whatnot," said Peyton.

"So you're okay then?"

"Yeah."

"Well, let's have some fun. Oh, shit, there's a party tonight, at the Stevens boys' house, and I know Abel's been asking about you like crazy, girl. Can't let him hang around too long, I might have to scoop him up," said Bailey, flippantly.

"Or his brother!" this was Trish.

"Trish, he wouldn't want you, he's like six feet tall, you would need a ladder just to get up there to kiss him," said Bailey.

"Whatever, bitch, he'd probably just think I was the perfect height to give him something else," she replied with a sexual tone. This made everyone laugh, even me. I was surprised how openly they talked to each other. I would never say anything like that. I was still in the phase where I didn't tell people who I liked.

"Who's this," asked Alicia speaking for the first time, performing a roundabout point at me. I looked at other things, hoping she wasn't talking about me.

"This is Danielle, the one who was with me from the accident," said Peyton.

"Ohhhh," they once again said in unison.

"So, you ran into each other here or . . ." asked Alicia.

"No, I went to her house and got her and brought her here."

"All right, just asking," Alicia replied with her hands up in an offensive gesture.

"I love your hair!" said Trish, grabbing my arm and smiling. "It's so cool. Who did it?"

"Oh," her words embarrassed me and I ran my hand through it. "I did."

"Fun!" she said with a big smile, "Do you think you can help me dye my hair, see I have this thing where—-"

"Trish, she doesn't even know you. She's not going to dye your damn hair," said Bailey in her commanding attitude that I was already growing tired of.

"Whateverrrr, Bailey, you don't know," she said, mouthing 'we'll talk' to me. I laughed and winked at her.

"So, party, or what later?" said Alicia.

"Yeah, totally, after the carnival?" asked Peyton.

"Well yeah, they're actually here now, so I don't know when they're getting started, but probably late.

"We should have a party at your house, Peyton!" said Trish.

"Ha ha, maybe someday," said Peyton with a look indicating she didn't think that was a good idea.

"Well, let's go take on some rides," said Bailey.

We all headed in the direction of the activity; they crowded around Peyton in a circle as they walked. I followed behind just outside the circle. I tried to glance over their shoulders and listen in on the conversation, but I began to realize it didn't concern me. Distance began to be created between us and as the group continued walking, I lagged further behind. Bailey looked back at me, noticing I wasn't keeping pace with the group, then quickly averted her attention back to the conversation.

A loneliness crawled under my skin, and sadness sank in. Should I try to catch up to them? I felt as if I didn't belong and out of place. No, I didn't fit in with them.

I had the option of just heading home, but I needed to clear my head so I remained at the carnival for a long time, figuring I would eventually run into my parents and they could give me a ride home, or I could just walk if I didn't find them. I passed many booths, and could only smile at all the convincing calls from the people running them. They eased my racing thoughts.

"Hey, good looking, you look like luck is on your side tonight."

"Why don't you win something for your beautiful girlfriend?"

"Show us how strong you really are."

There were also booths selling goods: clothing, toys, jewelry, sunglasses, and much more. I noticed a small booth selling jewelry and feigned interest. I only had ten dollars, so it was unlikely I would be able to buy anything till I could hit my parents up for more cash if I ever ran into them.

There was a small, purple tent, with a light inside, and a hanging wooden sign stating 'Psychic Readings $5'.

I listened covertly to a couple of readings. They weren't done as you would expect: by an old wrinkly lady. It was a middle-aged woman, with long black hair, and eyes so blue they were not concealed by the darkness. I figured she had to be wearing contacts, for a more intense effect.

Two boys sat inside the tent. I recognized them from school; they were both tall, one with a near perfect muscular build, tanned skin, light brownish blondish hair and a great smile. He was obviously an athlete. The other was tall and thin with equally significant features, glasses, dark brown hair, but much lighter skin.

"Okay, tell me how many times I will get laid this year," says the athletic one.

"Ha ha, boys, it doesn't work like that, I cannot tell you your future to a T, I can just tell you what is suggested based on your current outlook."

"What? I wanna know who gets more girls?" he replied. The reader sighed.

"Three and two," She said pointing from the muscular one then to the thinner one.

"Oh yeah?" he said, raising his hands above his head.

"Yes, isn't that great . . . perhaps I should also inform you that there's going to come a point in this next year when someone will need you to be there for them and if you are not . . . the consequences will be severe."

"She's going to need me like sexually," he retorted sarcastically and began laughing.

"Abel, really dude?" said the other as he half pushed him off his seat, "Let's get out of here. Thank you for your time, ma'am."

He fumbled for his wallet and pulled out a twenty, "Please keep the change."

They begin to leave, and she grabbed the arm of the boy wearing glasses. "Do be your brother's keeper. His unborn child's life depends on him being there when he is most needed."

He turned around, clearly bewildered, while the other boy seemed to not hear what the woman had just said, and dragged his friend away, back into the crowd. I was quite entertained by the reader and thought there might be some more interesting things to see around the carnival. I started to leave then heard something behind me.

"You," I turned around to see who the woman was talking to; she stepped out of the tent and was staring right at me.

"You're here. Huh, that's ironic, I wasn't expecting you, not yet. Come inside."

The woman beckoned me inside. I went in slowly. I was happy I had ten dollars because I think she was expecting me to get a reading. Inside, the tent was like a whole new world. The noise outside seemed to fade to insignificance. I wondered how I had ever heard the conversation that had just ensued. I sat across from her on a fluffy pillow, legs crossed, taking everything in. Smoke filled the tent from burning incense; the smell was intoxicating and relatively nice. It was comfortable inside. The woman seated herself on a small stool and stared across at me. I noticed she had several tattoos covering her arms; they were quite exquisite. In spite of being inside the tent, she lit a cigarette which filled the air with more smoke. She stared at me from the corner of her eye.

"Do I pay by the minute?" I asked, thinking my money would run out fast, at this rate, "'Cause, I only have five dollars."

"You come with many questions," she said without looking at me.

"Is there something I'm supposed to know?" I played along with the charade.

"There are so many things I can tell you right now, but I fear what effect they will have on your perception of this life. I can tell you this: I know that you will suffer more than you already have. This will be the worst year of your life, and I don't think you are prepared to deal with it emotionally. It is going to break you, and your recovery is undetermined."

"Wow. I thought you were supposed to tell me that riches awaited me," I said, feeling let down.

"I'm sure that's not what your great-grandmother told you."

I snapped my head up so fast I think I pulled a muscle.

"What?" I said rubbing the back of my neck.

"You know what I speak of. I fear just being in the same room with you. I felt the same way when I was around her, but I couldn't resist. You guys are two of a kind, and a bane to the psychic community. You see, when you step into my world it's a rush, your emotions run unbounded through this room, like a wildfire. They speak for themselves when you are silent."

"Are you the same way?"

"Ha, heavens no, I mean I have my gift, for most, it's like a whisper in your ear, and you just, know what is coming. For you, your life is screaming at me," she raised her hands to her temples, "it's almost deafening."

"What's wrong with me?"

"Nothing yet. You've barely scratched the surface of this thing you have going on inside you. It's strong and all-consuming. If you let it, it will take control of your life. You can hurt, you can heal, you can kill."

"Kill?" I repeated, laughing to myself in disbelief. "I don't think anything could make me go to that sort of extreme."

"Have you ever been in love?" she asked, "Believe me, it will take you there. Hate is not the opposite of love, no. Hate is so much like love the two are basically two halves of a whole. The worst kinds of hatred come out of a place where there once was love."

I was perplexed yet intrigued by this comment. My mind slowly processed it as I tried to remain present in the conversation.

"I just don't want to hurt anyone," I said trying to choose my words more carefully.

"Oh, I know you don't want to, but if you can't constrain it after it gets control of you, you'll be helpless."

"You sound a lot like my great-grandmother, you know that?"

"Well, we were friends. Although she might not agree with that definition," she said, "Look in that address book you have for Jasmine Thine. I'm in there, page four third from the top. She came to me regularly, looking for answers, looking for a light that was never there."

"I don't think we're all that alike," I said decisively.

"Well, you hardly knew her. A visit once a year, that's an acquaintance, not a relationship."

"So, what's coming next? What am I supposed to prepare for?" I was becoming irritated and impatient.

"Have you seen your shadow yet?"

"Uh yeah, I generally see it every day . . ."

"Oh my goodness, child, that's not what I'm talking about."

"Then no. Why are you asking me? Shouldn't you know already?" I ask in faux concern. She laughed as she exhaled her cigarette smoke.

"Two of a kind, you know– " she shook her head, then stopped abruptly, "Oh, you lie."

I felt myself grow tense.

"You have seen it . . . twice." she looked at me in surprise.

"But you're so young. The second one you felt an obligation for, but the first . . . the first you felt something else. A girl?" she asked with a raised eyebrow. I shrugged my shoulders, unwilling to elaborate. She smiled, stubbed out her cigarette while blowing out the smoke, and immediately lit another one.

"Must be some girl, what are the odds?" she said facing me directly and getting closer, "The day of the accident. Something unusual happened to you?"

"Yeah, it was so weird, like the world stopped and everything had this like purple tint to it."

"You mean blue."

"Blue? No, like purple."

"Like purple, or was it purple?"

"It was purple," I asserted, humored by her interest. She accidentally dropped her cigarette, but immediately retrieved it while brushing ash from her clothes.

"Why did you save her?"

"I don't know," I said, "I felt . . . something."

I shook my head not really knowing how to explain it to her.

"A connection?"

"Yeah, she said she felt something too."

"And right now you think that she doesn't care about you," she said and scrutinized my reaction. I was sure she didn't care.

"You're wrong, she cares and the awareness she sensed between you will always be there, for reasons I believe are not my responsibility to divulge. With you two, though it is different, there's more. Your shadow . . . it's so unusual," she said, but offered no further explanation, "You think she doesn't understand, but she does. She's going to bring you a world of hope and a world of pain."

"I don't think I'll be seeing her anytime soon," I said.

"You will, but listen to me now. That voice you hear in your head, whispering to you about that girl; whatever you do, don't ever act upon it. It will get more persistent every day. Not that I have a problem with people's lifestyle choices, I don't. I can feel your energy toward her, it's strong now, and as much good as you may want to do, you always have to understand you can cause that much pain to a person. Don't take her down with you."

"I don't think that's going to be a problem," I said, only half understanding what she was talking about.

"You'll come across all kinds of people in your journey through life," she said.

"People like me?"

"I suppose it's possible but unlikely. I was referring to an assortment of different personalities. You have readers like me, not rare, but not common. Then you have the 'intuitive,' these people are unpredictable, I'm not even sure if their art is real. They are said to feel people's energy; be able to tell how dark someone's soul really is. Then there're parasites, as I call them. These are the individuals that feed off of the goodness inside others. They are the worst, nearly impenetrable by your abilities; they can suck the life right out of you. I do not recommend using your 'talents' on these people. You have a lot more to lose than they do. See, everyone has some sort of gift, and in the presence of a dual soul it becomes magnified — "

"Dual soul?" I repeated.

"Yes. Did your grandmother tell you anything?"

"Well she gave me her journals — " I began.

"Oh, see that outlines a lot for you — "

"But I didn't actually get them," I said.

"You mean you don't have them?"

"Nope."

"Unbelievable. Okay, well a dual soul, you, for example, has the ability to project their soul. I call it a mirrored spirit."

"I'm confused," I said.

"Have you ever heard the old wives' tale that you should not let an infant see its own reflection?"

"I think so, or they'll be conceited or something?"

"So they say now, but it stems from the belief that if an infant sees their reflection, a portion of their soul will remain in their reflection, thus splitting their soul into two parts. As a result, they would develop a fondness for their own reflection, leading to the assumption that they are conceited."

"Okay," I said struggling to keep up.

"This is obviously not true, although it will help me explain. You are like a mirrored soul, except there is no absolute divide. Your soul is split, but it can embody itself as one when necessary. It can escape the body when necessary. It can get up and leave when it desires, but it rarely acts as one vessel. Normally, the personalities of the two parts of your soul are night and day. Typically split into good and evil, love and hate, et cetera. See, with everyone else, the body cannot typically survive without the soul for a long time. It's not impossible for one's soul to leave the body temporarily. For example, when people have 'out of body experiences,' their soul leaves the body to protect itself, however, this does not keep the body from being damaged. You can. When your soul leaves the body, it is impervious to the environment. Such was the case with your 'accident.' Though your body should have been mutilated, you remained unharmed. People who meditate can train their soul to leave the body. They say it's enlightening; I view it as dangerous. Then, there're people who can do astral projection. I'm not too clear on the specifics of their gift, but fundamentally their soul leaves their body and wanders around, but remains tethered to their body. Their body cannot function without their soul. They claim to experience some quite literally 'out of this world' encounters."

"Whoa, this is a lot," I said feeling my imagination running wild, "So you're saying I have special powers?"

"I guess you could use that terminology," she replied.

"Well, what else can I do? And how do I use them?"

"It's not like learning your ABCs or building a house."

"But how do I deliberately make it happen when I want it to?"

"It's something I cannot explain to you. Let me put it this way," she took a long drag of her cigarette and exhaled. "Pretend for a second that this smoke is your emotions, it floats around, takes no specific shape, and is difficult to contain. Now, sometimes I can manipulate the smoke."

As she spoke, she cut through the center of the smoke cloud. She then put the cigarette to her lips, inhaled once more, and blew three perfect smoke rings.

"Sometimes I can manipulate it very well, but what you're basically asking me to show you, is how to turn this smoke into a flower. It's impossible, yet somehow you have the ability to do it. All I know is that it is, in simple terms, a physical manifestation of your emotions. That's why your biggest concern should be learning to control them. What are you capable of? Well, no two people feel things the same way, so no one really knows. For all I know, you could have the ability to fly. The only consistency is the 'rules' your great-grandmother came up with, and we see how well they served her. She imprisoned herself to protect the world."

"So . . ." I began but trailed off, not being able to think of my next question.

"That is it. You have dual souls like you, you have parasites, readers like me, the ' intuitive,' and of course 'believers,' an interesting species."

"How do you mean?"

"They don't necessarily have powers per se. Their faith is their power."

"Faith?"

"Yes they believe relentlessly in God," she said.

"Well, isn't that a lot of people?"

She laughed out loud at this.

"Few and far between, actually. Believers, real believers, well, they are the ones with faith so strong they could walk on water if instructed to do so. The woman in the hospital, the color you saw was green, am I right?"

"Yes."

"Of course it was, see green is when you are being used as a catalyst for their power. They have the power, you have the machine that makes it work."

"So what does purple mean?"

"I wish I knew. Your great-grandmother never spoke of this color. Just red, blue, green, orange, and yellow."

"So, if there are believers does that mean God is real?" I asked curiously.

"Don't be foolish child, of course she's real," she said. I was confused by her choice of words but didn't care to question them at the time.

She gave me a wink and appeared to be done talking. I took this as a chance to leave and dropped my money on the small wooden table that lay between us.

Once outside the tent, I had to adjust to the surrounding sounds. Everything seemed much louder from before.

"Danielle!" I heard a voice call. I looked around and eventually saw Peyton and her crew hurrying toward me.

"Hey," I responded.

"Where did you go? I've been looking for you," she asked. I watched as Bailey rolled her eyes dramatically.

"I was just looking around," I replied.

"Well, I came here to hang out with you, so don't go running off again," Peyton replied with a sound relief, "Unless, of course, you don't want to hang out with me?"

"No, of course I do," I said.

"Good," Peyton said with a smirk.

"Hey ladies," interrupted the boy who had been talking with the psychic, accompanied by his friend.

"Abel!" said Bailey and Trish in unison.

"Hey Abel," said Peyton.

"What are you guys up to? Peyton, I haven't seen you in forever, are you feeling okay," he asked, seeming genuinely concerned.

"I'm okay, just got a little banged up."

"Well, it's really good to see you," he said giving her one of those gorgeous model smiles.

"You too," she said, returning his smile. "Danielle, this is Abel and his twin brother Cain. Guys, this is my friend Danielle."

"What's up," said Abel.

"Nice to meet you," Cain said, sticking out his hand to shake mine. He was obviously the 'gentleman' of the pair.

"Nice to meet you too," I said.

"So, you guys going to come to the party tonight?" asked Abel.

"Yeah, of course, totally," chorused the other three girls.

"Yeah, I don't know. I'm kind of tired, I was just going to hang out here a while then head home," said Peyton.

"Oh, come on! You gotta come. I'm throwing it just for you!" Abel joked.

"Nah, not tonight."

"Well, at least you can go on a couple rides with me then," said Abel, encompassing Peyton in another smile. Everyone was looking at her. "Yeah, of course."

"Sweet," Abel grabbed her hand, anxious to take her away, "We'll catch up with y'all later."

She pulled back for a second, "Danielle, meet me here in a half-hour?"

"Oh, sure," I said.

We were all left standing around, unsure what to say.

"Sooo Cain, are you still with that girl?" Trish asked, eventually.

"Uh, what girl?" Cain appeared confused.

"Oh, no one. So you're single?" She batted her eyelashes at him.

"Very," was all he said, then changed the subject. "So Danielle, how do you know Peyton?"

He had switched his attention toward me, catching me off guard.

"Oh, uh, we met the day of the accident," I had no idea how else to explain it.

"No way, are you the one who was with her?" he pressed.

"Yeah . . ." I said, not really wanting to get into details. Thankfully, he didn't pry further.

"Wow, yeah, I bet you guys will be inseparable. I've seen you around school for years, I just didn't know anything about you. We had geometry together sophomore year."

"Oh, yeah, that's right," I was surprised he would remember something like that.

Once again, Bailey began rolling her eyes. Trish appeared to be waiting for a moment to say something.

"I had geometry too." clearly, this was the best she could contribute.

"Oh yeah, with Miss G?" Cain asked.

"Oh, no, but I had it," she professed with a wide smile.

"Ugh, come on, I'm bored, let's go get something to eat," said Alicia. Bailey took Trish's hand, dragging her away.

"Oh, okay. Bye, Cain. See you later," she said, waving.

"Bye," he said, returning her wave. "She's nice."

"Yeah, I think so too."

"Bailey on the other hand," he laughed, "She can be unpleasant . . ."

"Yeah, I would have to agree."

"I like your hair, by the way, it looks great," he said as we began making our way around the carnival.

"Oh, thanks," it was weird engaging in a near flirtatious conversation with a boy, but Cain seemed so kind-hearted, it was impossible not to like him.

"Looks like my brother finally got to Peyton," he said, "He's been talking about her since she came into town last year."

"It seems that way," I agreed.

"Are you with anyone?" he asked candidly.

"Ha, uh . . . no."

"I feel for you on that. I feel like I'm never going to find someone," he said.

"Well, Trish just loves you, apparently a lot of girls do," I said, thinking he really couldn't find it that surprising.

"Really? Hmmm. I guess you never really know if people notice you until they say something."

"Yeah," I said, wondering if I should have said what I had about Trish, maybe it was a secret. I suddenly felt nervous. I didn't want to be perceived as the person who couldn't keep a secret.

"Don't worry, I won't tell her you told me," he promised. "You look worried."

"Thank you," I said with relief.

"It's good to see Peyton hanging out with more down-to-earth people and not just space cadets," he said laughing.

"Yeah, who knew," I replied thinking it was somewhat unbelievable for someone on the outside looking in.

We sauntered around a few more times before we wound up back where we started and found Peyton and Abel waiting for us.

"Hey," Abel called, waving his arms as if we might have difficulty spotting him. We joined them.

"Hey, it looks like it's going to rain, you want to head home?" Peyton asked.

"Oh, yeah, sounds good," I hadn't expected to head home together since our homes weren't exactly close to each other.

"Wait, where's your car? We can give you guys a ride home," Abel offered.

"Thanks, but I think we'll just walk," she said, "It was good seeing you."

"All right, well if you change your mind about the party tonight, swing by."

"For sure," Peyton said with a nod. "Ready?" she asked me.

"Yup," I said, then turned back to Cain, "It was nice meeting you, see you around."

"Definitely, it was nice meeting you too," he said, smiling. Abel was clearly puzzled.

Peyton and I left the carnival and started heading homeward.

"Sorry about my friends, and getting caught up in conversation with them," she said.

"It's okay."

"And sorry about leaving you."

"That's okay too."

"And sorry —" she started.

"Don't worry about it. I had fun," I interrupted, smiling.

"So I see, seems like Cain took a liking to you."

"And Abel to you."

"Yeah . . ."

"Do you like him?" I asked, curious because she didn't seem to care for him at all.

"He's nice, he's good looking. I just have other stuff going on and I don't know if I'm ready for all that," she said.

"Well, maybe it's better to not go through stuff alone," I suggested.

Peyton smiled and slipped her arm through mine.

"That's what you're here for."

It occurred to me we weren't taking the quick way home; we were following the route that passed through the park. It was secluded at this hour. Then, rain drops started falling.

"We should find some cover," I said as the rain started coming down harder.

"What's wrong? It's just water," she extended her hand to catch some. I didn't know how to respond to that.

"All right," I said shrugging my shoulders.

It quickly began to pour. Peyton stretched out her arms making sure as many rain drops fell on her as possible. We became drenched in minutes. Like a child, Peyton began jumping through every puddle.

"Come on," she said grabbing my hand. She led me to one of the park's playgrounds. Letting go of my hand, she ran up the ladder to one of the slides, and slid down, creating small waves as she descended. It looked like fun. She began ascending the ladder again, and when she reached the top, she waved for me to follow. I reluctantly climbed the ladder. It was actually a really high slide that swirled as it went down. There wasn't much room at the top. When I joined her, there was little space between us, so I was able to get a good look at her. She was drenched. Her hair had become wavy and stuck to parts of her face. She didn't wear much makeup, which was good because the little eyeliner she was wearing had run slightly. Her hoody was unzipped, and her T-shirt had become see through, which I tried not to notice. It seemed she didn't notice and didn't care.

"Your turn," she said smiling.

"Uh . . ." I started.

"Go," she said, pushing me forward. I sat down on the slide and slid down. It was a mini-rush on the way down, similar to a water slide. I came to a stop at the bottom, realizing I wanted to do it again. Then, suddenly I felt Peyton's body smack against my back, hitting our heads together and knocking us both off the end of the slide. She fell on top of me laughing hysterically. I laughed too.

"What were you doing?" she said still laughing, "You're supposed to get out of the way."

"Oh," I said on my back, laughing.

I glanced toward the merry-go-round thinking that would be fun. Peyton caught my glance and began to get up to run toward it. I grabbed her, pushed her back toward the slide, and began running.

"Oh, hell no!" I heard her laughing from behind me. She caught up to me in no time and plopped down on it first.

"Track star baby," she said winking, "You push first."

"What?" I said laughing but impressed.

The merry-go-round was a big circle that had bars extending from the end toward the middle for kids to run around and hang on to.

I grabbed one side and began running around it as fast as possible, trying to make her dizzy. When it began to slow, I jumped on the side, throwing it off balance slightly, but it still continued to spin rapidly. She laughed as I jumped on and leaned her head back.

"Your turn," I said as it slowed to a stop. She got off and commenced running around it as fast as she could, which was obviously faster than I managed. I felt dizzy almost instantly. It began to slow down. I saw Peyton grab it with both hands, and jump up, but her foot slipped. She took a nasty fall, right on her butt.

I stopped the ride as fast as I could.

"Are you okay!" I asked, worried. She was laughing again.

"I'm fine, oh man, I forgot . . . It's raining!"

"Are you sure you're okay?"

"Wait," she said clutching her ankle, "I think I twisted something, oh man."

She looked to be in pain.

"Oh man, you're going to have to carry me home," she said, extending an arm.

"I don't think I can carry you. Should I call someone?"

"No, no, no, just here," she said beckoning me with her hand, "My house is like a block away from here, just give me a piggy back ride."

"Oh, okay," I tried to help her up, as she avoided putting pressure on her ankle. I turned around so she could get up. She wrapped her arms around my shoulders and gave a small jump. I caught her legs with my arms and leaned forward. She was exceptionally light, thankfully, because I would have felt bad if I needed to take repeated breaks.

"That way," she whispered into my right ear, as she rested her head on my shoulder, pointing to the road. I felt a chill of nervousness and excitement rush through my body.

Although she was light, and her house wasn't that far, it was still quite exhausting having to carry another person on your back in the rain, soaking wet. It was weird having someone so close in proximity to me. Other than Cindy, I had almost never touched another non-family member. I could tell she was a track star because her legs felt taut against my hands, and her arms gripped tight across my shoulders. She rested her head on my shoulder and I could feel her breath on the back of my neck. In that moment I felt like I could walk five miles.

We arrived at her house in less than ten minutes, and I let her down at her front porch. Her house was massive. Her parents had money, and lots of it. It reminded me of Christian's house, but with class.

"Are your parents going to be mad that I'm here," I asked. Not wanting to wake them up or disturb them, considering I had never met them.

"Um . . . they're not here . . . Actually, they're never here," said Peyton in a sad voice, and looked back at me with an insecure expression as she unlocked the door.

"Oh," I said thinking back to the hospital, how her parents never came for her.

"Yeah," she stepped into her house. It was definitely what you would picture for rich people, chandelier in the entry, huge staircase, beautiful marble, and perfectly clean as if no one lived there. In fact, it was hard to believe anyone did actually live there. There were no family pictures or anything else on the walls. I stood close to the entrance door, not wanting to make tracks in the house.

"Come on," she said starting up the stairs much too quickly.

"Wait a second, I thought your ankle–" she adopted a 'caught in a lie,' expression, and laughed.

"Oh, my God, do you have any idea how exhausting that was?!" I said laughing, but not regretting it.

She ran up the stairs and I followed her. Her room was huge, modeled to fit her, even including its own bathroom. It had trophies for track, pictures of her and her friends, a huge four poster bed.

"This is my room," she said extending her arms.

"Wow," is all I could think to say.

"Yeah. it's something else." She took off her shoes, and hoodie, "I like it?"

"Yeah," I said, thinking I should take off my shoes, too, and followed her lead.

"I think I got some stuff that might fit you," she said, pulling out a pullover, hooded sweater, and some track shorts she obviously used for working out. She handed them to me and continued to undress. She removed her top, and I averted my eyes, till something caught my attention. She had two discolored marks on her sides that extended round to her back. I couldn't avoid staring at them and she noticed immediately.

"You want a closer look?" she asked.

"Oh," I said, shaking my head, "I'm sorry."

"No, really," she came closer to me, "They're my only souvenir from the accident, I'm not really sure what they are. It doesn't hurt, it's just there. They are lighter now."

That piqued my curiosity. As much as I tried, I couldn't drag my eyes away. She approached closer to me, running her hand across the blemishes. Her stomach was perfectly sculpted from running, which also did not escape my attention. The marks looked more like light bruises than scars. She reached down and grabbed my hand and ran it over one of them. They were smooth. I hoped she couldn't feel my hand shaking in hers. As she turned, one went horizontally across her back, the other more vertically reaching just to her neck.

"Crazy right?" she said grabbing a shirt and putting it on, "Do you have one?"

"Uh, no, I don't think so," I said, changing my clothes quickly while her attention was averted.

"Any?" she asked.

"No." I thought it was unusual.

"You're telling me you don't have any scars?"

"Nope," I said.

"Well, I like mine, reminds me of that day."

"I try not to think about it," I said honestly.

"Sometimes it's all I can think about. What do you think really happened to us? Do you think we died?"

"I sure hope not, but this next life doesn't seem so bad if we did."

"No, it's not so bad," she said.

"Well, I guess I should let you sleep, and head home," I said, "Thanks for letting me borrow the clothes."

"Oh yeah, well, I have my car, I can give you a ride home, or you could just stay."

I was left with the distinct impression Peyton feared I would say no. I looked at her, assessing her expression, and noticed a distinct emptiness in her eyes that wasn't apparent before.

"Oh . . . all right, just let me call my parents and let them know."

When I called, my mom answered. "Danielle? Where are you? Are you okay?"

"Yeah, I'm fine, I'm at a friend's house," I said.

"Is it that boy I saw you were talking to at the carnival?" she asked, "He's cute, Dani."

"What? No, why would I be at a boy's house? And if I was why would I tell you? Actually, I'm at Peyton's house. Can I stay the night?"

"Is it okay with her parents?"

"Uh, yeah, they don't care."

"Aw, a sleepover, you never sleep-"

"Is that a yes?" I asked, not wanting my mom to expand on how I have no social life.

"Yes, just call me if you need a ride home," she said.

"Okay, love you, bye," I wanted to get off the phone fast.

I returned to Peyton's room. She was now fully dressed, and halfway dry.

"Yeah, they said I could stay," I said.

"Awesome," she beamed, obviously delighted.

We spent several hours talking and getting to know each other. I enjoyed listening to every story she told, the good and the bad. I just wanted to know everything there was to know about her. We laughed for hours and finally got ready for bed. Her bed was big so there was plenty of room for probably four people.

"Here, you can have one of my pillows," she threw one to my side.

"Man your bed is so nice, I bet people love staying over here," I said, anticipating possibly the best night's sleep ever.

"I wouldn't know. No one else has ever stayed here."

After some time, I fell asleep. In the middle of the night, I felt Peyton back into me and grab my arm and place it around her. I felt her shaking softly against me and could hear her breathing heavily. I wrapped my other arm around her and held her, her body slowly began to relax against mine and she drifted off to sleep.

* * *

"What was it about you that she clung to you so much, you guys really seemed to connect from what you say," Doctor Joy remarked, as she soaked up the story.

"I wish I knew the answer to that," I confessed.

"She seemed to have a lot of issues, I fail to understand what would draw someone in."

"What do you mean?" her words puzzled me.

"She just seems so . . . broken," she replied, appearing almost ashamed at these words.

"Her beauty was in her brokenness," I said.

Dr. Joy paused for a second and looked at me in the most unusual way. I thought I caught a glimpse of admiration, but she quickly broke eye contact and changed the topic.

"And what were her parents like?" she asked, "What did you think of them?"

"I don't see why that matters."

"Indulge me," she said.

"Hmmm, well, I guess I would describe her parents as ungrateful."

"Explain."

"Well, they had everything. A nice home, cars, money. Not that any of that matters, but they had safety and security. They had a family that had the potential to be happy, but they never appreciated it. They always wanted more things, more money. They never even saw each other, never talked to one another. I wouldn't even call them parents. Peyton did everything for herself. I met her father once in a little less than a year, and her mother, well, I never saw her at all. I think she only remained married as a duty. I think she'd found someone else she thought would make her happy. She'll never be happy though."

"What makes you say that?"

"Everything she could ever need to make her happy was waiting for her already at home, but she was too damn blind to see it."

"You said you never met the mother and met the father once. Did you ever stop to think that maybe there were things about them that you didn't know? Perhaps there were things about Peyton that you didn't know either?"

"I knew everything about her," I asserted defensively.

"Just like she knew everything about you?"

This stumped me. It was a circumstance I had never considered.

Chapter Seven:
Everything About You

"Wow, nice place," said Peyton parking in the driveway. I found out after our walk to the carnival that Peyton had a car, a Mercedes. It was beautiful, but it seemed Peyton only drove it when she thought there was no alternative. In fact, she still rode the bus to school; something I went along with but found rather unsettling at times.

"Yup . . ." I said, starting to feel sick to my stomach with anxiety.

"Relax," Peyton said reaching over and giving me a small smack on the arm, "I won't do anything to embarrass you."

"That's not what I'm afraid of."

"My favorite niece!" Christian materialized with his arms outstretched. I still did not enjoy this inside joke but gave him a hug, happy to see him.

"Hi, Christian," I then hugged Cindy. Was it my imagination or did she cling longer than usual? "Hi, Cindy."

"Wow, who is your friend?" Christian asked.

"This is Peyton, my friend from school," I said.

"Hi, nice to meet you guys," Peyton said, shaking both of their hands.

"You're so pretty," Cindy conveyed the smallest hint of bitchiness, that I think only I caught.

"Oh, thank you, you too," said Peyton, glancing over at me momentarily, as if asking how she should interpret that.

Although it lasted only a microsecond, the tension was already starting to get under my skin. People exchanged glances, smiles, nods, handshakes. All the while their mannerisms revealed their hidden undertones.

"Where's Nathan?" Christian asked.

"Oh, he stayed home, he said he wasn't feeling well."

"Oh, that's too bad. I had a whole boy's night planned, so you ladies could hang out. Well, how 'bout we get ready to eat? I'm cooking some steaks tonight, special occasion for our special guest," said Christian.

"Sounds good," I wanted to get inside, separate the energy in this place.

As we entered the house, I exhaled a deep breath. Peyton nudged me.

"What's up with you?"

"Nothing, just feeling a little uneasy," I said fidgeting.

"You seem more than uneasy," her voice communicated concern.

I didn't respond, what could I say? My mind was caught in a weird loop where things weren't processing as they should. I sat down with them in the living room and pretended to watch whatever was on the TV. I tried to focus on one thing, just one thing, but my mind was running wild. It jumped from one thing to another, and then to three things at once. It was starting to become overwhelming. We were staying here all night, so I needed to snap out of it. I noticed Peyton sitting next to me on the couch, trying not to make it obvious that she was glancing over at me, not knowing what to say.

In a flash, I realized what the problem was.

"My medication," I exclaimed, panicking, and reaching into my pockets for my cell phone. I hadn't missed a dose since I'd started taking them almost three months ago.

"What's wrong?" Peyton said.

"I didn't take my medication, I need it," I said dialing my mom's number. "Mom, can you see if my medication's in the kitchen?"

"What?" said my mom, obviously not expecting a question so quickly.

"My medication, is it in the kitchen?" My hands starting to shake as I spoke.

"Yeah, it's here. Why?" she asked.

"Cause I forgot to take it, and I need it."

"Dani, it's past five already, you can miss a dose for once," my mom's voice was unconcerned.

"No, you don't understand. I need it now, mom," I noticed I was becoming more agitated by the second.

"Dani, we're eating dinner, then your brother needs to shower and get ready for bed. Your dad's not here, so I can't just leave," she said.

"What do you mean you can't leave? Just put him in the car. He can sleep in the car. There's no school tomorrow, what's the fuckin' problem?" I saw Peyton's shocked reaction as I spoke this way to my mother.

"What did you just say to me?" she asked. "Dani, it's past five, you're not going to take it. Just wait till tomorrow."

"When I wake up tomorrow is it going to appear magically here when I need to take it? No!" I became irrationally furious, "If it's not here, then how the fuck am I supposed to take it?"

After this outburst, I clenched my phone as hard as I could and slammed it down onto the floor, shattering it. I slumped onto the floor beside it, striving to calm down.

"Fuck," I repeated through gritted teeth.

Apparently, everyone was listening. It would have been impossible not to overhear. Christian and Cindy were peaking in from the kitchen. Peyton knelt down next to me.

"It's okay, Danielle, I'll drive you over there. We can go get it, it's not a problem," she said, cautiously. I dragged my fingers through my hair trying to get a grip. I held my hands out in front of me, and they shook uncontrollably. I clenched them into fists and closed my eyes.

"I got this." I heard Cindy's voice. She inserted herself in front of Peyton.

"Get up," she said. She reached down and pulled me up by one of my arms. When I was standing, she wrapped one arm across the front of my body over my shoulders.

"We'll be right back." I glanced down for a second to see the worried and confused look on Peyton's face.

Cindy half pulled me up the stairs into her room, and then into the bathroom where she sat me down on a seat. I remained there staring at the ground, trying to comprehend how I had just spoken to my mother; how I had just behaved in front of my friend.

"What's going on with you?" Cindy asked, fidgeting with something by the sink, not turning toward me. She didn't seem at all worried. In fact, she seemed perfectly calm.

"I don't know," I said, honestly.

"You always act that way in front of your girl?" she asked, turning around to face me.

"She's not my girl."

"But you want her to be?" she asked. I stayed silent.

"No offense, Dani, but you can't go around acting like a fucking idiot if you want her to stick around," she said. "Is she worth it?"

I didn't respond.

"Well, I don't know if I like her, but you obviously do. So, before you go out there you need to put on a different face. Call your mother and tell her you decided to stop acting like a bitch, and then we can get on with tonight. I'm not looking forward to this charade any more than you."

"I don't know what to do. I can't control it."

"Well," Cindy said with a smirk, "I know something that always calms you down, puts things into focus for you."

"Yeah?"

"Yeah," she said winking and stepped aside to reveal her surprise for me.

Laid out on the granite counter, sat a little pile of white powder.

I smiled.

I remembered the first time I'd encountered this substance. I'd walked in on Cindy snorting multiple lines off the counter in that same bathroom. I remembered the terrified expression on her face when she noticed I was there and asking her what it was and what it did. It seemed she wanted to decriminalize herself more than distract me. I'd grasped the opportunity and told her I wanted some and remembered how reluctant she was the first time she handed me that straw. I will never forget that first experience. It had given me the peace I sought every waking moment. I knew the way I felt when I used it was different from everyone else's experience. I felt calm, collected, safe, and focused.

Cindy appeared more high-strung and agitated. I always wondered why she even bothered, but I would never forget that first time. After that, our bathroom get-togethers had become more frequent. Our little secret. We would stay up all night talking about anything and everything, smoking cigarettes indoors, and philosophizing about life and the universe. I hadn't had any since I met Peyton, which had been almost four months ago.

After probably twenty minutes we emerged from upstairs. I'll admit: I was feeling much better. I felt numb to the things that made my mind run wild. I was calm, and I had called my mother and apologized profusely. She said that she would come over right away; that she didn't know I would have such horrible withdraws. I assured her it wasn't necessary.

As we walked downstairs, Peyton and Christian sat in the kitchen, clearly on edge. I smiled reassuringly.

"All better?" Christian asked.

"Uh, yeah," I said, then switched my attention to Peyton, "Can I talk to you for a minute?"

"Yeah," she said, getting up.

We walked out onto the back porch by the pool; she sat down on the bench outside. I cleared my throat. Feeling residue running down the back of my throat brought more comfort to me.

"I'm sorry for how I acted," I said.

"It's okay," she replied.

"No, it's not, I shouldn't lose control like that," I said, "I just uh–" I tried to continue, but began to drift away a little. What I wanted to say made sense in my mind, but at that moment I just wanted to enjoy the feeling pulsing through my body.

"Look at me," Peyton said suddenly, reaching up to my face and gazing directly into my eyes. I tried to give nothing away.

"You're different," she said, searching my eyes.

"Different? I usually don't get that upset . . ."

"I don't mean then, I mean now. I saw you before, as upset as you were, but I don't see you now. Your eyes don't look at me the way they normally do."

"And how's that?"

"Like . . . what did you do upstairs?" she asked, changing the subject, her eyes penetrating.

"We just talked," I tried brushing it off.

"Right . . ." she turned away from me.

I wanted to know what she needed to say but didn't want her to question me further, so I dropped it.

We all congregated inside. I prayed that Cindy wouldn't be obnoxious and make it obvious that something had taken place. We sat around Christian's huge table, set just for four. Christian sat at the end, Cindy on one side, and Peyton and myself on the other. The food looked amazing, but I no longer had an appetite.

"Wow, looks wonderful," I said.

"Why, thank you, Danielle," said Christian. "Sometimes I know what I'm doing. Oh, I forgot drinks. Sodas or . . ?"

"Yeah," I said.

"Yes, please," said Peyton.

Christian fetched four drinks from the kitchen. He set them all out in front of us and saved one for himself. My eyes fixated on him for a long time, not wanting to believe what I saw.

"What's that?" I asked, indicating his can.

"This?" Christian said, holding up his can. "It's a beer, pretty standard domestic if I'm not mistaken."

"You're drinking again?" I asked in disbelief.

It suddenly became quiet and extremely awkward at the table. Christian didn't seem offended by the question.

"It's not like before, Dani. I've got it under control. Tell her, baby," he said, nodding over at Cindy.

"He really does, Dani, just a couple every now and then," she said with a smile.

"I don't understand," I said, wondering how he would ever even consider drinking again after it ruined everything for him before. Peyton put her hand on my leg as if to say 'calm down.'

"Dani, it's okay, relax," said Christian with a smile, raising his hands in supplication.

"Yeah, Dani, who are we to judge?" Cindy said, winking at me.

I knew I was stuck. She was right. How could I judge Christian after the performance I'd just given? The remainder of dinner was mostly small talk. I didn't have much to contribute.

As I got ready for bed in the room I normally slept in, I felt Peyton's eyes on me. From the other room, I could already hear arguing in low voices. It reminded me of how it used to be, except back then Christian didn't have someone to take it out on.

"Come sit with me," Peyton said from the bed, already in her sleepwear.

I walked over to the bed and sat on the side.

"No, come over here," She said, dragging me into the bed. I put up a token resistance as she tried to pull me further into the bed. Eventually, I gave up and sat next to her.

"Tell me something," she said running her fingers across my knee.

"Tell you what?" I asked.

"Is this why you didn't want to come," she asked.

"What do you mean," I asked, even though I knew the answer.

She let the room get quiet so that we could hear Christian and Cindy arguing in the other room, "That."

I was quiet. I felt so embarrassed for bringing her here. I knew she would never want to come again. Who would? Not that I cared. I just didn't want her to see what it was like. What I was like. Not to mention, I didn't know Christian had starting drinking again, which added insult to injury. This was probably the worst way her visit could have gone.

"Hey," she said, "it's okay."

"No, it's not," I said, with frustration, "It's really not."

"Listen, you know the worst parts of me. Do you think I expected everything about your life to be perfect? Do you think that matters to me and our friendship? I want to know who you really are, and if this is a part of it, then I need to know that too. No matter how bad it is."

I stared at her, realizing why I cared for her so much. She was the most genuine, most unselfish human being I had ever met.

"Got it?" she asked with a flicker of a smile.

"Yeah."

I lay back on the bed, and she lay next to me, propped up on one elbow. She began to brush my hair away from my eyes with her fingers, then continued running her fingers through my hair. This always relaxed me.

I asked her, "What if there are worse things about me? Things that you don't want to know?"

"There is nothing you could tell me that would make me doubt who you are. I've seen the best part of you, and as long as I know that exists, I will always believe that there's a way to go back to it again."

She patted my chest in a reassuring manner, then slid her arm down so it was across my waist. My left arm was behind my head, gripping the sheet tightly to prevent any reaction registering on my face. I looked up at the ceiling trying to avoid Peyton's stare. Her fingertip strayed across the skin between where my shirt and pants met and I turned to face her, our faces inches apart. I could have sworn she inched closer to me.

"I'm not sure what you think you see in me, but I just don't see it."

"You don't have to see it," she said rolling over and grabbing my arms to wrap around her. "Just know that I feel it."

I pulled her close to me, and my arms rested around her.

"This right here, being in your arms. This is the only place I feel safe. This is where nothing else in the world matters," she whispered to me.

I awoke later that night and tossed and turned restlessly. I attempted to fall back to sleep with no avail. Eventually, I got out of bed and went downstairs for a drink of water. Just as I had reached the bottom of the stairs, I noticed Christian was in the kitchen. I reluctantly continued to the kitchen, knowing it was too late to turn around to avoid him.

He stood at the sink emptying beer bottles into the drain with a look of frustration. I avoided his gaze and grabbed a cup from the cabinet. I pressed it against the water dispenser and watched the glass fill ever so slowly. I prayed that it would fill faster as I could hear Christian huffing and puffing like he had something he wanted to say or wanted me to ask him. Just as my cup reached half-full, and I determined that there was enough water, he spoke.

"Do you ever feel like no matter what you do, you always somehow end up doing the wrong thing?" Christian asked in a mildly drunken tone.

This seemed to be a hypothetical question, so instead of responding, I leaned against the fridge to listen to what I hoped would be a short conversation.

"Sometimes I just feel like I can't be a good person, like I wasn't meant to be good. All I am good at is hurting people, disappointing them, and destroying myself . . . Who knows maybe that's the answer."

"What's the answer?" I inquired, curious as to what he could be insinuating.

"Nothing," he says waving off his last comment, "I just thought that there's this part of me that I would eventually grow out of. I thought I'd get older and wiser. That I would change and one day be able to forgive myself for what I had done and actually be able to ask forgiveness. You can't ask forgiveness when you just keep doing the same things wrong over and over again. I just can't stop."

I was caught off guard by his admissions. Although I had disdain for Christian and wanted to ignore his drunken self-loathing, my dark side empathized with him.

"All I can say is: I know it's easier, and it feels better to let that side win. No matter how much you think you despise it, part of you loves it. I think if you let that side win enough it becomes who you are."

"Do you think it's too late for me to change? Do you think I'm stuck being this person?" He asked.

"I don't have any answer for that," I replied, exiting the kitchen and leaving Christian alone with his thoughts.

* * *

"Why do you think you had such bad withdrawals from your medication?" asked Dr. Joy, jumping right into the questioning.

"Maybe because I'm one of the few people who really needed it," I said, as if the answer was obvious.

"You were relatively okay until you realized that you didn't have your medication or access to it."

"Well, yeah, because I knew it would go from bad to worse."

"You don't think you viewed it as some kind of safety net, an excuse to control, or in this case, not to control your emotions?"

she asked. It seemed for the first time she might actually be doing the work of a 'doctor.'

"I knew I felt better when I was on my medication, whether it was physiological or psychological, I don't know if I could tell you the difference. I felt as if people were safer around me when I took it," I said, trying to choose my words carefully.

"So, you thought people were in danger when you weren't on your medication?"

"When I'm not on my medication, I'm more than a nightmare. I despise the person I become." I tried to make her understand the severity of what I was saying.

"Don't get me wrong, Danielle, I have no doubt of your need for medication. If anything, it reassures my theory about you."

"How do you mean?"

"Well, from what you've told me so far, your 'episodes' seem to only occur when you don't take it, or before you took it. When you're on it, you have no special abilities, experience no supernatural circumstances, no outbursts of rage. If anything, I would say the medication is doing exactly what it's supposed to, and limiting your psychotic episodes and stabilizing your mood."

I sat quietly for a second, waiting for an example to come to me to disprove her theory. The smallest incident would have sufficed. Nothing surfaced.

"I'm guessing this makes sense to you?"

"So, I just imagined all those things?" I asked defensively.

"I don't think you imagined what happened. I think your mind just exaggerated what it saw and interpreted it in a way that made the emotional sensations you went through seem like a real physical experience."

"No," I said, shaking my head, "You're wrong."

"Danielle, I'm right, and you need to see that!" she slammed her hand down on her desk, harder than she probably intended. She was visibly frustrated.

"I didn't imagine it!" I retorted. I almost didn't believe my own words, but I remembered those experiences. They felt so real, and I could not live thinking that those events never actually happened.

"Dani, you need to come to terms with this," she said.

"No, that stuff really happened, I know it did!"

The doctor stood up suddenly, pulled open her desk drawer, and snatched something from it. She then went to her door and locked it. This made me nervous. Doctors were never supposed to lock the doors to their office. This was for their safety, mostly. I sat up straighter in my chair not knowing what to expect. She strode over to my chair and began undoing the restraints around my wrists. She freed my hands, and I laid them to the sides of the chair, trying to show that it was okay, and I posed no threat.

"Look at me," she said, "You do not have super powers, you cannot heal people, you cannot hurt people, it is all in your head."

I was beginning to become angered by her actions but remembered that I wasn't restrained, so I used all my self-control to remain in my seat.

"I'm telling you, it happened," I said in an almost pleading tone.

She snatched something out of her pocket and held it up to my face. I had to move back to realize she had a knife in my face. The blade was bright, reflecting off the light coming in the window. I caught my reflection for a second and noticed the amount of doubt that was showing through my expression. She held it there for a second then said the words I was expecting.

"Then prove it."

I sat there for a second. I didn't know what was going to happen next, all I knew was, that no matter what, I was afraid.

"I won't," I said.

"Who said you have a choice?" She responded.

"I thought you said you could, that it was real. Isn't that what you've been trying to prove to me this whole time?"

"I don't control it," I gripped the chair arms as tightly as I could.

"Right . . . it controls you . . . Well, what if you had to make a choice?" She slid the blade lightly across my wrist, "What if you had to save yourself? You don't have any scars, right?"

"You're sick," I said, disgusted by her.

"Better yet, what if you had to save me?" she sat back and held the knife against her own arm, "What would they think if they came in here, and I was bleeding all over the floor. I'm not sure if I could remember what really happened. What would they do to you?"

"You wouldn't."

Before I could react, or comprehend, she flipped the knife in her hand and dug it into her arm. For a second, I wasn't sure she had cut herself. There was just a thin slit in her arm. She stared at it for a second. Then, blood suddenly came rushing out of her arm, dripping onto the floor.

"Oh my God," I said, I could barely look, "Oh my God."

"Do something," she said, paying no mind to her bleeding arm, and grabbing the collar of my shirt.

I sat there waiting, but nothing happened. I began seeing flashes of the worst day of my life in red and blue. I tried to remain focused but was consumed by the thoughts of my past swirling in and out of my mind. I knew I had to save her this time, but I felt nothing like I had said I once did.

She was right.

I saw her begin to sway, and I knew that she was losing blood too fast. I jumped up and quickly got behind her and pulled off the thin sweater she was wearing and wrapped it around her arm to slow the bleeding. She resisted.

"No, do what you said you could do," she said.

I tried to apply pressure to her wound and reached over the desk and slammed on as many buttons on the phone as I could without looking. Then, I finally got a response.

"Dr. Joy? Do you need assistance?"

"Get in here, fast," I yelled, "The door is locked!"

They didn't wait for further instruction. The force they exerted removing the door from its hinges seemed to shake the room. They were inside within seconds. I was snatched away from the doctor and slammed face down on the floor with at least three people holding me down. I felt knees in my back, and someone's heavy hand pressing my face hard into the linoleum floor.

"Why are you unrestrained?" about three people shouted at me.

"What did you do? Why was the door locked?" another asked.

"What happened?"

I remained silent. I had no idea how to explain what just occurred and knew nothing I said would be believed.

"It wasn't her," Dr. Joy said in a low voice. They all continued to yell, demanding answers.

"It wasn't her!" She repeated as loud as she could manage. They fell quiet and turned their attention to her. One of them continued to wrap her arm to suppress the bleeding. No one knew quite what to do at that point, not even me. They eased off a little and allowed me to sit up.

"I was opening that letter, and my hand . . ." she glanced at me, "slipped. She was only helping me."

"Doctor, you know it's against policy to have weapons in the building; much less around patients, dangerous patients at that," one of them remonstrated, while looking at me as if I were garbage.

"Dangerous? I wouldn't be so sure." She looked at me with evident disappointment.

Chapter Eight:
A Bad Day for Everyone

I replayed every memory I had in my head for the next two days. I kept trying to locate the line between what was real and what wasn't. Which of my memories were genuine, and which were just figments of my imagination? I began to wonder if I not only imagined occurrences but people as well. Was the way I viewed people even the way they really were? Was everyone as sick and twisted as I thought, or was I the sick one? If I imagined things so vividly, perhaps the people I thought no longer walked this earth, waited behind the doors of this institution. This was the only thing that gave me hope about the doubts I harbored concerning the reality of my life.

When my door opened a couple days later I was surprised.

"What?" I asked, wondering why the escort staff was interrupting my thinking time.

"It's time for your session," two escorts said, looking at me as though I was indeed crazy. This did nothing to reassure me. However, I knew what I had experienced my last session, and there is no way that Dr. Joy had any further business with me.

"Excuse me? With who?" I asked, confused.

"Same one as always, Dani."

I was escorted to the usual office and sat down in the usual chair, feeling so tense my muscles began to ache. When Dr. Joy walked in, I tensed up even further. She began setting her stuff down in her usual fashion.

"Relax, Danielle," she said, not looking at me, "We won't have any repeats of our last session."

I observed her relaxed manner as if our little incident never happened. I noticed she had her arm tightly wrapped and tried to push the memories out of my head.

"Why am I here?" I asked.

"What do you mean?" she said before she finally sat down.

"Well, you were here last time. You saw what happened," I sighed. "You were right, there's something wrong with me, and it's not exceptional or unbelievable. I'm fucked up in the head, right? What else is there to know? Except you might be quite fucked up too."

"Oh, Danielle, we're just getting started. Admitting you have a problem is just the first step. There's so much more to figure out about you. More than I thought."

"What's the point of talking, when I'm not sure if what I'm saying really happened or if I just think it happened."

"It's about more than simply what happened. What did you feel when these things happened? What triggered these responses? Then we have to go through them and sift through reality and delusions. Until we can reach a point where you know who you are and what you are really capable of."

"I'm nobody," I said.

The doctor looked at me with pity.

"Do you really believe that?"

"It just feels like nothing matters anymore. I don't care about anyone or anything. I don't care if I don't wake up in the morning. I don't care if I spend the rest of my life in this place."

"Why is that?"

"Because it wasn't real. What I saw, what I felt. What I thought other people felt."

Dr. Joy was quiet for a minute, surveying my emotions.

"You need to finish your story, then we'll figure out if it really doesn't matter."

"If I'm not ever sure what my story is, how can I possibly tell it?"

"Tell it exactly as you remember it, just like before."

I was exhausted at the thought of even trying to tell any more of the story. I knew I would question every word that escaped my lips. I knew I would question every expression she might make. I would wonder if she knew better than I did what really happened in my life.

"Are there things about me that you know that I don't?"

"Since you claim to think that you are nobody, I would say, yes. There's a lot about you that I know that I think you don't know. I want to know something."

"What's that?" I asked.

"When did things start to go downhill with Peyton?"

I cringed at this thought.

* * *

"Dammit, I hope we don't miss all of it," I said as we were driving through town, trying to locate the complex.

"I'll get us there," Peyton said and winked at me, as she sped through a stop sign. I gripped the door panel, thinking we should definitely be driving slower, or at least more carefully. The other half of me wanted us to go faster.

It was the night of my little brother's baseball game, and I had promised I would be there. Now, I don't do a lot of things I should or have many values, but when it came to my brother, I always kept my promises.

I saw the lights of the complex over the trees as we rounded a sharp corner. We drove onto the gravel and parked in a spot not necessarily designated for cars. We both jumped out and ran full speed to his field. I think Peyton must have held back because she was a few paces behind me.

I sought out my parents and located them seated in the bleachers. Their expressions displayed an air of mild embarrassment.

"What's going on?" I greeted them.

"Hey, you made it!" my dad said, trying to change the expression on his face as best as he could.

"Of course, how's he doing?"

They both gave me a 'you don't want to know' look.

"He's . . . struggling," my mom said.

"Yeah, and all these assholes in the stands aren't helping," my dad added.

"What do you mean?" I asked.

"He's struck out every time; the ball's gone past him twice, and everyone keeps telling the coach to take him out of the game," said my mom.

"What? He's one of the best players on the team. What's going on?"

"He probably just lost his confidence," Peyton said.

"I'm sure we haven't seen the worst of it yet either, this is the bottom of the last inning, and we've got one person on base; another up to bat, then he's next. I just know they're going to rip him to shreds."

"Maybe we should just pull him out," my dad suggested out of pity.

"We can't. The only reason he's even playing is that there's barely enough to have a full team. If we pull him out, they'll have to forfeit," my mom said.

"Yeah!" the crowd erupts as another player got on base and goes to second.

One on second, one on third, and Nathan was up. I could see him dragging his bat to home plate, his face dejected.

"Oh, you gotta be kidding me, Coach!" I heard a parent shout.

"Make him walk, coach!" shouts another.

"Hey, they're just kids," I hear Peyton call back to them.

"Well, my kid wants to win a game every once in a while," some guy shouted back to her.

I looked down at the field and saw the pitcher getting ready to throw his first pitch.

"All right, Nathan, this is it. Just like practice!" I hear his coach shout to him.

The pitcher throws.

"Strike," the umpire shouted unnecessarily loudly. I saw tears of frustration attempt to escape Nathan's eyes.

"Oh my god, get him out of the game!" the same man shouted again.

I become overly anxious for my brother as I watched the events unfold.

"What do you think?" Peyton asked.

They had two outs, we're down by two, and Nathan was up with one strike.

The pitcher wound up and delivered a ball hard toward Nathan. Everyone held their breath. Nathan didn't budge an inch.

"Strike!" shouted the umpire.

"That's right Nathan, just wait for your pitch!" the coach shouted, a little less hopeful.

The catcher threw the ball back to the pitcher. The pitcher composed himself and wound up. Peyton gripped my hand as tight as possible, and I squeezed hers back just as hard. Three, two, one. The pitcher released the ball.

Nathan didn't move at all; he didn't do anything. He just stood there as the ball flew past him.

"Strike three," the umpire announced, less loudly this time. The other team ran onto the field in celebration of the game's end. Nathan's teammates straggled to the dugout with their heads down. As they came back out to shake the other team's hands, Nathan finally made his way to the dugout expressionless.

My heart ached for him. We avoided the glances of the other families and comments uttered under their breath. Some of them seemed dazed and saddened by Nathan's performance, others were furious.

One by one the boys came around and found their families and headed off until there were only a few families left. Nathan had still not appeared.

"I'm going to go check on Nathan," my dad said starting to get up.

"No," I said putting out my hand, "I'll go get him."

My dad sat back down with slight relief in his expression.

"Do you want me to come?" Peyton asked.

"No, it's fine, I'll be right back," I replied.

I walked around to their side of the dugout. It was dark, but I could see Nathan sitting inside alone in the dark. I walked inside and sat next to him. He did not acknowledge my presence. He just remained slumped forward.

"Nathan, don't worry about the game, everyone has a shitty day every once in a while. You just have to brush it off and keep going," I said, attempting to be encouraging.

He continued to stare vacantly at the floor.

"Nathan, it's just a game . . ."

"I hate my life." He said, glancing over at me for a moment before averting his eyes again. He shook his head, and I saw a tear roll down his cheek. He immediately wiped it away.

He spoke those four words with such darkness and intensity. I was convinced that he sincerely meant them. I knelt down in front of him.

"Nathan, look at me," I said. He lifted his head slightly, "Things are going to get better. I promise. Everything you are feeling right now, you are not going to feel forever. Some days you're going to get knocked down or feel like you can't take anymore, but you can. You can endure it, and when you get to the point where you feel like you can't anymore, you tell me. No matter what it takes, I'll make it better. When you get older, you're going to face some dark days, and on your darkest day I will be there, and I will help you. I will make any sacrifice to help you. You never have to go through anything alone."

"Everything okay?" came Peyton's voice from a safe distance back, so as not to appear to be listening in.

"Yeah," I called back to her, "We'll be right there."

I looked back at my brother.

"Are you going to be okay?"

"Yeah," he said nodding his head, "Yeah, I'll be okay."

* * *

I lead him back to my parents, and we all headed back to the house in separate cars.

"How's your brother?" Peyton asked as I got in the car.

I bit the skin around my thumbnail as I looked out the window without response.

She started the car and headed toward home.

We pulled up into the driveway. My parents and Nathan were already home, and Christian and Cindy had arrived as well.

"Hey, someday, right?" Peyton remarked.

"Yeah," I said.

"Are you all right?"

"Just thinking about my brother," I said.

"He really looks up to you."

"Sometimes I wish he didn't."

"What do you mean?"

"I just worry about letting him down."

"You are the kind of person, Danielle, who when you have no choice but to not fail . . . you won't," she said.

"I hope so," I said. "I'm going to change shirts real quick before dinner."

"Okay."

I went upstairs thinking about what Peyton had said. I doubted her words. Perhaps because I knew a million things about myself that she didn't. I just couldn't shake the feeling that I didn't want that kind of responsibility. Or, not even that, I was worried, because I felt the power I had to help someone, was equal to the power I had to hurt them. I knocked on the door to the bathroom.

"Hey, it's me. Let me in," I said.

Cindy cracked open the door and pulled me inside.

"I need some," I said, seeing she'd already started without me.

She passed the straw to me without saying anything, still trying to get the remainder she had already snorted to clear her nasal passage. She was standing next to the counter, and I put my hand on her back to reach around her to grab the card. I felt her twitch almost imperceptibly.

"What was that?" I said.

"What?" she appeared bewildered.

I stared at her hard. She stared back trying to portray confusion. I took a step toward her, and she pushed her back closer to the counter. I put my hand on the bottom of her shirt right above her belt line and she tried to push away, turning away with tears in her eyes. With both hands, I rolled up her shirt revealing her stomach. It was a hard sight to look at. My throat tightened, and I felt like I had just had the wind knocked out of me.

Bruises lined her stomach. They were dark; clearly, he didn't hold back. There were deep scratch marks, welts, intimating she had been struck by something. I turned her around, and her back was even worse.

"It's all I had," she whispered. "I'm not smart, I don't have a job, I can't fucking have kids, all I have is my body. Now, look at it . . . It's ruined."

She began to cry uncontrollably.

"I'm not even good enough for him. The one thing he wants, I can't give him. What the fuck is wrong with me?" she sobbed.

"Nothing," I assured her. "There's something seriously wrong with him, Cindy. Nobody deserves this."

"I'm nothing, Danielle. I'm worthless. Even to you. What kind of person am I, giving this shit to a kid?" she laughed mirthlessly at how ridiculous it was.

"I'm not a kid anymore," I said, fully aware that statement probably wouldn't help, but not knowing what else to say.

She lifted up her shirt while looking in the mirror. She had an expression of disgust as she scrutinized herself; tears running down her face.

"You're still beautiful," I said.

She turned to look at me with a different expression on her face as if she needed something. She pulled her shirt back down, moved across to me, put her arms around me, and hugged me. I hugged her back, then she whispered something in my ear.

"Tell me again," she pulled back and looked me in the eye, both of us still with our arms around each other, "Tell me again," she begged.

"You're beaut . . ." I started, but before I could finish, she put her hand behind my neck, pulled me in, and kissed me. I reacted immediately, and unexpectedly. I pulled her close to me. I hadn't kissed many people in my life, but even if I had, there would be no precedent for this. I knew it wasn't a normal kiss, and I knew it wasn't right, but nothing would have stopped me at that moment. I didn't kiss her because I wanted her, I kissed her because I wanted her to feel wanted.

Our lips collided in chaos. I felt her tongue against mine, and it unleashed something inside of me. I pushed her back to the counter and pushed her up to where she was sitting on it with my waist between her legs. I felt as if I couldn't get her body close enough to mine, and I could tell she felt the same way. Her nails dug deep into the skin on my back. Reality began to catch up to my very slow mind, but not fast enough; the door opened.

"Um . . ." Peyton said, staring in complete disbelief, "Dinner's ready."

She turned and left the room before I could even put half a syllable together. I pulled away from Cindy, who looked horrified. She pushed me back.

"I'm so sorry," she said, with her hand over her mouth. She, nor I could believe what just happened. I wasn't too concerned about explaining the situation till I glanced down and noticed a pile of coke was still spread out on the counter in perfect miniature corn rows.

"Oh fuck," I said.

Cindy grabbed me by the arm, "Go fix it."

The look in her eyes was completely different from when I came into the bathroom. She was back in control.

"Go, I'm okay," she said, I began to grab my jacket and reached for a smaller bag that still had some white powder inside, holding it up questioningly.

"Take it," she said with the wave of her hand.

I raced down the stairs and out the front door. When I got outside, Peyton was just sitting in her car. She looked as if her brain had just powered down because it had seen too much. I knocked on the passenger window. She didn't look at me, she just unlocked the door. I climbed inside slowly, not knowing what to say. She started the car, and we began to drive away.

We drove to the park, and she turned off the engine and got out. I followed her. She walked about ten feet and sat down in the grass. I sat next to her, looking at her, not knowing what to say.

"I don't understand," she finally confessed.

"I don't know what to say."

"Be honest with me. What exactly was going on in there, Danielle?"

"What do you mean?"

She gave me the 'fuck you,' look, "Don't play stupid."

"I'm not, I just don't understand what you want to know," I said.

"What were you doing?" she asked.

"Stuff. I wasn't doing anything wrong."

"Listen, I'm not here to judge you, I just don't understand why I just saw you nearly fucking your uncle's girlfriend with a bunch of fucking drugs on the counter," she said, clearly angry.

"Okay, I went in there, and she was crying, and it just happened, I don't know why," I pleaded.

"Has it ever happened before?" she asked.

"What? No, this was the first and only time."

"And the drugs?"

"They were hers, I didn't do any," I lied.

"Don't! Don't you dare fuckin lie to me, Danielle!" she nearly screamed at me. "You think I can't tell?"

"You know what, you're not my parent, you're not my girlfriend, and even if you were, it's my life my body. You do what you want to your body," I said pointing at her wrist, "and I'll do what I want with mine."

"You really want to go there?" she asked in a threatening tone. I wasn't sure if I did, but I nodded.

* * *

"Okay . . . okay . . . um . . ." The doctor looked over her notes repeatedly.

"Yeah . . ." I said, knowing how crazy it all was.

"Well, this story is like a bad day for everyone. Unbelievable, all of that could occur in one day," she said.

"Well, if you were there, it would be even more unbelievable."

"I don't understand, it seems like you had a lot of um, how do I say this, 'love' feelings for Peyton. Why would you do that with her in the house? In fact, why would you do that at all?" she asked.

"I don't know. At the time it seemed to be something I had to do. Not because she wanted it, because I felt like I could actually alleviate someone else's pain. I just wanted her to know that she wasn't worthless; that someone thought the world of her."

"No offense, Dani, but she kind of hit the nail on the head. How could she be considered a good friend, or even a good person to you when she's been supplying you with highly dangerous and highly illegal drugs since you were barely a teenager? I mean, fourteen years old, that's about the age of your brother now."

As she continued to talk I began to space out. Fourteen? She's correct, that is how old my brother is now. Since I'd been here, he'd just been in a time capsule in my mind. I had never considered the fact that he'd grown older, probably much taller, and probably was starting to forget me.

" . . . Dani, are you listening?" the doctor asked, "Or am I just talking to myself?"

"You said that you talked to my family?" I asked.

"Yes, that's correct," she sounded cautious.

"My brother, what did he look like?"

"I don't think discussing your family's circumstances at this time is such a good idea."

"What do you mean?" I didn't understand.

"Well, I'm sure a lot has changed since you've been here, at least it seems that way," she said.

"A lot has changed?" I repeated.

"You're not there, Dani. It's not the same. The people you remembered have gone through hell and back since before you left up until now. They've experienced loss, they've struggled, they're alone. Their daughter and sister has been in a mental institution for three years now with no signs of recovery, and at this point, pretty much no hope that they will ever see you again."

"And what do you think?" I asked, "Do you think I'll ever be out there again?"

"Sooner than you think," she said plainly, "Now, I'm curious, how did things change between you and Peyton?"

"That was the beginning of the end. It was from that point that everything started falling apart. I began to push her and everyone else away. I pushed her away at the time because I felt I had to in order to protect her. If I had still been there for her as I had always been, then she never would have gone away. I was supposed to be her best friend, look out for her, want what's best for her. She just wanted to be close to me, and I couldn't allow that to happen. I couldn't let her get too close because every time she saw a glimpse of what I really was, I felt like I didn't deserve her, more and more."

"And is that how she treated you?"

"No . . ." I said, "She always treated me like no matter what I did, no matter how bad I screwed up, no matter how much I lied to her, blew her off, pushed her away, I still meant the world to her. Until the last time. I just couldn't get over the idea that she was missing out on the life meant for her by being around me."

"So, you deliberately pushed her into the arms of another lover?" she asked, already knowing where the story was going.

"I thought he could give her more than I could, or just give her something normal, something good, and something she deserved."

Chapter Nine:
Toxic

I was in my room, getting ready to go out. Peyton would be here soon to pick me up. I didn't really put in much effort; parties weren't really my thing. I just didn't want to be alone with Peyton at this point. I didn't want her to look at me with questioning eyes as she had been doing for the last week. I just wanted her to be distracted by something else. So, I suggested we go to the boys' party that night. I knew this meant all of Peyton's friends would be there, welcoming her back into their world with open arms. Cain would be there, and I liked being around him. Most importantly, Abel would be there, and he would be waiting for Peyton.

I heard a knock at my door, simultaneously I heard my phone beep. It was a text message: 'I'm here.'

"Come in," I said, and began to grab my things, and get ready to head downstairs.

"Hey," my brother said, poking his head in and closing the door behind him.

"Hey, Nathan, what's up?" I asked.

"Nothing," he said, "Are you about to leave?"

"Yeah, did you need something," I asked. It was kind of unusual for Nathan to come into my room at this stage in his life, but since the game, he seemed to want to be a little closer to me. So, naturally, I distanced myself from him.

"No, I just wanted to talk . . ." he said.

I waited for a moment, then when he seemed to have nothing in particular to say at the time, I walked over and gave him a quick kiss on the head.

"Tell you what, I'll be around tomorrow. We can talk then, sound good?"

"Yeah, okay," he said, "Well, I have baseball practice in the afternoon, will you be here in the morning?"

"Yeah, yeah, I'm pretty sure I will be. If not, we can talk whenever I am here."

"Okay," he sounded disappointed but smiled.

I stopped when I saw him do this. I knew it was a fake smile. It broke my heart to see him do that. It was something I did, and here he was doing exactly the same thing, and I knew no one else would notice. For a second, I wondered how long he had been doing this and why. But instead of an interrogation, I gave him a hug and headed down the stairs.

"Don't forget your medication if you're staying at Peyton's!" my mother called to me. I slowed up, trying to avoid this conversation.

"Oh right . . ." I said, and I grabbed it off the counter, "Thanks."

I had avoided telling my mother all week that I had stopped taking my medication. I didn't think that moment was a good time. I headed out the door.

We arrived at the party, and Peyton stayed seated in the car. I removed my seatbelt waiting for her to follow my lead, but she remained seated.

"You know, I'm not really sure if I want to go. Can't we just go somewhere to be alone?" she said.

"What do you mean, we're already here?"

"I know, I just . . . I don't know. It's like going back in time. I'm done with this part of my life," she said, rubbing her hand across her forehead in frustration.

"Well, maybe you're not. Maybe there's something you missed," I said.

"Why did you want to come tonight, Danielle?" she said, with a frustrated expression on her face.

"Hey Peyton, you made it!" I heard Abel's voice from the front porch. "Come inside!"

He stood there, smiling as if his birthday had come early. He had obviously put extra pride into his appearance today because he was looking quite handsome. I silently thanked him.

"Hey Abel," Peyton said as we walked up. He hugged her, then hugged me.

"Do you know how hard it is to get you ladies over here?" he asked, laughing, "Come inside."

We entered the boys' house. It was beautiful with a log cabin feel to it, but modernized. You could tell their family was into the usual: having money, hunting, fishing, and raising athletes. Several animal trophies lined their walls. There were a couple of deer heads, some fish, a bobcat, trophies, and pictures. It was very homey and welcoming. It was an open-plan layout. From the entrance, you could see the living room, the kitchen, and the entertainment room, which had an exquisite pool table that was obviously only used for get-togethers like this. Several people sat around in that room waiting for their turn, drinking beers from their little red cups.

"I really like your house," I said, looking around. "Nice animals."

"Right? See that buck right there," Abel said, pointing to a massive deer on the wall, "I shot that one when I was twelve years old."

"Oh, that's nice," I said, not knowing how to be properly impressed.

"See that, right there?" he pointed to a tiny fish that had somehow been preserved to look like it was still partially alive.

"Yeah," I said.

"Cain caught that when he was fourteen, and he felt so bad he cried because my dad wouldn't let it go," he laughed hysterically. It was kind of funny.

"Seriously?" Cain said, walking into the room, "Are you going to tell everyone that story?"

"What, I can't brag about my baby brother?"

"Well, I'm actually older than you by several minutes, so no," Cain said.

"Well I guess 'cause I was in the womb a tad longer, I was the only one who developed the ability to grow muscles, and get a tan, and grow facial hair," he was still laughing. This made others laugh too.

"Well, I think it's a lovely fish," Peyton said with a smile.

"Thank you, Peyton," Cain gave her a hug, "good to see you."

"Danielle," he hugged me too, "always good to see you."

"You too," I said hugging him back.

"I'll get you guys a drink," Abel said, heading to the kitchen.

As soon as he took off, Peyton's girls walked over.

"Oh my God, look who's here!" Trish exclaimed.

"Finally," said Bailey.

"No way!" Alicia remarked.

"Hey, girls," was all Peyton said.

"You've been keeping her all to yourself, Dani," Trish said, giving me a little tap on the shoulder.

"Yeah, sorry."

They all hugged her and began talking nonstop about school, track, boys, Abel, Cain, the party, and many other things. I took this chance to slink away. Those girls produced way too much energy; it was difficult to be around all of them at one time.

"Hey, got you a drink," Cain said. He was holding one in his left hand and offered the second one in his right hand toward me.

"Thanks," I said, taking it.

"It's cheap, but we might have some shots later if you're into something a little more hardcore."

"Oh, you have no idea . . ." I said, not wanting a shot but definitely wanting something a little more 'hardcore' as he put it. I slipped my hand in my pocket to make sure it was still there. I felt a small lining of a plastic baggy and was reassured.

"So, how's school?" Cain asked.

"Uh, almost over, thankfully."

"Ha, ha true. Hey, we should play beer pong, me and you versus my brother and Peyton," Cain suggested.

"Let's do it," I said. Actually thinking this might be some fun.

Abel cleared out everyone else playing as soon as he heard the idea.

"The championship of all championships!" Abel announced to the entire party. "In corner number one we have Dani and Cain. Team Save the Fishes with a record loss of 5 out of 5 games, will they be able to compete against the undefeated, relentless, extremely attractive, badass of all badasses Abel, and his newly acquired, exceptionally beautiful, new teammate, Peyton Deason!"

We laid out a triangle of cups on each side of the table and filled them with beer. Everyone began to gather around.

"I feel a bet coming on," Abel said, rubbing his hands together. "What do you think, baby bro?"

"Ha ha, I think I was expecting that. What are you thinking?"

"Hmmm, whatever I want?" Abel asked.

"No, not whatever you want, something that's legal," Cain said, as he finished pouring the beers.

"Okay, okay, I've got it. If I win, Cain, you have to kiss three boys in here," the crowd laughed out loud. "To prove that you are in fact, actually gay. Three of my choosing. Boys, if you don't want tongue from my brother, please leave now, otherwise, you are left with no choice. Hey, and this never leaves the house."

"Oh my God, you're sick!" one boy shouted from the background.

"I see we have our first volunteer!" Abel said. Again, this made everybody laugh, "Now, shut up. Three boys, and then your partner has to finish this bottle of whiskey."

He held up a bottle that was mostly empty, but still the equivalent of about three shots.

"Beer before liquor, bro!" another guy shouted from the crowd.

"Our second volunteer for my brother, okay!" Abel was grinning like he was so impressed with himself. "Sound fair?"

"Ha, you're so funny. Okay Abel, but if I win, I want the exact same thing. You, three boys, and Peyton, one shot, not the whole bottle."

"Oh my God, you're so fucking lame, Cain, but you got yourself a deal," Abel said, putting out his hand. Cain shook it.

"Trish, get us three volunteers," Abel shouted. "Like I said, if you want to leave, you can, but I think we're all in agreement, that the ones who left, made out with boys. Am I right, everyone? Otherwise, this never leaves this room."

"Yeah!" everyone said. It made several boys heading for the door change their mind and turn around. People were laughing hysterically at the thought of either of the boys making out with anyone else here, already forming scenarios in their head about what it would be like. Trish picked out three relatively attractive, extremely nervous looking boys, and led them to the front of the room by the table.

"You like what you see, Cain," Abel said, laughing.

"Let's just play," Cain said.

Cain turned toward me, "Oh my God, what the fuck was I thinking?"

"It's okay. If we lose, we lose," I said.

"But you don't have to make out with a bunch of dudes!" he said, "Oh man, I'll never live this down."

We started the game, and Abel wasn't exaggerating, he was exceptionally good at it. With his first three turns he threw his ball into a cup, fortunately, Peyton missed all of hers. I got two of mine, and Cain got one of his.

"Come on, Peyton, I'm counting on you," Abel said, standing right behind her.

She tossed the ping pong ball out of her hand and it actually went in.

"Hell, yeah!" Abel said, grabbing her and kissing her right on the lips. She was impressed with herself too.

Me, not so much. I didn't think it would sting that much seeing her kiss Abel. It was what I wanted, why we came here, but it still hurt.

Suddenly, the game turned extra acrobatic, and people were bouncing the balls off the table, the floor, and the walls. I think everyone was getting a little drunk.

Cain and I sunk both of ours in one turn. This put an expression of extreme anxiety on Abel's face. We had five to go, and they had four. We were only behind by one.

He suddenly became very focused, and hit one of ours, leaving only three for them to make; Peyton missed hers.

We got the balls back, and both got in again; leaving only two for us and three left for them.

Abel shot and missed, but Peyton sank one. Then, it was two left on each side. We shot back and forth three times, with no one achieving a shot. Then, Abel scored one, leaving one for them, two for us.

Next, Cain shot and succeeded in scoring, leaving one cup for each side. The crowd was on edge, especially the boys whose fates were sealed either way. They stood at the front looking apprehensive.

"Okay, okay, here's the deal, last cup. No overtime. If one team makes both their balls in the cup first they win, but if they just make one, then the other team gets to try to score with both of theirs with one try, then they win. But, the second shot has to be a trick shot. Fair enough?" Abel was talking to the crowd.

"Sounds good," Cain said.

Once again, we went back and forth with several tries with no result. Then, it happened. Abel sank the last cup. My heart sank, not for myself, but for Cain. I glanced at him, and he looked miserable.

Abel was cheering and picked up Peyton and hugged her. I was repelled by the sight, even more so because we lost.

"Why are you so happy?" Cain asked. "It's still our turn."

"Seriously, Cain?" Abel said, laughing. "It's a slam dunk!"

"Whatever," Cain said, tossing his ball that somehow managed to fall perfectly into the cup making a small splash.

"Oh shit," he said in a kind of unbelievable tone.

"Oh shit," I said realizing it was my turn.

'Trick shot!" Abel shouted nervously. "It has to be a trick shot!"

I turned to Cain, he looked hopeful, but terrified.

"Okay, now I want you to focus real hard, Cain," I said. Abel was standing right next to the table, laughing, but visibly edgy. "There's a point on that wall right there, that if I bounce it off, it should go right into the cup. I need you to find that point for me."

"Okay," Cain said, he appeared tipsy. He stared at the wall for a long time. He made some projections with his eyes and fingers before he eventually placed his finger at a point on the wall.

"There?" I asked. He shook his head, then moved his finger about six inches to the left.

"There?"

"Yeah," he said.

I looked at the cup at the other end of the table, it now seemed miles away. As I stared at it, I watched Abel smiling and wrapping his arms around Peyton from behind, his hands over her stomach.

I sensed the red pigment of the cup engulf the entire room with its hue.

"Ready?" I asked Cain, who still seemed to be moving his finger every few seconds.

"Hurry up, there should have been a time limit!" Abel said, laughing.

Cain moved his finger one last time, and without taking my eyes off Peyton and Abel, I flung the ball to the left, it bounced almost exactly where Cain's finger was placed, and zoomed right into the cup, spinning as it went down.

"Holy shit!" Cain and Abel said at the same time.

The Crowd went crazy, cheering and laughing.

"Your rules Abe," Cain told his brother.

"Well," Abel said, leaning back with his hands in his two front pockets, "a bet's a bet."

The three boys winced as Abel approached them. He looked back at all of us, who were wondering if he was really going to do it.

"A bet's a bet," he said again, and kissed the first two boys in about point five seconds, possibly not even touching them. They both wiped their mouths and spit. He winced as he reached the last boy.

"Oh Trish, you picked a good looking one," Abel said, laughing nervously.

"I swear I thought it was for you Cain!" Trish shouted. Everyone laughed at that, "I mean . . ." her voice tailed off.

"This is for you, baby brother," Abel grabbed the last boy and gave a long hard kiss in somehow, the most non-sexual way possible, then pushed him away. The crowd roared with laughter.

"I need a shot," Abel said, wiping his mouth, then gagging as if he was almost going to throw up, "quick."

"Let's not forget the lady," Cain said, winking at Peyton and pouring her a shot, and setting the bottle next to the miniature sized glass.

"Of course," Peyton said, holding the glass up, "to the champions!"

Peyton threw back the shot without wincing. Everyone cheered. Cain reached for the bottle and Peyton moved it away from him, shaking her finger at him, "Huh-uh."

She held the bottle up to see how much was left. A couple of shots worth. She glanced at me. I looked at her, implying it was definitely not a good idea, and shook my head. She winked at me and threw it back. As it went down, the crowd fell silent. Small amounts escaped down the side of her mouth. I held my breath as she took it down, thinking how disgusting it must be. When the bottle was all gone, everyone clapped. Abel went up to her and hugged her.

"See why I love this girl? She's badass!" He said. She put her hand up against his chest to steady herself.

"Now that I need to get the 'dude' taste out of my mouth, and Peyton has provided us with a perfectly empty bottle, who wants to play another game?"

About ten or so people were completely into Abel's idea and raised their hands, and everyone began moving furniture to make room for a spin-the-bottle circle. I walked over to Peyton.

"What are you doing?" I asked, concerned.

"Nothin' . . ." she said, shrugging.

"You don't think this is kind of excessive?" I asked, making a drinking motion with my hand.

"I can do what I want with my body, right?" she said matter-of-factly, "Let's play!"

I reluctantly found my way into the circle. There sat Peyton, Abel, Cain, Bailey, Trish, Alicia, two of the three boys Abel had kissed, and a couple others I didn't know.

"Okay, now no more dudes kissing dudes, that shit's done. But ladies, I highly encourage dual participation, and I think we all will agree that it is highly appropriate," Abel said. This made the girls roll their eyes, and the boys high five and fist bump.

"I'll start it off," Abel said giving it a spin. His first land was on Trish, who was clearly nervous and blushed, then proceeded to shove her tongue down Abel's throat. I, too, became nervous at this point. I hadn't realized what was involved. Everyone clapped as they separated.

"That's how you do it!" Abel shouted, pointing at Trish who smiled back at him.

Cain was next to spin and landed on Bailey. She gave him a sweet, seductive type kiss, which seemed nice. Peyton was next, and she landed on Abel. My stomach churned.

"Yes!" Abel said, pumping his fist in the air. Peyton scooted closer to him and kissed him. I tried hard to pretend I wanted to watch and wasn't trying to look away. She began to draw back after a short kiss, but he pulled her closer for more, till she put a hand on his chest and lightly pushed him away.

Everything was slowly fading into more and more of a red tint. Next, it was my turn. I landed on Cain. He gave me one of his sweet gentlemanly kisses with a little tongue. It was nice. I could tell he was a good kisser.

The bottle went around and around. Almost everyone kissed everyone. I kissed Cain, Abel, Trish, someone I didn't know, and Alicia. At my next turn, my stomach sank when I realized it was slowing down. It stopped, directly on Peyton. I looked up quickly at her and saw her swaying a little from how much alcohol she had consumed.

"Oh shit," Abel shouted. Everyone whooped and clapped, "The moment we've been waiting for."

"Come on," Peyton said, motioning with both her hands for me to scoot closer to her. I was still sitting cross legged and pushed nearer. She looked at me with a proud drunken smile and began to lean forward; I got up on my knees, leaned in, and gave her a quick kiss, then moved back to my seat. She opened her eyes and gave me a look of complete confusion.

"Aww, come on, what was that?" some people said. I shrugged.

"All right, next!" Abel said, sliding the bottle to Alicia.

"Hey, where's the bathroom?" I asked Cain.

"Across the living room, down the hall to the left."

"All right, I'll be right back," I said, getting up.

"Hurry back, maybe I'll get another chance," Cain said, seeming to get a lot less shy the more he drank. I just smiled back at him.

I found my way to the bathroom after opening a couple of the wrong doors and finding it was actually on the right side. I locked the door and fumbled inside my pocket. I needed some peace of mind. I poured a small pile onto the counter, not even bothering to line it up, and inhaled it as quickly as possible. I hurriedly used the restroom and washed my hands. Just as I was about to open the door I felt it starting to take effect. My nerves calmed, and a peace began to run through my veins. I opened the door and Peyton was standing there, seemingly about to knock. She seemed a little drunk, but not as bad as I expected after how much she had consumed.

"I was going to knock this time," she said with a drunken laugh, and pushed her way in, closing the door behind her.

"What's up?" I asked, glancing in the mirror to make sure I didn't have a guilty face. It looked fine.

"What's up with you, I mean what was that?" she asked leaning against the wall and crossing her arms.

"What was what?"

"That bullshit kiss, Danielle?" I was completely shocked to hear her say those words.

"I don't know, everyone just made a big deal about it, I got nervous I guess," I avoided eye contact with her.

"Yeah?" She approached me, grabbed my hand, and put it under her shirt, onto her stomach. "Well, they're all in there now so . . ."

She began to unbutton her shirt and pushed herself clumsily against me. I put both hands on her shoulders, trying to keep her back and give myself more time to confront this rationally.

"What are you doing?" I asked, nervously.

153

"Kiss me, Danielle," she said looking into my eyes, "Kiss me like you kissed her."

I knew she spoke of Cindy. She looked at me and put one hand behind my neck and pulled me to her lips and kissed me. Before I could even think to stop her, I felt her grip tighten on my neck, as soon as our lips touched. I felt her take a deep breath. I instinctively wrapped my hands around her and pulled her close to me. As many times as I thought about it, I never thought this moment would happen. I had wanted her from the first moment I saw her, and could only fantasize at the thought of her wanting me too. A rush of adrenaline shook my hands as they ran over her body, taking in every inch. I did everything in my power to hold back. I was afraid of letting go and revealing to her how much I craved her. She pulled me closer to her and began kissing my neck. She kissed softly at first, then began sucking on my neck. I felt the blood rushing through my body a trillion cells at a time. I dug my nails into her; softly enough as to not hurt her, and hard enough to keep me grounded. All I wanted was to be in that moment, but my mind began to get in my way. Red flashes began to invade my vision like a strobe light. I grabbed Peyton harder and pushed her up against the wall. I began kissing her neck as she slipped her hands under my shirt grabbing my waist.

I saw bright red flood the room. I felt Peyton's breathing become louder in my ear, this only fueled the fire inside me. I felt all control quickly slipping away from me.

I looked up into Peyton's eyes for a second and saw nothing but desire. I kissed her and felt her pull my waist in closer to hers. I felt her tongue sliding against mine and her body rubbing up against me.

I suddenly felt a surge of energy transfer between us. It was painful and dark and immediately invaded my body like a poison.

I felt Peyton reach for my pants and began to unbutton them. I grabbed her hand, and pulled back immediately, thinking I had somehow done something to her that I had not intended. As soon as I let go, I felt the pain dissolve from me, and the room returned to its former color.

She seemed surprised and confused by my reaction. I looked her over quickly to ensure that I hadn't done anything to hurt her.

"What?" she said, stepping closer.

"Nothing," I said, taking a step back. She proceeded to grab me, began kissing my neck. I stood there paralyzed with indecision. She sensed my absence.

I went there to do the opposite of what I was doing. I needed to follow through with the original plan.

"I can't," I said.

"Why not?"

All I could think of was what the psychic lady said. How all I was capable of doing was hurting her. I felt that line, and I knew I was crossing it. I told myself I never would, and today I won't.

"I know you feel the same way about me, Danielle, you're not fooling anyone. I feel it in the way you look at me. I feel it in the way you talk to me, and I feel it every time you touch me. I've always felt it, and I've been waiting all this time for you to do something about it. Then, I realized you were too scared, and if I kept waiting, that day would never come. Now, I'm telling you that I want you. I want all of you and you're telling me you can't? What a fucking joke," she said, buttoning her shirt.

"And you know what?" she approached me quickly and shoved her hand into my pocket. She pulled out the remnants of the small bag. "I never judged you, but this shit is going to kill you. Is this why?"

"No," I said.

"Whatever." She opened the bag. I knew she intended to get rid of it, and I grabbed her arm, much harder than I intended to. I surprised myself. She looked at me in disgust and tried to jerk her hand back to no avail. I tried, but I couldn't let go. I felt the pain I

155

was inflicting on her, coursing through my veins, coursing through her stare.

"You better let go of me right now," she said with anger and pain in her eyes.

I did. Straight away, I saw deep red indentions on her skin. I turned away. The air slowly began escaping the room. What was I doing? Peyton dumped the contents of the bag in the toilet and flushed it. She threw the bag in my face and it floated onto the countertop. She left the bathroom immediately after that, saying nothing.

When I finally organized enough courage to leave the bathroom, I headed straight for the door, needing to get out of there. I slipped out unnoticed, or so I thought. I'd reached the bottom of the steps of the porch when the door opened.

"Hey, Dani," Cain called behind me, "Where are you going?"

"I just gotta get out of here," I said. I felt my hands shaking as I tried to sound calm.

"Something up with you and Peyton? She seemed upset."

"No, I'm just not feeling well."

"Hey, I'm a guy, but I'm not dumb. Is there something going on between you two?"

"No . . ." I said, truthfully. He surveyed my neck, obviously seeing marks that made it appear I was lying.

"I can tell by the way she looks at you. She loves you. You know that, right?" he asked. I was surprised by his intuition.

"Yeah."

"So, what's the problem?"

"I am," I said, "and I'm always going to be."

"You know, I wish you wouldn't go," he said, "I'm sure I've made that clear by now."

He had made it clear.

"You have," I said, smiling at him, "but I gotta go."

"All right, Dani, please take care of yourself."

"I will," I walked away, then turned around, "Hey Cain."

"Yeah."

"Make sure your brother takes care of her," I said.

He nodded, and I walked away.

I walked around the neighborhood, not wanting to go home. I just wanted to get away from myself. The one component I knew there was no escaping from. I found my way to the park where Peyton and I ended up after the carnival. I climbed up one of the structures at the playground and sat under one of the small coverings. I took off my sweater, rolled it into a ball, and shoved it under my head. I heard my phone ringing and looked at it for the first time since I'd left. It was my parents calling. I dismissed the call and scrolled through the texts and missed calls. Six calls from Peyton, four calls from my parents. I began scrolling through the texts.

Peyton:

'where are u?'

'I'm not mad just tell me where you are'

'I called your parents. I'm worried about you'

'just tell me you're okay'

'I know what I said and did was way out of line. It's okay if you don't feel the same way. Maybe I was wrong'

'I almost wish I could go back in time and change this, but I had waited so long . . . '

'I really need-'

I stopped reading, turned my phone off, and went to sleep.

* * *

"So, what happened then?" Dr. Joy asked.

"My parents were worried. They called the cops, and they found me the next morning walking home," I said.

"And Peyton?" she asked.

"I never called her back. I did what I could to eradicate her from my life. She came over a couple times, but I didn't respond. She sent over seven hundred text messages before I asked my parents to change my number."

"And her? Did she . . . this other guy?"

"Abel? Yeah, she did eventually."

"So, you got what you wanted?"

"I did what I had to do to protect her. You see, everyone is always under the impression that they love someone so much, and that means that they have to be with them."

"But she loved you too," she pointed out.

"She did. But if you really, really love someone, don't you think that if being with you means hurting them, the best thing you could do for them, is to get them as far away from you as possible? It's so selfish to put yourself before the well-being of someone you claim to love."

"I wouldn't argue with that statement, but what could you have done to hurt her more than you did that night?" she asked, "There's more pain than just physical pain."

"I know."

"Well, we're out of time for today, we'll pick back up on Thursday." She closed her notebook.

"Hey, I was going to ask you something," I said.

"What's that?"

"Could you increase my medication? I don't think it's working as well as before. I haven't been feeling all there, and my mind has just been running wild," I said, rubbing my hand behind my neck, avoiding her gaze.

"I would love to help you, but I can't."

"Why not?"

"Danielle, I'm sorry, but I can't adjust your medication at this time."

"What?" I said, surprised, "I thought doctors loved to push medication. With the way I've been feeling, I can't help but think I need more, a lot more."

"With what you are taking, you shouldn't feel anything," she said, with a humor I didn't understand.

"Well, then could I at least not get the generic brand?" I asked, "This shit doesn't work at all."

"I don't regulate the budget here. The director says we can only afford generic, so generic is what we have to give. I'm sorry."

"What am I going to do when the medication stops working entirely?"

"We'll cross that bridge when we come to it." she said.

Chapter Ten: The Parasite

I spent a lot of time at home, or over at Christian's house over the next few weeks. I missed half of school, and when I was there my mind was somewhere else. I did everything I could to avoid Peyton, and when I saw her I made sure she didn't see me. Sometimes, I would see her with her friends, sometimes I would see her with Abel.

I spent a lot of time with Cindy. I wanted to make sure she was okay. I knew Christian wouldn't do anything if I was around. She told me he'd never done anything that bad before, and she didn't expect it to happen again. I doubted this, and as the words escaped her lips, I knew she had no conviction in her own word either.

Nathan and I were over at Christian's for the weekend. Nathan wasn't speaking to me much since that night either. I wasn't there for him that morning, and I didn't feel like talking the next day, or for many days after that, and when I was finally ready to converse, he didn't want to talk to me. When I stayed over, Cindy stayed in my room.

"So, what's going on with your girl?"

"What do you mean?" I asked.

"You know . . . I haven't seen you with the girl in a while. Did you mess things up or what?"

"I guess you could say that," I said, not really wanting to get into the subject.

"Well, you should just tell her how you feel. I know for a fact that she feels the same way about you."

"I know how she feels, that's not it. I just choose not to be with her."

"Why? You worried about what your parents are going to say?"

"Surprisingly, no. I mean, I don't think they would really be surprised. I just know that us being together isn't good for her," I said.

"No offense, but it seemed like the best part of both of your lives was every second that you were together. I've never seen anyone, much less a couple, share the energy that flows between you two. You're young, but your love seems ancient. Your souls know each other so well they communicate in silence. People can feel the glances exchanged between the two of you, and it makes them know that there's hope for every lover that's with some sorry piece of shit. As I see it, there's no force in this world that can dissolve that kind of connection. I'd do anything to know that love."

It was silent for a moment. I knew all too well the words she spoke, and how she described the things I could never have put into words. I knew my soul would always long for Peyton, she was something that filled the cracks of my imperfections, and made me whole. I was broken without her.

"I think you've had a little too much," I said, dismissing her with humor and taking the tray we had the drugs on away from her.

"I'm serious!" she said, laughing, "Oh my God. What time is it?"

"It's 4 in the morning."

"Oh my God! I'm not even tired, this shit is strong," Cindy laughed.

As we lay down to go to bed that night, my mind was reeling. This was a distraction not a solution, but I knew the only thing that would make this pain go away, was gone. I'd made that happen. I spent forever trying to fall asleep. Every time I tried, it was as though I were dreaming, but I was never asleep. My body rested, but my mind never took a break. Dreams flooded in and out like small glimpses of 'what if?'

I dreamed that Peyton told me she already knew what I was, and that she was the same way, so it was okay. As far as my heart soared at this unrealistic thought, it crashed twice as hard when I realized it wasn't real.

I dreamed that she told me she was with Cindy, then I watched them kissing each other passionately, asking me if I was okay with it. Peyton was saying that it could have been me. I woke to this extremely angry, even as I thought of how unlikely it was. I was still angry at Cindy, who had done nothing wrong as she slept soundly next to me. I selfishly pulled the covers off of her with the dream still lingering in my mind, but in her deep sleep she didn't seem to notice or care.

I drifted off once again and dreamed of my brother. We were in the living room of Grandma Elizabeth's house, but there was no furniture, and it was dark and uninhabited. He stood with his back to me, crying. I tried to no avail to ask him what was wrong, but every word I tried to speak came out as a whisper, inaudible above the sound of his crying. He turned around finally, and he had bruises all over him, and he said: "You let this happen to me!"

I began to shake my head, "No," I said, regaining my voice, "I didn't know."

"I tried to tell you, now you're too late."

"No, I can fix it, I can make the pain go away," I pleaded.

My great-grandmother entered from the next room, regarding first my brother, then me. He continued to cry as she began to speak.

"You can't fix him. His soul is damaged, I don't think he's going to make it,"

Next, I was holding my brother as if he was just born, looking down at him. He resembled baby Alex.

"I need a doctor in here!" I heard my voice echo through the now empty room. I looked down and my arms were empty.

"Nathan . . ." I entreated through the silence.

"You can't save anyone," I heard my grandmother's voice right next to my ear and shot upright in the bed. I tried to gain my composure as quickly as possible, breathing in every second that assured that it was a dream. As the dream left me, and pieces faded quickly, the emotions remained.

I got out of bed and headed for the garage. Cindy seemed to be up already, but was nowhere in sight. Everyone in the house seemed to be awake, or just waking up. I didn't care whether I was heard or not. I had a sudden need to know about the things my great-grandmother spoke of so many years ago on her death bed. I needed to fill in the missing gaps. As I went into the garage, I noticed it hadn't changed much. In fact, the box I first rummaged through remained half open. I reached in, knowing what I was looking for. I couldn't care less about the rules, I needed to know what my great-grandmother had seen. I grabbed her journal, tucked it in my pants, and covered it with my t-shirt, then headed back inside.

I ascended the stairs quietly, hoping to sneak into the bedroom while it was still empty and get some time alone to explore the pages. Just as I was about to sneak into the room I saw Christian in the hallway, unaware of my presence. He was standing outside of the bathroom door, waiting, I assumed. I expected him to call out to Cindy and tell her to hurry it up, but he just stood there, apparently fidgeting with something in his pocket before he pushed the bathroom door partly open. When I realized what he was actually doing, I was disgusted and embarrassed and immediately tried to sneak into the bedroom without him noticing. I had no intention of providing him with an opportunity to explain playing with himself while his girlfriend showered. If he couldn't control himself, why didn't he just walk inside and join her, and do whatever it is they do in private.

Just as I was about to open the door to the room, I heard a voice from behind me, but not the voice I was expecting.

"Hey, Dani, you up already?" Cindy called from the bottom of the stairs looking up at me.

It took me about three seconds to register what was going on. If Cindy's downstairs, the only other person who could be taking a shower was Nathan.

I remembered his face the night of the game, I remembered him wanting to talk to me about something for the first time. I remembered the smile that he faked, and now I realized exactly what his reasons were.

Christian glanced at me from down the hall and smiled nervously, obviously unsure how long I'd been standing there.

"Hey, Dani, I didn't know you were up," he said, hopeful that I would play along; pretend to be oblivious, say nothing and do nothing.

I felt the heat rising through my body, my hairs standing on end, my heart working overtime. My body began to shake with the deepest rage I had never thought possible.

"I was just waiting for your brother to get out of the bathroom," he began to say, but slowed as he noticed my expression, "It's not what you think."

He raised his hands slightly as if in surrender. I felt like I was holding in check an explosion that was growing exponentially within me every second I stood there. I watched as the color of the room faded into a deep crimson red. Then I saw it.

From within me my shadow stepped out and crossed to stand behind Christian. It was as if I were looking into a mirror; I felt like I was watching myself, or a part of myself. It looked at me, and with the same rage, I directed it at Christian. He continued to talk, but I didn't hear anything else except the pounding of my pulse in my ears. He was mid-sentence when my shadow placed its hand on Christian's shoulder. He immediately stopped talking, stopped moving, as if he were paralyzed. A smile spread slowly across my shadow's face and it nodded at me.

Nathan's baseball equipment had been left out in the hallway and had caught my attention. I grabbed his bat. I advanced down the hallway toward Christian and began to swing. I remember the bat feeling heavy and smooth against my hands. I remember the harder I gripped it, and each time I brought it down against Christian's head, the heavier it felt. I remember the sound of metal colliding with his skull, his jaw, his chest. What I don't remember is if I hit him three times or three hundred times. Eventually, I threw it to the side and gripped his neck with the remainder of the strength I had in my body. I didn't even have to squeeze to feel the life leaving his body. It flowed directly into my soul, like an elixir. I remember how it brought a smile to my face to feel his soul leaving his body through my hands.

I felt two strong hands come up from behind me wrap around my stomach and tear me away from him. As I was pulled back, I felt his soul escape me and drive itself back into him. As I looked down at him, I saw his wounds healing before my eyes. Color returned to the room, and I saw that blood covered Christian, the floor, the walls, the ceiling, and me. His mangled face began to return to its original structure. His jaw reattached; the concave structures made in his face began to close up.

"No!" I cried out, "You don't get to live you piece of shit! You fucking parasite!"

I knew now what the palm reader spoke of. Christian was a parasite. I could not use my gift against him.

"Dani, Stop!" Cindy said, turning me around. I pushed her off of me, knocking her to the ground.

"Dani?" I heard my brother's voice behind me. Every angry emotion in me disintegrated at the sound of his voice. I turned around to see the horrified expression on his face as he looked down at Christian. I had never wanted him to see something like that, but I would do it again if I had to.

"We're leaving," I said, reaching over Christian to grab Nathan's hand and pulling him toward me.

I lead him down the hallway, passing Cindy in the process. Suddenly, I stopped, turned around, and knelt down, putting my face close to hers.

"Don't ever let me find out that you knew about this," I said, still reeling with anger that I knew I would project at anyone who stood in my way. I heard Christian begin to moan as he regained consciousness. I whipped around to look at him and let go of my brother's hand.

"Go downstairs, get the keys to one of the cars, and I'll be right out," I said.

"Come with me," he pleaded, grabbing my hand, terror evident on his face.

"I'll be right down," I promised, leading him toward the stairs with my hand against his back, "Hurry."

He reluctantly did as I asked. I heard him grab a key, and the door close behind him. I returned to Christian as he writhed on the floor groaning. He had no idea of the things I wanted to do to him. I knelt next to him and turned his face back and forth to see if any of the damage I had inflicted had stuck. There were some bruises and minor cuts. It wasn't enough. I stood back up and ground my foot against his face. He had barely opened his eyes when I brought my foot back. Then, with all the strength I could muster, I connected with his face. His head whipped in the opposite direction, and more blood splattered on the wall. Cindy screamed and covered her eyes. As I passed her to leave, she had her face in her hands crying. For a few seconds, though, she parted her fingers and gazed at me with a terrified expression. I looked back at her and I felt no remorse.

I ran downstairs, jumped in the car, and sped off. Luckily I'd had some practice driving Peyton's car, but it proved only mildly helpful in my state of mind. I tried to maintain my speed and obey traffic signals, but I was so amped up. It was difficult to focus on things that seemed so insignificant at the time.

"You know?" Nathan said as he gripped the door handle and the seat, trying to brace himself.

"I know," I said, my hands still shaking and perspiring, slipping on the wheel as I tried to steer. I looked down at them for the first time and noticed they were covered in blood. I could only imagine how scared Nathan must be.

"Is he dead, Dani?" he asked. I turned toward him, wanting to say I wished he was, but responded instead with the truth, and what I knew he wanted to hear.

"No."

"Are you sure, there was so much–" he stopped and changed the subject, "I wanted to tell you."

"What did he do to you, Nathan?" I asked knowing it probably wasn't safe for me to know the answer.

"I don't want to tell you, you'll tell dad," he said.

"Of course I'll tell dad and mom; Nathan, they have to know!" I said, more emphatically than I intended.

"She won't believe you . . ." he trailed off.

"What do you mean? What are you talking about? Of course she'll believe us," I said as we pulled up to the house, and I turned off the engine.

He sat silently for a second, not wanting to answer.

"Nathan?" I prodded. He looked at me.

"I already told her," he said, and began to cry, "She didn't believe me, she told me not to tell dad."

My heart sank to the floor for Nathan. How could this have been going on? How could I not know? My mother . . . How could she?

I hugged my brother as I led him inside and told him to go change his clothes, and stay in his room, that I would talk to our mother.

I sat at one end of the kitchen table trying to digest everything that had just happened. At first, I expected to hear sirens at any second. Then, I remembered Christian was smart, and surely knew better than to draw attention to the situation. I drummed my fingers on the table and readjusted constantly in the chair. Leaning back, I felt something pressing against my back. Then, I remembered I had the journal. I whipped it out, threw it on the table, and flipped the pages to the only passage I needed to read at that moment; the one I had originally turned to months ago, the one I knew my grandmother spoke of when she rejected Christian on her death bed.

Chapter Eleven:
Turning a Blind Eye

December 1980

I have never been filled with such disgust as I am today, I cannot even comprehend to myself the things that have transpired. I ask God for strength and forgiveness, but these feelings feel so far from me. The only thing that courses through my veins is hatred, for my grandson, and for my daughter. I felt that I could have killed that boy tonight; I knew I had enough of the hatred in my heart to do so without a regret. I don't know why I didn't, and I have a feeling I might regret not doing so for a very long time.

Everyone was gathered at my daughter's house for the usual Christmas Eve dinner. I was staying there for a few days and unpacked my things in Bridget's room. Her room had hints of pink and purple with animal stencils lining the walls. It was the perfect room for a little girl. I wished I had dedicated such time to ensuring visual entertainment in Ivy's room when she was a little girl. I wished I had the luxury of being close to my children. A visit for the holidays was not enough, but it was all I could give. I remember hearing commotion from the living room. I knew that meant that another guest had arrived. I glanced out the window to see Christian lugging his bags toward the front door. He was on break from college, and here for the next week. Christian was young, strong, charismatic, handsome, and unusual.

I went into the living room to greet him with his mother and little sister as he came in the front door. Bridget ran up to him and greeted him with a big hug. He scooped her up in his arms and hugged her.

"Hey little lady!" he said, hugging her, "Whoa, you're getting big. How old are you now?"

"I'm eight," she said, pushing him.

"Eight?!?! Wow, you're all grown up," he said, laughing and hugging his mom.

"Hi Christian," I said to him.

"Grandma Elizabeth," he said with a nod, and proceeded to give me a hug for show, then turned to his mother. Christian had resented me since he was a small child, but he always had clever ways of hiding it.

"Hi Mom," he said, giving her a great big hug, "You look amazing, not a day over 30."

He gave Bridget a wink and smiled at his mother.

"Well, I'm going to unpack my stuff and get settled in. If that's okay?" he said with raised eyebrows.

"Of course, sweetie," his mother told him, gesturing him up the stairs.

Our eyes met as he walked by with a smirk on his face.

"I'll help you!" Bridget exclaimed behind him, following up the stairs.

"You will?" he replied, laughing.

Christmas celebrations dragged on, through the days. Family came and went. They all talked about how surprised they were to see me, how it was such a rare occasion. I felt guilty, wishing it was just over. It was the day I was going to leave, and the house had mostly emptied out of visitors. I had taken a stroll through the neighborhood that afternoon while Ivy went to a half day of work. I wanted to be back before she got home so that she wouldn't think I was completely neglecting spending time with my grandchildren, so I shortened my stroll with nature.

I got back to the house and slowly made my way up the stairs, slightly tired. I grasped the railing at the last step and heard Bridget giggling from Christian's room.

I started to walk toward my room, then I heard something, and it was just the way the words escaped his mouth. I stopped.

"Did you miss me?" Christian asked.

"Yes," I heard Bridget say with a giggle.

"You did?" Christian said with a false surprised voice, "How much?"

"That tickles!" Bridget exclaimed, continuing to giggle.

I proceeded to walk toward Christian's room.

"What's that?" I heard him say. Bridget laughed loudly.

"Shhh, shhh, you remember what to do?" I heard him ask with my ear close to the door.

"Uh-huh," Bridget said.

"Good, and you can't tell ,right?" he asked, "It's our little secret."

I ripped open the door. I was overwhelmed by the sight. Bridget lay completely naked on the bed, Christian in only his boxers, propped up over her with his face close to her stomach, his bottom half slightly covered by the sheet.

"Grandma Eliz —"Christian began, but before he could get the second word out I had made my way across the room. Red tint invaded my vision. I snatched him up by his neck and slammed his face into the wall.

"You son of a bitch," I said, pulling his head back and smashing it into the wall again, "You sick snake!"

Anger consumed me. Bridget had wrapped herself in the sheet, and began to cry and scream, "Stop, you're hurting him!"

"Get your clothes on, sweetie," I said, looking her way.

She continued to cry, but did as I said. Just as she had finished putting her shirt on I heard a voice behind me.

"What the hell is going on in here?" It was my daughter, "Mother, unhand my son!"

"You don't understand. I caught him in bed with Bridget," I walked closer to Ivy and said in a lower tone, "He was trying to perform sexual acts with her."

"Oh Mother, that's ridiculous!" she said with a laugh.

"Ivy, this is not a joke. Your son has been preying on your daughter," I said, angrily.

"What proof do you have of this, mother?" she asked in a dignified voice.

"I just told you, I saw it with my own eyes," I said in disbelief.

"I don't see anything unusual going on here, except you using violence against my children. That appears to be the only unacceptable behavior here."

"Bridget, tell your mother what Christian was doing to you," I said.

"Bridget, tell mommy, was Christian hurting you?" she asked with a smile on her face.

I wanted to slap my daughter so much in that instant.

"No," she said in a low tone.

"No?" Ivy responded, "Has he ever tried to hurt you?"

"No," she said again.

"Well, there you have it. I think you're mistaken, Mother, and I think it's time you leave," she said with a serious expression.

Christian, who had been silent in the background, put his hand on my shoulder, "It's okay. I'll help you get your things, Grandma Elizabeth."

I grabbed his hand and pushed him away from me, "Don't you ever touch me, boy, and if I ever find out that you even so much as think about what you were doing today . . . I will come back and I will finish what I started."

I left the house that day with more regret and rage than I had felt in years, and guilt within myself. Had I made this monster?

* * *

When I finished reading I felt so many emotions: anger, sadness, pity, and confusion. I closed the journal and was still absorbing the words when I heard the garage door open. My hands began to shake as I tried to plan how to approach talking to my mother. I prayed that my hands stayed put this time. She opened the door and smiled at me. I knew that she was still oblivious to what had transpired today.

"Hey Dani, is Christian here? I saw his car outside," she asked, putting groceries down, not looking closely at me.

"No, he's not, Mom," I said, hoping that she would stop moving, and pay attention to me, "I need to talk to you."

"Okay, let me just finish getting the groceries and then–"

"No, I need to talk to you now," I said, shaking uncontrollably at this point, and becoming more frustrated every second she avoided me.

"Okay, okay, just let me–" she began.

"Stop! Stop moving! Stop talking! Look at me!" I screamed at her, standing up.

She stared at me, horrified.

"You're bleeding! Oh my God, what happened?" she said with her hand over her mouth, crossing the room to examine me.

175

"I'm not hurt, Mom," I said, shaking her off, "I'm fine, it's Nathan."

"Nathan's hurt?" she said, looking even more horrified.

"No," I said, raising my hands up to make her stop talking.

I wanted to explain what happened, I wanted to tell her what I saw, what I did, but that's not what came out.

"Why didn't you believe Nathan, Mom?" I asked. She got a shocked look on her face, and glanced at me sideways, pretending that she didn't know what I spoke of. This began to fuel the flame of fury within me.

"What are you talking about?" she said.

"Don't do that, don't act like you don't know what the fuck I'm talking about," I said, "He told you about Christian, and you told him not to talk about it. Why is that?"

"Honey, sometimes children think that things happen to them that don't really happen. It's common for a child to exaggerate or fantasize about things like this, especially at his age. I just . . . I just didn't want things to get out of hand without any proof."

"Proof? He told you, his mother, that he was being molested by your brother, and you still thought it was safe for him to go over there to see him? Are you fucking kidding me?" I said, becoming more enraged.

"Well . . . you were there," she said in a low tone. This put a knife through my heart.

"How dare you put this on me! I didn't know, and if I did, I would have done what I did now, a long time ago," I said.

"What did you do, Danielle?" she asked, "Is Christian okay?"

"What the fuck is wrong with you? That man has been molesting your son! I wish he was dead right now! In fact, I hope he is!" I said.

"He didn't do it, Dani! He would never do that! I know him, it's not true!" she screamed back at me. I didn't understand how she could say that so plausibly.

"How can you even believe that?" I asked in despair for her.

"You don't understand," she said with a helpless inflection in her voice, while refusing to meet my eyes.

"Don't understand what?" I asked.

"He's not like—"

"How can you not believe Nathan when I know Christina did the same thing to you!" I yelled.

Her eyes jerked back toward me with a glare I'd never witnessed on her face before. I didn't even have the time to string together a thought when I felt her hand collide so hard with my face that it knocked me off my feet. That was the only time in my life my mother had hit me, or anyone for that matter. I was speechless.

She pointed her finger at me with tears streaming down her face, "You don't know what you're talking about."

She left the kitchen and closed herself away up in her room. She turned on some music and remained there for the rest of the night, and for days to come. My dad was out of town, and wouldn't be back till Wednesday, so there she stayed. My anxiety rose as I thought about what would happen when my dad returned home. What would we say, what would we do, how would we put this back together? I comforted Nathan, almost constantly. He felt so guilty about everything, even though he was the last one to be blamed; my mother not only avoided me, but him as well. She wouldn't even leave her room to go to work or eat. I felt guilt rising up in me, I felt like I had broken her, and I knew it was the kind of broken that I couldn't fix. All Wednesday at school I couldn't focus. I became more and more anxious about my father's return. I knew he must be worried. In our phone conversation, no one had much to say, except that we couldn't wait till he was home, and that everything was fine, but I could tell he knew otherwise. I knew if there was a way, he would have been back sooner. He wouldn't be home until around 6 pm, by the time I arrived home it was 4 pm.

I entered the house and Nathan was sitting on the stairs. He looked uneasy.

"What's up?" I said, putting my stuff down right by the door.

"Something's not right," he said.

His unspoken words were clear to me. The energy in the house was intrusive to my being. You could feel it, like a chill that cut through the stagnant air. I heard music from upstairs creeping from under the door of my mother's room.

I looked up the stairs, then reached into my pocket, and handed my phone to my brother. I meant to tell him something. I meant to explain to him . . . that this wasn't his fault.

I ran up the stairs, three at a time. I hit the wall when I reached the top, and I plunged down the hall to my mother's room. I threw open the door. It led to a small hallway that led into the main bedroom area. The door to the bathroom was in that small hallway. The music was coming from behind the door. It was so loud at this point. I could barely hear anything. I banged my fist on the door hard.

"Mom! Open the door!" I screamed with my voice cracking. I didn't care if the fear showed.

I banged harder and harder with no response. I knew, despite the loud music, there was no way she couldn't hear me. I stared at the door in frustration. Light seeped out from the bottom of the door, thrown from the interior window. My eyes focused on where the tile in the bathroom met the carpet of the hallway. Blood.

It leaked out of the bathroom and had begun to leach into the carpet. My heart stopped. I reached down, and with my finger tip, touched it lightly, just to make sure it was real. It was still wet. I pulled myself up by the doorknob and began to throw myself against the door with all my strength. The door stood strong.

"Mom!" I screamed. I threw myself again and again. I began to kick the door. I braced my back against the wall opposite and kicked the door four times before I felt it begin to give. I pushed my back against the wall, and with all that was left in me, charged at the door. It gave way.

In a split second, I took in everything: my mother sitting with her back against a wall with a vacant expression on her face. Her hair looked like she had spent all day working on it. She sat wearing a beautiful dress. Her makeup was perfectly placed on every contour of her face, her eyes, nearly lifeless. Her arms were at her sides, her left wrist cut deep down the middle extending vertically up her forearm. The pool of blood ran from one side of the bathroom to the other. The bathroom reeked of fresh blood. It smelled like copper.

I knelt down next to my mother, trying to comprehend what was going on.

"What did you do?" I asked her.

I tried to grasp her other wrist to see if there was a pulse. I suddenly felt a presence standing in front of me, and looked up to see my mother, or at least a vision of my mother staring down at herself. It was her shadow, her soul. I reached for my mother and clutched her hand. I felt the energy flow through me and into my mother. I knew there was still a chance to bring her back. Just as the room began to fade into a light blue tint, and I began to be reassured that hope wasn't lost, my mother's shadow spoke.

"How could you let this happen?"

I froze at those words, and sick guilt shot through me, and the room faded into blackness. As I felt myself drifting I reached for my mother's hand, but to no avail.

* * *

I awoke in my dreamland the way one would awaken from a nightmare. I was in a nightmare. I had to get back to my mother. There could still be enough time to help her if I could just get out of here. I sat up quickly in the peaceful bed that I had once found so comforting, it now only sickened me. I looked around.

"Danielle, you need to relax," said a voice behind me. Anarah stood next to the bed.

I sprang up and began pacing the room.

"How do I get out of here?" I said, clenching my fist, looking for a door that I knew didn't exist.

"You can't leave, your soul needs to heal," she said in a concerned tone, "Danielle you need to stay here."

Her voice was changing from concerned to cautious. I didn't care. I wanted more than anything to be out of that place, and I would do anything to leave. Anarah tried to put a hand on my arm and I pushed it away.

"Dani, it is important that you calm yourself right now," she commanded.

"Dani," I heard an unexpected, yet familiar voice, and turned toward it quickly. There, sitting on the side of the bed was Peyton.

"Peyton?" I said, in disbelief.

Anarah hastened across the room to stand between Peyton and me.

"Danielle, you need to listen to me very closely right now. Whatever you do, do not talk to her, do not welcome her presence in this place."

Peyton got up from the bed and walked past Anarah.

"Dani, your mom, she needs you," she said, grabbing my arm.

"I don't know how to leave," I said.

"You have to make it happen," she said, looking straight at me, "She's trying to keep you here, but time is running out. If you stay here any longer, you won't be able to save her! Dani, you have to go."

"Don't listen to her, Danielle, she's an illusion, she's not real. You can't leave here till your body is ready, it will tear your soul apart!"

Nothing logical crossed my mind at that moment. Nothing mattered except getting back to my mother.

"Get me out of here. Get me out of here now!" I screamed. "I want to go back!"

"Don't do this, Danielle," Anarah said with pity in her eyes.

"I have to," I replied.

Peyton smiled at me, and Anarah hung her head.

"Then so it is," she said.

* * *

When I awoke I expected a commotion. I expected to be back where I left. I was ready to act, to save her. I tried to move, but my body could barely budge. I opened my eyes, but still only saw darkness. I struggled to gain my bearings. It was like being suffocated by emptiness. I turned my head left and right and then looked up. Above my head, I noticed a small chink of light. Like the moon in an otherwise dark sky. I continued looking at it for several minutes trying to understand what it was. I began to free my hand from my side and reach above my head. I reached for this moon, but it wasn't far away at all. My hand covered the light, and it created darkness. Around this light, I felt metal. I put my finger into the light and pulled. The sound that resulted was unsettling, the light unzipped through my fingers and air filled my lungs. My arms became free, and I unzipped this thing that imprisoned me. I sat up and looked around.

A body bag. I was in a body bag, sitting on a metal autopsy table.

That was my resting place. I looked around at what appeared to be an empty laboratory with metal beds and medical equipment. The morgue. To my relief, I noticed I was still clothed. I investigated the room, and to my left something caught my eye, another bag. I stared at it for several minutes. I waited for something, that sick feeling, that uneasiness, that despair, that loss, that emptiness. I waited for these feelings to invade my being and incapacitate me. I'm not certain I told myself; that's why these feelings alluded me. I rolled to the side of the metal table and lowered myself onto the floor. I noticed my shoes were missing, and the floor was cold. I walked toward the other table and stood next to it. I knew what was in there. I reached to the top of the bag and pulled the zipper down.

My mother laying lifeless in her bag was revealed. I looked, and I looked. Her eyes closed with darkness around them, the color drained from her body as the blood settled elsewhere. I continued to scrutinize her face and reached out to her shoulder and placed my hand on it. I felt no life moving through her veins, no emotions, just hollowness. She was truly gone.

My mother laid there dead in front of me, and I felt nothing. There was no sadness or longing. I stood there for a long time, expecting the shock to wear off.

In my mind, the only emotion that resonated toward my mother was anger. Anger for what she had done to herself and what she had done to us. Some diabolical characteristic in me wanted to hurt my mother, more than ever before. I noticed how my grip on my mother's shoulder had tightened as my nails began to dig into her arm. I pulled my hand back and noticed an affliction on her flesh from where my hand had been placed. The skin shriveled and become darker.

"You coward."

I spoke these final words, turned from her body without a second glance, and proceeded to leave the death room.

I exited the room through two heavy double doors. Immediately to my right was a reception window. A young woman looked up from the phone she had been talking into. It immediately fell to the desk, and she turned white as she saw me. I approached the desk.

"Can you tell me something?" I asked. She did not respond, she only looked up at me with her mouth partially opened.

"Is this part of the hospital?"

She remained frozen.

"When did I get here?" I asked, more impatiently.

" . . . Two hours ago," she responded.

"Is this part of the hospital?" I asked again.

"Yes, let me call a doctor – " she began, and reached for the phone.

"No, don't do that," I said hastily, my voice cautionary.

"He can come—" she said, reaching again for the phone.

I reached through the window, grabbed the phone, and rested in the cradle, holding my hand tightly over it. At this point, I was extremely close to her.

"Don't call anyone, don't tell anyone, don't do anything. Just tell me where the exit is," I said.

I attempted to escape from the hospital as inconspicuously as possible. I inspected my pants and saw how much blood had dried on them from when I found my mother. Other people seemed to notice as well. The situation wasn't helped by my missing shoes. I departed to the outside hastily through the automatic doors. The sun was still out, and my eyes were sensitive to the bright light. I trudged along the sidewalk for miles toward my house. Walking from the hospital had become so common; I knew the route well.

After nearly an hour of my trek, I arrived on my doorstep and reached for the handle. All along my route, I had not prepared myself for the chaos inside, what to say, or how to react. As I closed the door behind me, I felt the coldness in the air. The foreboding scent of death lingered. It was like a reminder of reality, and I found it undeniably comforting.

I immediately turned toward the stairs, wanting to escape to my room for solitude, but as I turned I saw my brother sitting at the bottom, gaping up at me. He blinked hard and stood up. He remained silent as he slowly approached me. He put his hand out to touch me and barely brushed my arm before quickly pulling it back as if he had touched a dead body. He retreated a step back and scrutinized me with an expression of absolute bewilderment.

"Nathan, who's at the door?" I heard my father's voice from around the corner. He sounded strained and exhausted.

"It's . . . Dani," he said, barely able to string the words together.

"Nathan, that's not . . ." my dad began, as he walked around the corner. His words trailed off at the sight of me.

"Dani . . ." he choked back his tears as he rushed toward me and embraced me. He hugged me tightly as if I might escape back into the afterlife. He tried to speak as tears escaped his eyes.

"They told me you were gone . . . I . . . I saw your body. I can't believe you're here," he said in wonder. The happiness seemed misplaced, considering the circumstances, and my mother's body lying in the mortuary.

"There . . . was a mistake," was all I could come up with.

I stood there with my dad's arms around me, still hugging me. I wanted to return the relief of seeing him again and embrace him as well, but no affectionate emotion overcame me. His arms around me began to make me feel uncomfortable, so I stepped back to free myself. He appeared slightly put out by this response, but an expression of understanding came over his face.

"I'm so sorry, Dani . . . your mom," he began.

"I know," I said abruptly, " . . . it's fine."

I headed back toward the stairs, tentatively making my exit.

"I'm just really tired . . ." I said, trailing off and started upward. My brother quickly moved out of my way. I reached my room without another word being spoken, and without an explanation given or asked for. I locked myself in. I had no inclination to be disturbed by their emotions. I sensed a distance from my family, a disconnect. It felt like they were actors portraying this tragic story, and I was an unconvinced audience.

* * *

"With you, it's like you became a completely different person. When you became the person you are today," Dr. Joy began at the end of my story.

"I lost it. Not my mind. No . . . something much worse. I lost my ability to connect and my ability to forgive. I never cried for my mother after she died. I still haven't to this day.

"Although, over time, many emotions have returned to me at least in part, I've never felt close to complete since that day, and now I just feel like the time to grieve for her has passed. I feel so guilty about not being able to be there for my family when she was gone."

"I'm sure they didn't expect that from you, Danielle, you were only eighteen," said Dr. Joy.

"I expected it from myself. I could tell they knew I was different after that day. They kept their distance, and I kept mine. Sometimes they would try to connect with me, but as much as I wanted to seek that connection, I was unable to. For a long time, I didn't want anything to do with them. It was like living with strangers. Who would have ever thought that the pain you feel when you lose someone close to you is something that you would want to feel, something that you need to feel? Most people would give anything to relieve that pain they feel when they lose a loved one, but I would have given anything to feel it. It was impossible for me to experience those emotions. At times I couldn't help but think I wasn't supposed to feel that way, and they were weak because they did. The only emotion I was able to embrace was anger."

"You should have stayed," she said.

"What?" I asked, confused.

"Maybe if your soul had taken the time to heal, it would have been different, maybe if you hadn't left right away . . ."

"But that's not real . . ." I said. "That was my imagination creating an illusion."

"Something you need to understand about the mind, is that when the mind is broken, the person is broken as well. If your subconscious is under the impression that something is one way, the body will react physiologically to what the mind believes to be true."

"I guess that makes sense . . ." I admitted, still a little confused.

"That's all the time we have today, but I'm curious as to how this story ends," she said.

"You've read the journals, you know what happens next."

"I think there's more to it than what I've read."

Chapter Twelve: Provocations

I spent a lot of time in my room reviewing the conversation I'd had with the doctor, and something wasn't adding up, although, I couldn't put my finger on exactly what. She wound up canceling our next visit. I hated it so much when she did this. It was always when I was prepared to discuss things, and I felt we were close to achieving answers when she interrupted the flow by canceling our appointment. My mind started growing fuzzy, and I didn't know what was real and what wasn't. I would see something one way, then remember that I didn't necessarily see things how they are, but in some skewed perspective, and I would wind up dismissing every thought I had.

Rachel, the same female medication dispenser, entered my room. I was so lost in the words inside my head, the door opening startled me.

"You look like you were deep in thought," she said, pushing her cart of medicine into the room.

"Yeah, kind of . . ." I answered, attempting to recapture my train of thought.

"What were you thinking about?" she dismissed her duties and leaned against the wall.

"I don't remember," I said, reclining back onto my bed, trying to hide my irritation.

"Well, maybe if I leave, then come back in, it will return to you?"

"Yeah, I don't think so," I said.

She walked over and sat on my bed. I didn't move, but shifted my eyes to look at her. She leaned back on her elbows the same way I did. The bed was small, so she seemed to be sitting annoyingly close to me. I felt her knee brush the side of my leg. I sat up.

"These beds aren't so uncomfortable," she said, pressing down on the mattress.

"Try sleeping on them for years, you might change your mind," I said, not looking at her.

"Perhaps."

I looked over at her questioningly.

"What goes on inside of your head? It seems like it's so loud in there."

"It can be."

"Can I ask you something?"

"What do you want to know?"

"Why do they keep you separate from the other patients?"

"What is it about the answer to this question that intrigues you? I'm sure you've heard the stories."

"I have heard the stories. I heard them several times with many variations. In this place, it is not unusual to hear crazy or unbelievable stories. It is truly our day-to-day job to deal with such situations. However, when patients or staff tell me what happened with you, they seem like they believe something that's impossible. They talk of the day as if they had seen the devil himself. They blame you for what they did to that patient. They think you're possessed or evil."

"Can't say I blame them for thinking that. It was better in the jail, they knew better than to put me among other people."

"They beat him senseless with metal batons and turned his brain to mush during an altercation you two had. They were unable to control the situation and took unnecessary measures. I hardly see how that could be considered your fault. I know there is something peculiar about you. I don't deny that. I felt it, that terrifying chaos. There was so much darkness . . . so much guilt,"

"What happened to that patient is exactly what I wanted to happen to him," I said, "You're right, I have a darkness inside me, caged up like a rabid dog. Should you ever encounter such a creature, heed my advice, the last thing you should ever do is —"

"Provoke it," she finished.

"Exactly," I gave a devious grin.

Rachel inched her leg away from mine.

"I'm surprised they let you come in here alone," I said.

"Well, they said since they've segregated you from the other patients there have been very few incidences. However, I am equipped with a very shiny whistle in case of emergencies," she said, pulling out a necklace with a purple whistle attached at the end," Apparently self-defense devices, sharp objects, including sedatives are not allowed. They said I stood the best chance if I just called for help."

"Does that make you feel safe?" I inquire.

"You don't make me feel as scared as I know I should."

"I see that."

"So, then tell me, Danielle. What provoked you that day?"

* * *

As the memories of that day lined up like dominoes waiting to be knocked over, my mind returned to that day. Coming to the mental institution was easy. I had cut my ties with all the things that bound me emotionally to the outside world. Every person I excised from my life was a burden lifted. My inability to connect turned the

189

loss into emptiness rather than pain. When I first arrived, I thought I was completely void of emotion. I was wrong.

"Okay, we're almost done with the intake process; I just have a few more questions. Then, afterward we will take you to the cafeteria, and get you something to eat before your meeting with your doctor, then show you to your living quarters," said a man sitting in the chair across from me in a tiny office with no windows. He was an older Hispanic male with dark hair and a five o'clock shadow just starting to gray. He scribbled on his clipboard as I answered each question.

"I understand."

"Excellent, tell me, have you ever seen a professional before regarding any mental health disorders?"

"Yes."

"Have you, or do you know if you have been diagnosed with any mental health disorders?"

"Yes."

"Can you tell me what they are?"

"Bipolar II."

"Okay, anything else?"

"No."

"Have you ever been prescribed medication for this?"

"Yes."

"What kind of medication have you taken?"

"I don't remember."

"Are you currently taking any medication?"

"No."

"Is there any history of mental illness on your father's side of the family?"

"No, not that I know of."

"What about your mother's side of the family?"

"Yes."

"Do you know how or what they were diagnosed with?"

"My great-grandmother was also diagnosed Bipolar II later in life."

"Okay, anyone else?"

"My mother had depression . . . I believe."

"You believe? Do you know if she saw a doctor or had an official diagnosis?"

"I'm not sure, but she . . . committed suicide earlier this year," I said, hurrying the end of my sentence.

I could hear the doctors writing halt momentarily. He looked up at me over his glasses, "I'm so sorry to hear that."

I did not respond, he appeared to have almost a sense of relief that I did not immediately wish to explore the topic further.

"I want you to know that although this is a long-term facility, it is our intention to provide medical care, counseling, and the tools needed to reintegrate you back into society. Rarely do our patients stay here more than a year. You seemed to have experienced a great deal of trauma in your life, and we plan to work with you to start the healing process. How does that sound?" he said with a smile.

"It sounds fine, I guess."

"Good, now let's take you to the cafeteria and get you some food. I will have the orderlies escort you. Then, after you eat, you will have a meeting with your doctor. At that point, she will prescribe any medications she or he feels like you might need or benefit from."

"Do I have to take medication?"

"Medication is part of the treatment process, so yes it is very likely that you will be prescribed one or more medications."

"It's just I've taken medication before, and I'm worse off now than when I started taking it. I'm not saying it doesn't help, but there is no cure for what I have, so why do we receive medical treatment?"

"We are not trying to cure your mental health disorder, we are trying to cure the temporary disorder in your life that your condition has caused. Regular treatment, counseling, as well as the various other tactics we use here, can make your disorder manageable," he said, getting up from his chair. He opened the door and motioned for the staff to retrieve me. I took this as my cue to get up.

"It was very nice meeting you, Miss Blake, and I wish you the best of luck," he said, shaking my hand, "this is Ryan, he will be your escort to the cafeteria. As a protocol for new patients who have not yet met with their doctor to ascertain their risk level, we require wrist wraps. These will make it difficult to eat, but I expect after your meeting with your doctor they will no longer be necessary."

"Oh, okay," I said, sticking my wrists out as to be handcuffed.

"Just put your hands about six inches apart with your wrists facing the ceiling," said Ryan.

Ryan was a smaller guy, even shorter than me. He was young, probably in his early twenties. He had black hair arranged in a messy fashion and dark eyebrows. He had a kind face and friendly disposition. I found interacting with him pleasant.

He latched what seemed like a short thick dog collar onto my left wrist and buckled it. It was heavy and made holding up my wrist less pleasant. He quickly buckled the other one. A sort of rope, almost like you would find at the end of a backpack strap ran between the two, almost a foot in length.

He fastened it about two inches, then lowered my wrist.

"I won't tighten it too much, so you'll have less trouble eating."

"Thanks."

He walked me down a hallway, through double doors into the cafeteria area. It had a serving line much like a school, and about ten tables with chairs attached to the tables. There were approximately fifteen other patients in the room, eating or talking to one another. While some of them had an unease about them, the majority seemed to be typical people. As I walked in, some turned their head, others continued about their activity. One patient, however, made a beeline for me and Ryan. He strode over flamboyantly, exaggerating every step and expression.

"Ryan, Ryan, Ryan!" he exclaimed as soon as he arrived, attempting to clutch Ryan's free hand that Ryan pulled away.

"You know the rules, no touching," Ryan said with the shake of his finger and a smile.

"Of course, of course," this man said with a bow of his head in apology, "Ryan, who is this?"

"William, this is Danielle, she is just about to get something to eat. If Danielle is okay with it, you may join her. Are you okay with that, Danielle?"

"Of course she's okay with it," William said excitedly, clutching my arm with his hand.

Ryan quickly removed William's hand from my arm with force and placed it at William's side.

"I said no touching, William, you need to listen. Do it again, and I will write a report. Now, I didn't ask you, I asked Danielle if she would like to eat with you. Danielle?" he asked, looking over at me.

"Yeah, that's fine."

William smiled and clutched both of his hands together, "Wonderful."

Ryan took me to get a tray of food then sat me opposite of William at the table. I looked down at the styrofoam tray with a mixture of carrots and peas, a slice of some sort of meat product with gravy, mashed potatoes, completed with an apple juice, and a spork on the side. I slowly consumed some of the mashed potatoes with no interest in the rest of the meal. They were not terrible. As I ate, I noticed William's eyes examining me, and him fidgeting continuously. I tried to ignore it.

"So, can I see it?" he said at last.

"See what?" I said, shifting my eyes back and forth, thinking he must be some sort of pervert with his question.

"Your gift, silly. You're a dual soul if I'm not mistaken. Is that right?"

I stopped eating and placed my utensil on my tray, "What do you know about dual souls?"

"Oh, I've heard things, learned things . . . seen things," he said with an unnerving smile "I never thought in all my years I'd be in the same room with one, but I heard you coming a mile away."

"How?"

"Your thoughts are like sirens, like the tortured crying for help, I've never felt so high in my life."

"You're a reader," I said, remembering a similar description of my thoughts from the palm reader.

"Yes, but here I'm no reader, or so they tell me. The voices I hear, the whispers, and the future depictions I see are not real they say. Schizophrenia is what they call it. I don't mind being here though. At times the voices get misinterpreted, mixed, and transposed. Sometimes the things I hear are lies. This is where I come to rest. To sort out my voices, put them back in their proper place. They are always quieter here, except for yours."

I hesitated with my next question, but curiosity coaxed me, " What do you hear?"

This drew another repulsive grin from William. I averted my eyes slightly.

"What do I hear? The gift consuming you, the rage of a thousand wrongs, the guilt of a cold body. I hear your mother crying as you pushed her to the edge. I feel Abel's family shattered by the light you took from them. Your father lost and alone, feeling like a failure in every way imaginable."

"Okay, that's enough," I said, sensing the heat rise in me at his words.

"Show me and I'll stop."

"No."

"I hear Cindy being beaten for her infertility. Your great-grandmother's relief to leave this cruel world and pass her gift to you knowing that you would suffer every day, but she still willingly did so."

The familiar strobe light of blood laden lenses began. I looked around for Ryan to come to my aid. I saw him standing across the room, and he seemed to notice my discomfort and began to walk over. However, another orderly stopped him for something.

"I'm warning you," I said, glaring at him.

"I see your brother being preyed upon, asking you for help, asking you to listen . . . but you're too busy. And of course Peyton, Peyton, Peyton! Let's not forget about her. You're her savior, her love, her everything. Oh my God, if she could just make you see."

I stood up from the table. I needed to remove myself from the situation. Just as I rose, Ryan noticed and began heading my way once more. I started toward him and just as I felt I had dodged disaster, William spun around in his chair and lit the match that would lead to his demise.

"Danielle, you shouldn't have so much pent up hatred for Christian, at times, Nathan liked the things that Christian did to him," he smirked and turned around.

I changed direction to walk the other way. I had almost taken my second step, then my instinct took over, and I turned back.

I slipped my thumbs under the rope of my wrist wraps, and in one motion slipped it over William's face and around his neck. As soon as I jerked the rope back, I heard an immediate choking noise from William. I then slammed his face against the table, making an immediate blood spatter, splitting his nose open.

As I was about to pull him back toward me again, he slipped a hand between the rope and his throat. I pulled back hard and removed him from his chair. In these three seconds, Ryan had caught up to me and was attempting to pry me away from William. I tightened my grip so nothing could get between us. Ryan grabbed my arms, even lifting me off the ground, but it did nothing to alleviate the grip I had around his neck. William repeatedly pulled at the rope in an attempt to gasp for air, at which point I tightened my grip more and more.

Two more orderlies arrived to assist, grabbing and punching me. All the other patients were moved along the walls.

"We're going to have to do it!" one orderly shouted.

"Get a fucking sedative, now!" shouted another.

Three of them pulled out metal batons. With an apprehensive swing, the first blow struck the back of my right leg. Another, on my lower back; others hit my arm, my shoulder, my side, my stomach, my ribs.

All the while, no blow penetrated my body, but I absorbed all the pain and held onto it.

"You wanted to see my gift, right?" I whispered in William's ear as he tried to gasp for breath. A noise that could have been a 'no' crept out of his mouth.

"Yes, you did," I said angrily into his ear.

"What the fuck is going on!" a shout came from behind me.

"She's not falling!"

"Harder, hit her harder!"

"You want to know what I can do?" I said as someone laid a blow to my head, and another to my leg knocking me off balance, "I'll show you."

I quickly loosened my grip on the strap and pulled it over his head. I plugged both of my hands forward into his back, releasing all the brutality intended for me onto him. Rays of red light filled my vision as William was thrust forward, face first onto the floor. I, as well as the six orderlies around me, were thrown backward.

There was silence for a moment. Everyone looked around in confusion. Then, cries of torment began to erupt from William. The most anguished disturbing noises I've heard to this day.

He lay on the ground, as blood began to drain from his body across the floor, filling the cracks in the linoleum as the pools expanded. His body mangled, blood splatter showed through his pants across the back of his legs, more on his back, a bone beginning to protrude from his arm. And the blow they attempted to lay on me, had blood gushing from the back of his head.

"What did you do to me?" came cries between his screams of pain.

All of them rushed to assist, but every inch of him they touched only inflicted more pain. They began fetching towels, blankets, anything to slow the bleeding; attempting to ascertain the extent of the damage. I felt something in the back of my throat trying to escape. I let out a small laugh, then another, and in moments, my laughter became uncontrollable. I did not think it was funny, perhaps a different side of me thought so, but nothing could stifle my uncontrollable laughter.

"Can someone shut her up!" one of the men assisting William yelled.

Another man grabbed my arm to pull me up off the ground and immediately jerked his hand away.

"What the fuck!" he said, gripping his hand in pain. He attempted to grab me again and pulled his hand right back. I continued laughing harder.

"What are you doing? Get her out of here!" the same man shouted again.

"I can't touch her," he shouted back, holding up his hand that was bright red, and starting to rip like an open blister.

Another orderly tried to grab me with the same response.

· "Well, do something!"

"I have an idea," Ryan said, running out of the room and returning moments later with what appeared to be a device that dog catchers use. A long pole with a metallic circular rope on the end.

"Everyone stand back," he said. Everyone quickly obliged and went to help William, or wrangle distressed patients.

I stopped laughing as Ryan knelt in front of me, attempting to figure out the contraption. He glanced at it, then me every millisecond, and the pole shook in unison with his unsteady hands.

"Please put your hands together and place them away from your body," he requested.

I complied.

He crept toward me and placed the noose around my wrist. I pulled in a downward motion to tighten the hold till it was completely secure around them. He breathed a sigh of relief as he stood up with the end of the pole in his hand.

"You got her?" someone said, ripping the end of the pole out of Ryan's hands, "I'll take it from here."

The man who took the pole from Ryan gave it a jerk, causing me to hit the floor.

"Hey!" Ryan said, attempting to regain control of the pole. The man shoved him back.

"I think you've already fucked things up enough today, Ryan, wouldn't you say? Why the fuck weren't her straps tightened!" he shouted at Ryan.

"I'm sorry," Ryan said with a guilt-ridden expression.

* * *

"So, it was you," Rachel said at the end of my story.

"Did you ever doubt?"

"No, I did not, I guess I wanted to. How did you become like that? How did you develop the ability to do those things?" she started as something seemed to catch her eye behind me.

"Joy – " Rachel began.

"Rachel," she said, raising her eyebrow, and crossing her arms, "Please step away from the patient."

She walked across the room to stand next to Dr. Joy. The doctor whispered something to her, and Rachel shook her head and walked away.

"Dani . . ." Dr. Joy said.

"Dr. Joy," I said, avoiding her eye contact.

"It's time for our appointment," Dr. Joy said, beginning to leave.

"I thought our meeting was canceled," I said.

"Oh no, we're still on," she said.

"Don't I need an escort?"

"Just follow me."

We arrived at her office and she jumped into the questioning.

"What were you two discussing?"

"The incident a few years ago with that patient."

"Ah, I see. The incident that almost got this hospital shut down and got multiple staff members fired. They would've had a big lawsuit on their hands had the patient had any sort of family, or anyone to worry about him, but no one came. No one cared. Why was she asking you about that?"

"Curiosity I suppose."

"Staff is not supposed to converse with patients about their history."

"Well, fire her then," I said, nonchalantly.

"Your sarcasm and humor are always such a breath of fresh air, Danielle."

"Yours as well, Dr. Joy, but she is really terrible at her job. Once, she almost gave me the wrong pills."

"She what?"

"It was an accident I assume."

"Do you know if you ever took the wrong pills from her since you have been seeing me?"

"Uh, I don't think so," I asked, trying to calm Dr. Joy's exaggerated irritation.

"You're sure?"

"I'm pretty sure."

"Okay," Dr. Joy replied, seeming to breathe a sigh of relief, "Putting that aside for now. From where we left off, tell me what happened next?"

Chapter Thirteen:
The Funeral

On the day of my mother's funeral, I sat as far back in the chapel as I could. I didn't want people to see me cry, or of more concern, see me not cry at my mother's funeral. I knew I was disrespecting her memory by avoiding showing my face on her last day. It was more troublesome being in the back than in the front of the church. I could hear all the people's gossip about what happened.

"Apparently, Alex said he wanted a divorce, so she killed herself."

"I heard that she was having an affair and Alex found out so she killed herself."

"The poor children."

"Yeah, I heard the daughter found the body, that's why she's not here, she lost it, and was committed!"

"I heard she was arrested!"

"Oh, I saw the cops across the street!"

I quickly leaned into the crowd of whispers and said: "Oh yeah, well I heard she killed herself because people couldn't stop gossiping about her life since their lives were so boring they had nothing else better to fucking do."

I leaned back hard into my seat as the people became silent at my comment. I checked my watch waiting for the ceremony to end. Several people went up to the front to speak on my mother's behalf. Even my brother was brave enough to say a few words. When they announced the final speaker, it captured my attention.

As Christian walked toward the podium and began to organize his papers, I felt my familiar friend overtake me. Anger. I immediately rose from my seat. As he started his speech, I walked down the middle aisle toward the front of the church. My mind was in disbelief that this man of all people was speaking at my mother's funeral.

As I reached the front of the church, he noticed my presence and paused.

"Dani . . . is everything okay? Did you want to say something?"

I stood for a moment, glaring at him.

"What are you doing, Christian," I said disgustedly.

Whispers reverberated through the crowd.

"Danielle, please don't do this," my father said, getting up from the front row.

"No, how dare you speak a word about my mother. Did you plan this?" I asked, glowering at my father. "Did you encourage this animal to be here, to speak at my mother's funeral?"

My father stared at me, shocked. He didn't appear to grasp the meaning of my words.

"I hate you, Christian," I shouted from the front of the church looking up at him, "Don't for a second think that I will ever forget what you did!"

I felt arms grab me from behind and pull me toward the back of the church.

"I will never stop, Christian! I will hunt you down! The next time I see you, it will be the last thing you ever fuckin' see!"

My final words escaped me as I was shoved outside into the open air.

"What the fuck are you doing?" came a voice from the person who had grabbed me.

I turned my head to see Peyton standing there. She looked so beautiful. She wore a black dress, just long enough to be appropriate, just short enough to remain stunning. Her hair was barely blowing in the light wind. I would never forget how gorgeous she looked that day. She had an expression of concern on her face, something she had grown to wear all too often around me.

"What are you doing here, Peyton?" I asked, leaning against the wall, sliding my sunglasses onto my face. I raised my eyes briefly and caught her eye for the first time. An intuitive perception rushed through me and turned my stomach. Something was different about her. I tried to look closer without her noticing. Something about her had changed.

"You knew I would come. I've been calling you and texting you and emailing you and messaging you for weeks. Why haven't you responded?"

"Because I don't know what to tell you," I said.

"They told me you had died. Can you imagine what that felt like?"

"Well, I'm here."

"Don't talk like that, Danielle. You act like our relationship was nothing, just some casual fuckin' friendship that didn't matter. You don't fool me, we both know that whatever we have or had is something powerful, and unmistakable. Danielle, give me something," she pleaded, her eyes locked onto mine, watching me intently.

I stared back at her.

"Danielle, I have been there with you, and suddenly you're pushing me away. I care about you more than anyone else in the world. It's been so hard to not be around you, it's like I'm missing a part of myself that now, I'm afraid it is lost inside you in a person I'm not sure exists anymore." She tried to hold back the tears rushing down her face, wiping them away in frustration.

"Say something!" she screamed at me.

She had taken me completely off guard. There was so much I wanted to say. She reached for me, putting her hands on my shoulders, then wrapping her arms around me. She reached up and removed my sunglasses.

"Look at me, Danielle, I need to see you," she said.

My eyes met hers. She searched for several moments, hoping to catch a glimpse of something she yearned for.

"Where did you go? I need you to come back to me, Danielle. You look at me and your eyes are empty," she said, placing her hand on my chest, "Danielle, what happened to you?"

I put my hands on her arms and then immediately pulled them away. I felt it, what I thought I saw in her eyes. She was different. I could sense something growing inside her.

"Why else are you here?" I asked curiously. She drew back from me.

"I'm leaving, Danielle."

My heart beat once, loud and hard, as though it had been struck by lightning.

"I'm moving with my mom. Apparently, she has another place apart from my dad a couple of hours from here. Danielle, there's something I really need to tell you," she said looking to the sky so her eyes might swallow the tears that persisted, "The only people that know are my parents and Abel. I knew that you were the only one I could tell who wouldn't freak out. I told Abel, and he wanted to break up, just like that. I know it's a lot for someone his age with his whole life ahead of him . . . I just didn't expect . . . I don't know what I expected . . ."

"Stop," I said, raising my hand and becoming more sick with every word she spoke. "I don't want to hear how you were stupid, and went ahead and fucked your boyfriend, and wound up getting yourself knocked up by that douche bag!"

"Excuse me? Are you fucking kidding me? You pushed me to him, Danielle! You—"

"And you come here telling me all this bullshit about how you miss me, and there's some big hole in your life when you couldn't keep your fuckin' legs closed – "

As I spoke, my dad exited the church.

"Fuck you, Dani," Peyton said as she shoved me, and turned away "Fuck you."

"You're just like everyone else," I said, turning toward her, "Selfish and stupid."

She looked back at me, disgusted, shook her head and walked away.

* * *

"That was the last time I saw her. She messaged me some, but I just ignored them. I didn't know how . . . to undo what I said. I wanted to take it back right away, but I knew it was something that words could never undo," I said.

"What made you react the way you did? I'm not saying I'm surprised. I just want to hear it from your perspective."

"I felt disappointed. It's so selfish and I know it is, but I wanted to think that if she couldn't be with me, then she wouldn't want to be with anyone else, no matter what. I figured she would date other people and try to find someone. I just thought there was no way she would be able to find anything even close to what we had, that she would always be disappointed, as I know I will always be."

"Explain that to me, because it is possible to be with someone in a sexual way without that kind of bond. You've proven that with the situation with your uncle's girlfriend."

205

I grew defensive once more.

"That was different."

"How? How is it different? Because it's you and not her?"

Unable to come up with a legitimate argument, I opted to end our session at that point.

Chapter Fourteen:
Empty Except for Anger

The night after the funeral I made my way back home and tried to keep to myself as much as possible. When my dad called me down for dinner, I dreaded every step I took down the stairs. I just didn't want to be around anyone. Everywhere I went I felt I didn't belong, and I didn't fit in. I didn't feel what anyone else was feeling, and I didn't know how to pretend that I did. It made every moment awkward.

I descended the stairs quietly and looked around the corner to see my brother and dad already seated at the table. They seemed awkward sitting there alone. Two empty seats. They had set out food that had obviously been prepared by someone else. It had been heated up in tinfoil makeshift dishes, and paper plates were set out on the table: four plates.

I walked over quickly, and snatched up the extra plate, holding it in the air.

"Are we expecting someone?" I said harshly.

"Uh . . . no," my dad said in confusion. "Just habit, I guess . . ."

I sat down and tried to consume my food as quickly as possible.

"Should we pray first?" my dad suggested.

My brother looked around curiously.

"I'd rather not," I said, "It's not like we ever have before, or have anything to be thankful for."

"Right . . ." my dad replied and began to eat his food with his head bowed.

"Peyton called . . ." my dad said, moving his food around his plate.

"Okay."

"She really wants to talk to you, maybe you should give her a call. Seemed you guys didn't end things so well the last time you talked."

"I don't have anything to say."

"Dani, I'm worried about you, you are seriously scaring me. Now, I'm not an expert on grieving, but your approach seems to be extremely uncharacteristic."

"I don't know what to tell you. I'm just doing what I feel. Is that not okay?"

"Listen, I know this has been a hard day for all of us, me, you, Nathan, Christian, and everyone. What you said during the service crossed the line. That's Christian's sister, he's torn apart over this. I just don't know what he did to upset you." My brother shot me a glance.

"Fuck Christian," I said under my breath.

"What was that?" my dad said, raising an eyebrow, clearly angered.

"I said, fuck Christian. He deserves way worse than that– "

"Oh my God, Danielle!" He ran his hands through his hair while trying to maintain a calm, constructive composure, "You don't mean that."

He directed his words at my brother as if to reassure him that I did not mean what I said.

"Of course I mean that! Fuck him! I'm glad I said what I did! I wish he was dead!"

"I know you're upset about your mom, but you can't say things like tha . . . "

"I'm not upset, I don't care. I don't give a shit. She did that! She let those things happen to Nathan, and she couldn't own up to the fact that it was her fault! I don't feel bad for her! She killed herself, she did the most selfish thing you can do, and the people who care about her are the ones left to pick up the pieces. No, no way!"

My dad had the most bewildered expression on his face. In a somber voice, he asked:

"Let what happen to Nathan?"

I paused. I hadn't even stopped to think that my dad had not yet been told about how everything had transpired in his absence. He was the one not only picking up the pieces but still trying to put them together.

"What?" I asked.

"What are you talking about, Danielle?"

My brother shook his head frantically at me while my dad's eyes were on me.

"Nothing," I said, getting up from my seat.

I passed them on my way out of the room. My dad reached out and clutched my arm. I immediately felt a hot energy rush to where his hand was. I quickly took his hand and removed it from my arm. As I gripped his wrist, I felt the flesh searing in my grasp.

"Don't ever do that," I said, pushing his hand away.

He pulled his arm to his chest quickly and began examining the damage, looking back and forth at me and then his hand, completely dumbfounded.

"I gotta get out of here," I said, walking out the door.

I left the house and began walking. I knew where I was going, and I was scared of what I would do when I got there. I could only feel anger, rage, and hatred pulsing through my body and trying to escape. I had a good idea what would happen when it did escape.

When I arrived at my destination, I rang the doorbell.

"Hey, Dani!" said Cain as he opened the door, obviously a little tipsy, but still smiling, "I wasn't expecting you, but so glad you could make it.

"Hey," I said, realizing I had walked in on one of Cain and Abel's house parties.

"Come in," he said, hugging me, "Hey, from the bottom of my heart I just want you to know I am so sorry about what happened with your mom. I can't imagine."

"Yeah . . . thanks" I said. Cain didn't have a bad bone in his body. I tried to be appreciative of his kind words.

"You want a drink?" he asked.

"Uh, yeah," I said in an attempt to get some space between us.

"Hey baby, can I get a drink too? Hey Dani!" said Trish from behind him, as she walked up and grabbed Cain around the waist.

"Hey Trish," I said.

"Of course, my love," said Cain with a smile, and gave Trish a kiss on the forehead.

Some infinitesimal piece of me was actually happy knowing they had found each other finally.

"Oh, my gosh, I know that you and Peyton haven't really talked lately, but can you believe she's leaving today? Like, she wouldn't even say why. Aw, I'm so sad," she said with an exaggerated sad face.

"Yeah, it's crazy," I said, not wanting to talk about Peyton.

"Can I ask you a personal question?" Trish said in a hushed tone.

"Uh . . . sure, why not?"

"Was there like something going on between you two?" she asked.

"What do you mean?"

"I won't tell," she raised one hand as if to swear, "There was just something about you when it came to her. I mean, we weren't close like you two. I don't think anyone was that close to her, but when you guys stopped talking she just like . . . shut down. She just cried all the time."

"I'm sure Abel fixed that," I said, wanting to escape the topic quickly.

"Ha ha. Please, that was the biggest joke ever, I mean no one is surprised they broke up," Trish said laughing.

"Who broke up?" Abel said, appearing behind Trish.

"You and Peyton," I said, plainly.

"Oh, heh, yeah whatever," Abel said, shrugging his shoulders.

"Why is that Abel?" I asked.

"Why what?" he asked.

"Why did you break things off with Peyton?" I asked.

"Abel, you said she broke up with you," Trish said, squinting her eyes questioningly.

"Not what she told me," I said, staring Abel down.

"Yeah, if you're going to lie shouldn't it be the other way around?" Trish asked, confused.

"That's what she told you?" Abel asked in a tone acknowledging that it was the truth. He ran his hand through his hair, obviously wondering how to approach the topic.

"Why did you break up with her?" I asked again.

He put his arm around me to lead me away from any listening ears and drew me to one side.

"Listen, I feel like shit about how things went down between me and Peyton, but she agreed with me that it was for the best. I don't mean to be an asshole but, no offense, she paid about as much attention to me as you pay to my brother. I feel terrible about the circumstances, but I don't think me being around would really help the situation."

"You're joking, right?" I said in disgust.

"Dani, I'm eighteen years old, I have my whole life ahead of me. I just . . . I can't be there for her the way she needs," he said sincerely, "Either way, she was leaving. What was I supposed to do?"

"You could have made her stay."

"No," he pointed toward me with his beer as he walked away, "you could have."

His last words echoed in my mind as I found a seat in the living room. People surrounded me, but the noise did not penetrate, did not distract me. I sat there, my eyes fixed on Abel. How dare he try to make her leaving my fault? Every second I looked at him fed the flame of rage smoldering inside me. I watched him laugh, drink, and have a good time with his friends. What was Peyton doing right now? I wondered how alone she felt right now. The room began to blur slightly. My heart raced under my ribs, making the room appear to be trembling. I felt my hands gripping so tight to the arms of the chair they began to go numb.

This sick, poisonous rage grew uncontrollably inside me. It wanted out, and never in my life did I feel more ready to release that pure hatred upon the world. This hatred was the closest feeling to love, and it fed my appetite for more.

Every smirk on his face, every laugh, every second I looked at Abel, the frenzy inside me grew.

I watched Abel walk up to Trish and put his hand on her waist.

"Hey Trish, care to see what the better half is like," Abel said, leaning into her.

Trish put up her hand and pushed him away, "Abel, I think you're a little drunk."

"Oh wait, you already have," he said more loudly, "Well, why not again, my brother's used to coming in second, so it's okay."

"What are you talking about?" Cain made his presence in the room known to his brother.

"Cain! There you are! I was just remembering a while back when I slept with your girl, ya know, right before y'all got together," he laughed, drunkenly, "Is that weird to you?"

"That's not funny, Abel," Cain said, appearing embarrassed, taking Trish's hand to lead her away from Abel.

"No, but it's true," Abel said, smirking at Cain. He grasped Trish's other hand, and pulled her harder than he probably intended back in his direction, "Wait, where are you going?"

"Dude!" Cain said and shoved Abel back into the counter.

"Whoa, whoa, whoa, calm down, baby bro. Why don't you let the lady choose?" said Abel, laughing.

"Abel, I'm serious," Cain warned in a lower but obviously frustrated tone, "fuckin' stop."

Cain turned his back to walk away. Abel shoved him hard in the back, and Cain's knee slammed into one of the end tables.

"What the hell's your problem?" Cain shouted at Abel.

"I'm just saying, why not let her choose? Oh, why? cause you know that there's no way in this world or any other that someone would choose you over me?" he mocked.

The room grew ominously quiet. People began whipping out their phones, knowing something was about to happen.

"Is that what you think?" Cain said, turning toward Abel in disgust.

"No," Abel said, taking a sip of his beer, "I know it."

"Yeah, well . . . Peyton didn't choose you."

Abel swung his fist at Cain and hit him hard in the face. Cain was taken off guard. Blood dripped off his bottom lip as he tried to regain his balance. He steadied himself quickly and swung at Abel, missing him as Abel sidestepped his punch, and pushed Cain to the ground.

Abel laughed hard, "Yeah, well, she was a dumb bitch." He kicked Cain in the stomach as he attempted to get up. Watching Abel laughing, I stood up. Immediately, red washed over the room and everywhere became a slow blur of noise and inaudible voices. I turned around and looked back to where I was sitting. My body was still there. I had embodied my shadow.

Time slowed. I approached Abel, unnoticed by the growing crowd in the room, and glanced down at Cain, barely getting to his feet again. I could feel the adrenaline pumping in their veins. As it coursed between the two of them. I felt it pass through me as well. Every instance of pain and suffering I had ever experience in my life felt like it had been burrowed up to the surface and permeated every part of my soul.

Cain stood, facing Abel. I positioned myself behind Abel. Out of the waves of inaudibility, I heard Cain:

"I hate you!" as he spoke, he swung his fist.

I could see Abel's shadow moving just underneath his skin, omitting a hazy white light as an aura. I positioned myself in front of Abel between the two of them. All my anger and hatred coalesced at that moment. I reached out and dug my fist into his chest and gripped his essence, wrapping my fingers around it tightly, and pulled back with all my strength.

I felt his soul rip from his body, it was like tearing a sheet of ice from him. As I pulled back, I watched his shadow fall to the ground. His shadow put his hand out to reach for his physical body, which stood lifeless in its absence. Abel's shadow looked at me in complete innocence and confusion.

In a second I was sitting back in my chair, watching from afar. Cain swung his fist and just as it was about to collide with Abel's left temple, Abel's expression went blank.

Smack! Cain's fist connected with Abel's head, he fell backward and collapsed onto the ground, his head smacking the tile on the kitchen floor.

Everyone cheered, impressed that Cain could manage such a feat. Cain looked around, surprised by his own achievement.

"Should have seen that coming," Cain said, kicking the side of Abel's leg with his foot, "All right someone get him an ice pack for when he comes to."

Cain reached down to grab Abel's hand and immediately let go.

"What the hell?"

"What is it?" Trish asked.

"He's ice cold," he said, looking up at Trish.

"You fuckin' killed him, Cain!" someone shouted from the background. Some cheered, unsure of what exactly the situation was.

"Hey, shut the fuck up!" Cain said, sliding around to Abel's side. He put his head down on Abel's chest, "Holy shit. Someone . . . Someone Call 911!"

Shouting consumed the room immediately. People began screaming, whipping out their phones, trying to dial those three simple digits, suggesting resuscitation. Others left the party as fast as they could.

I watched as Cain immediately began to try to perform CPR on Abel; he looked more worried with every thrust to Abel's chest.

"Oh my God. What the fuck?"

Standing next to Cain pacing back and forth was Abel's shadow. He walked with his arms crossed, looking down at Cain's fruitless efforts to revive him. He shook his head and looked at me, disappointed. He knelt down next to Cain and put one hand on his shoulder, trying to comfort him. He stood up once more, glanced at me, then he took a step back and was gone.

"He's gone," I heard myself say out loud.

Everyone in the room fell quiet.

"It was an accident. What did I do?" Cain asked bewildered.

"Nothing, I said," standing up addressing the crowd, "Cain didn't kill Abel, I did."

I exited the house. As I left, I heard everyone's confusion. I walked down the road in complete silence until I found myself at the park where Peyton and I had gone before. I stood there for a moment glancing up into the sky, trying to recapture that night in my mind. Hoping to feel the rain against my skin once more, and return to that moment. If I could have just gone back to that moment; I would have done everything differently. I collapsed on the grass in an open area, sitting Indian style for a moment, trying to comprehend the images in my head. There was an emptiness of emotion in my heart. I felt hollow. I took out my phone.

"911 dispatch, do you need police, fire, or EMS?"

"Police," I said.

"Please state the nature of your emergency," the voice on the end of the line said.

"I killed someone, I will be– " I began.

"I'm sorry, please repeat your last statement. Did you say you killed someone? Can you tell me the name of the victim?"

"His name was Abel . . . I will be at the park, you will find me there . . ." I said.

"Wait —" the voice on the other end began again as I hung up.

I sat there waiting. I put my hand on the grass and picked a blade. In the moonlight, I noticed the grass surrounding me had begun to die. A ring had formed around me and began to spread slowly as if the grass had caught fire. Death was exuding from my being, and engulfing any living thing I touched.

I began to hear sirens heading my way. I took a deep breath, knowing everything in my life was going to change . . . again. The dead grass continued to spread, five yards, ten yards.

Bzzzz bzzzz. I felt my phone vibrating in my pocket. Without looking I answered it.

"Hello," I said.

"Danielle? Oh, my God, I wasn't expecting you to answer. I'm here at the airport, about to get on my plane, and I . . . I thought I would try to call you one more time. Um, I had this whole thing to say and now I think I'm just in shock you're actually there. It's just so good to hear your voice. Where are you?"

"I'm at the park."

She was quiet for a second.

"I remember our first time at the park together . . . do you remember?"

"Yeah," I said. I felt a twinge in my heart. Sirens began to get closer, it became more difficult to hear Peyton through the noise.

"What's that noise, Danielle?" she asked.

"I gotta go now," I said.

"Wait, wait, wait . . . I have this sick feeling that I'm never going to be able to talk to you again, and if that's the case, I can't hang up without telling you that you mean the world to me, Danielle. You brought me back to life, and . . . and I will never love anyone the way that I loved you," she said, her voice getting choked up, "Do you hear what I'm saying?"

The dying grass stopped expanding, and I closed my eyes.

"Put your hands up!"

"Get on the ground!"

I put my hands up phone still wrapped in my fingers.

"Gun!" a voice exclaimed.

"Wait!" another person yelled, but it was too late.

I heard the gunshot. Hot metal ripped through my right shoulder, knocking me to the ground. I still held the phone in my hand as I fell back to the grass. I kept my eyes on it as I felt consciousness trying to evade me. Feet rushed up around me. One person kicked my phone away. I felt at least four pairs of hands grab me.

"You fuckin' idiot! It's a cell phone! I said wait!" I heard one person bark to another, "Get a goddamn ambulance over here."

"Sir, I'm so sorry, I could have sworn–" another voice began, but got cut off.

"I don't want to hear it!"

"Sir, the grass . . ." another a voice said.

Murmurs spread among them.

"We'll add an arson charge, get her up, and over to EMS."

I was carried to the ambulance on a stretcher. When they pushed the stretcher all the way back, I noticed the two paramedics assigned to care for me. One of them had a look of horror on her face. I assumed it must be one of her first days on the job.

"Single gunshot wound to suspect in a murder investigation," one paramedic began, "Lisa, are you here?"

"Yeah . . ." she said, averting her stare from me.

"We're going to have to sedate you," the male paramedic began.

"No, don't!" I said quickly.

It was quiet in the ambulance for a second. The male paramedic looked at the other confused, waiting for an answer as to what to do.

"I'm fine," I said, "Look for yourself."

The female paramedic reached for my shoulder slowly. Wet blood had soaked into my shirt, and there was a visible hole in my shirt.

She unzipped my jacket and pulled it apart, then began to cut my t-shirt underneath to reveal my skin.

"There's nothing," she said, rubbing her thumb hard across my skin, making we wince, "How is that possible?"

"It's not my blood," I said.

"It's probably from the victim. I'll go get the police back, and let them know that a stop at the hospital will be unnecessary," the male paramedic said, opening the back doors and jumping out of the ambulance.

The female paramedic stared at my shoulder for a long time, not saying anything.

"How is that possible?" she asked again, reaching toward my shoulder. I pulled back.

"I told you, it's not mine," I said.

"That's not what I was talking about. A week ago I was dispatch to a suicide and possible additional death. I arrived on scene and your body was lifeless on the floor, lying in a pool of blood. I attempted to resuscitate you for twenty minutes. Your body was still warm, but there was no pulse to be found. I called your time of death, I watched them cover your body. How is it that you are alive?"

I sat there quietly for a second, knowing what she was implying.

"You may not show any wound, but I can feel it. There's a big bullet lodged in your arm that didn't make it out the other side. I assume you will soon lose all function in your arm if it stays in there," she said.

I was unsure of the emotion she was attempting to portray, it was so mixed. I couldn't establish a connection with her. Her eyes said one thing, but her mouth said something else. It was most unusual.

"I could remove it," she said, staring at me waiting for a response.

I considered for a moment, it was unusual to have my secret kept for so long from so many others, and revealed in seconds to a complete stranger.

"Ok, do it," I said.

She reached over quickly and closed the doors to the back of the ambulance.

"I'm going to sanitize the wound, but . . . I won't be able to give you anything for the pain, and believe me, it's going to hurt." She said, leaning me forward.

"It's fine."

"Well, you say that now . . . Just try not to move too much," she said seriously.

"I won't."

"All right . . . here we go," she said, reaching for a knife of some sort, "Hold on."

As the knife entered my skin, I took a deep breath. It was the most unusual feeling. My body began to shake uncontrollably from the pain. It hurt so bad, I couldn't exhale.

"Oh fuck," I said, louder than I intended.

"Yup that's the usual response," she said.

I clenched my fist tightly.

"Breathe, sweetie, you're going to have to breathe to keep that blood flowing. If you pass out, we're going to have a big mess on our hands," she said, calmly, as if she had done this a million times.

I exhaled hard. I tried to steady my hands to quell my convulsions so that she could work quicker. I wasn't paying attention and gripped the paramedic's leg tightly. I could feel the blades moving beneath my skin as she searched for the hiding piece of metal. I felt her pull the equipment out of the massive hole she had made in my back.

Then I heard a clink.

"That's incredible," she said, looking at my shoulder. The wound had begun to close up right before her eyes, though blood now stained a large portion of the stretcher, "How?"

There was a loud bang on the back of the ambulance, and the doors opened. It was the male paramedic again.

"They said they will transport her in the patrol car—what happened in here?" he asked obviously noticing the increased amount of blood everywhere, including all over the woman's gloves.

"Bring the officers," she said.

He departed again, leaving the doors open.

"Why did you help me? Do you know what I did tonight?" I asked.

"Cause that's my job," she said.

"You didn't have to, but you did anyway," I said confused.

"This is what God called me to do. He called me to help people, no matter the person. He didn't call me to be the judge of one's soul. He's the only one that can do that. Now, although I have a major dislike for you, I cannot help but think that you've gone through more than one should. Not to mention considering what I just saw, I think God might have different plans for you."

* * *

"I confessed to the murder, and there was an investigation. I was found incompetent to stand trial, but with the videos that surfaced from the party, they found it impossible to believe that I was responsible for Abel's death. Cain was arrested, but he was never indicted, and charges against him were never pursued. Then, I was placed here, and here I've been ever since."

"I see," Dr. Joy stated, quietly. She studied the remnants of the story in silence, as she normally did, "Did you ever talk to Peyton after that day?"

"No."

"So you don't know where she is or what she's doing?" she asked.

"No, I assume she's living somewhere with her mom, and with a two-year-old now. She's probably working or something."

"You think?" she asked.

I had never really given it much thought up until that point.

"As extraordinary as you claimed she was, you think she's somewhere being a house mom and working or something?"

"I'd rather not think about it."

There was a knock at the door and some administrative looking employee poked their head in.

"Joyce, sorry to interrupt," said a girl's voice. Dr. Joy immediately shot her a warning look, "but you have a call, they said it's important."

"Okay, I'll be right there," she said, waving her off quickly. She closed the door quietly as she left.

I kind of laughed to myself, Dr. Joy seemed uneasy.

"That's funny," I said as the thought swam in my head, "Your name is Joyce Joy? What were your parents thinking?"

Dr. Joy sat quietly.

"Danielle . . ." she tapped her finger on the desk, "that is not my name."

"Really? You think patients are going to get out of here and try to find you so you give fake names or what?"

"No . . . Danielle, my real name is Joyce Deason," she said, avoiding my expression.

My stomach immediately became knotted, and my heart began to race.

"What?" I said, squinting one eye and cocking my head slightly to make sure I heard her right, "You're lying."

"I'm not," she said, shaking her head slightly.

"No, no, no, no. No fucking way!" I said, feeling more betrayed than ever, "You're— "

"Peyton's mother."

"You lied to me! You deceived me!" I said, trying to put the words together to express how I felt.

"I needed the truth. If you knew who I was, I knew that the version I heard would be tainted," she said authoritatively.

"I've told you things no other living soul knows. How could you do this to me?" I said, becoming extremely upset as I tried to run through in my mind all that I had told her. I felt disgusted.

"Danielle, calm down, we don't have a lot of time left," she said, her hand raised to try to quieten me.

"Dr. Joy," the same girl popped her head in again.

"Are you fucking kidding me?" Dr. Joy Joyce Deason, threw up her hands, "Now you get it right?"

"I want to go back to my room," I said, and the girl glanced at me, cautiously. "I want to go back!"

"Should I get someone?" she asked.

"No," said Peyton's mom.

"Yes!" I said.

"Okay, okay," Joyce tried to collect herself. "Wait a minute. We can meet again tomorrow."

"You aren't scheduled to meet again till Thursday," she said.

"No, we're meeting tomorrow," Joyce asserted.

"Oh okay," said the girl, "Oh, and you still have a phone call."

"I want a new doctor," I said to the girl.

"Shut up. Just stop talking," Joyce said, slamming her hand down on her desk, "I will be right there. You can leave now."

"Do I need to report what she just said?" the girl asked.

"No, Jesus Christ, get out!" Joyce replied.

As she was walking away, two people came in to escort me to my room.

"Arms up, arms down," they said, I followed their instructions, and they led me away.

"Tomorrow, Danielle," Joyce said, extending her hand toward me. I jerked my arm away from her.

"Don't you dare touch me," I growled.

I felt a push from behind by my escorts. I noticed they looked back at Joyce perplexed.

Chapter Fifteen:
The Things She Hid

I went back to my room, furious; I couldn't stop shaking for hours. Every time I replayed Joyce telling me who she was, I became more enraged. I dug my nails into my skin to find some release from this anger which seemed unavoidable when left with only four walls and my thoughts. I couldn't eat or sleep for the next twenty-three hours. When they finally entered my room to retrieve me, they literally had to drag me out and fully restrain me. They put clasps around my hands and feet, and a chain that ran between the two.

They sat me down in my usual chair in Joyce's office. She had not yet arrived. They slammed a small paper cup filled with water on the desk with a pill next to it.

"Take it," one said with a smirk.

"Fuck you," I said, rolling my eyes.

"I don't think she's going to cooperate," the other said with a laugh.

"No big deal," the other replied. He went behind me and pulled my hair, dragging my head backward. He squeezed his other hand on the sides of my jaw, roughly forcing it open.

The other male flicked the pill into my mouth, obviously trying not to touch any part of me.

I felt it hit my tongue. I swallowed air but not the pill. It stuck to my tongue and refused to go back. Yes, at this point I wished I had just agreed to take the pill. I pulled my head forward to try to swallow it. Finally, it slid back, creeping its way down my throat as slowly as possible. I could taste the coating of the pill, and it made my stomach attempt to reject it.

"Whoa, whoa, keep it down. Hand me the water," said the one who had been holding my hair. The other obliged. He poured it into my mouth. I was marginally grateful, though it did little to replace the taste in my mouth, it did make the pill go down a little faster.

"That should calm you down enough for Dr. Joy," one said, laughing.

"What's going on in here?" Joyce had entered the room.

"Just helping out a little, we got a recommendation for a sedative," one said in a much more professional manner.

"I didn't authorize that," she said with obvious anger.

"It came from the top, we were just doing what we were told . . ." the other said dubiously.

"She is only supposed to take what I prescribe, anything goes through me first," she said as if they were at fault.

"Okay . . ." they said, puzzled, and left the room.

Joyce closed the door behind them and locked it as she had done before. She returned to the desk and moved a trash can with her foot until it was in front of me. I looked at her perplexed.

"Fucking idiots," she said with a stone cold expression, "Get rid of it now."

I sat there for a second wondering if I should cooperate.

"Do it now, or I will stick my hand down your throat and fish it out myself," she said giving the trash can another kick.

I bent forward and stuck a finger down my throat, it didn't take much, and it came right back up. It was ten times as disgusting coming up as going down. The taste was so sickening, I threw up more than the pill. I threw up anything that remained in my stomach.

"Done yet?" Joyce asked. I shot her an 'are you serious' look. She put up her hands, "Let me know."

When I had finished, I wiped the tears that had run from my eyes.

"It's weird to see you appear to be crying," Joyce said, scrutinizing my expression.

"Why are we still here?" I asked, "And please don't lie to me anymore. It's exhausting."

She sat there with her hands folded in her lap, contemplating, while turning slightly in her chair, left to right.

"I need something from you . . ." she said, letting each word escape her mouth slowly as if it were carefully chosen.

"What? This is some kind of sick game you've been pulling on me," I said.

"It was necessary."

"Your definition of 'necessary' escapes my comprehension, Joyce," I said.

"I didn't tell you who I was because I needed you to be completely honest with me. I needed to know what really had been going on with Peyton the last year and a half I wasn't . . . around."

I laughed with disgust at this.

"You sure went a long way to eavesdrop on your child's life, when you could have just . . . I don't know . . . been around."

"Listen, I get that I wasn't there and there's nothing I can do to get that time back, but I am here now, and I will do anything it takes," she said.

"Where were you? Where was so much more important?" I asked. She began shifting in her chair again.

"I fell in love with someone," she said.

"Are you kidding me? See, I knew, I knew it was something completely selfish. You are a real piece of work. I want to leave."

I started to stand up, struggling with my shackles.

"I'm not saying that I never made any mistakes, Danielle, but I am here now to make things right—"

"I'm ready!" I began shouting, knowing no one was likely to hear me.

"Danielle, please sit down," she said, frustrated.

"Hello! Anyone?" I kept yelling as I made my way toward the door.

"Stop, Danielle, come over here for a second," she said, struggling to maintain her wavering composure.

"We're done in here!" I said, beginning to bang on the door.

"She's dying," Joyce shouted at me.

I stopped my banging immediately and jerked my head back toward her. My heart plummeted. I sensed she was telling the truth, but couldn't let myself believe it, because of all the lies I'd already lived through with her.

"Who is?" I asked, already knowing the answer.

"Peyton . . . Danielle, I don't have a lot of time . . ." she said with tears beginning to stream down her face.

"What happened, I don't understand," I was confused.

"Years ago when Peyton was still young, only thirteen, she was diagnosed with cancer. She was sick all the time. I quit my job and returned home to take care of her. I took her to doctor after doctor, we tried everything, every treatment, every medicine, every hospital. Sometimes it seemed as though something would work, then she would relapse. This went on for years. Eventually, we moved to find a place closer to the best medical care in the state. Every day was a battle, every day was harder than the day before. It is so hard being a parent, and watching your child suffer day in and day out, and there's not a damn thing you can do to help them. There's nothing you can do to make the pain go away, to make them feel better . . . There's nothing you can do to save them.

"One day Peyton insisted she wanted to leave the house and see the new town we had moved to. She didn't care what anyone thought of how she looked, or how sick she would be the entire time. She had lost most of her hair, weighed just under ninety pounds, her complexion pale, and the features of her face were sunken. She said she just missed seeing the world. So I looked in the paper and saw there was a football game at the high school. It seems dumb now to take her among so many people, but we went. We arrived at the end of the third quarter, so there wasn't much time left. The stands were packed, and there was nowhere to sit. She was mostly confined to a wheelchair at that time. I remember getting nervous trying to figure out where she could sit. Then this family sitting in the front row volunteered to make room for us. I remember in my mind counting down the seconds till I could get her out of there and get her back home to a safe place."

"Do you like football?" the girl next to her asked.

"Me?" Peyton looked at her, confused. Ever overprotective, I leaned over slightly to eavesdrop.

"Yeah, you?"

"Oh, I don't know, I've never really watched a game," she said.

"No? Wow, you must not be from around here," the girl said with a laugh.

"No, we're new to town," Peyton said. I found it unusual to see her engage in conversation with anyone other than myself or her father. It was like watching your child start school for the first time and seeing them interact with other children.

"Well, the best part of this game is the food, nachos to be specific," the girl said, "Cause our football team sucks."

Peyton laughed at this, it was the first time I had seen her laugh in ages. I felt my throat begin to get dry.

"Want one?" the girl asked, offering her portion in front of her.

"Oh, no thank you."

"Not just one?" she urged with a smile.

"Okay, maybe just one," Peyton said, making a selection. It was nearly impossible to get Peyton to eat anything ever, so I was mildly jealous that this girl made it seem so easy.

"Good, right?" the girl asked.

They talked the entire twenty minutes or so we were there. When the game was almost over, I insisted that we leave early to not get stuck trying to get through the crowd. I tried to pull Peyton's wheelchair out, but one of the bag straps was hung up on the bleachers. The girl she had been talking to reached down and untangled it and pulled the chair forward.

"There we go," she said with a cheerful smile. Peyton stretched across and brushed her wrist with her hand. Their eyes locked for what seemed to be forever. They looked into each other's eyes, appearing to be searching for something. I became nervous at this unusual interaction between two strangers.

"Thank you," Peyton said to the girl.

"Yeah of course . . ." the girl said, and we left.

The next morning Peyton woke me up early before the sun had even come up.

"What is it!?" I asked in alarm, still half asleep.

"I need to go to the doctor," she said. I woke up instantly and looked at her. All I could think was that taking her out probably made her sick.

"What is it? What's wrong?"

"Nothing is wrong, Mom. I'm not sick anymore," she said with a smile on her face.

"Oh, honey . . ." I said, with deep sadness in my voice.

"Mom, I know it, I'm better," she insisted.

I remember an urge to argue with her and not wanting to give her false hope, but I was so worn down that if she had hope, then I was willing to take that chance. I made an appointment with her doctor, and then four more doctors.

She was right, it wasn't completely gone, but she was in remission.

After her story was over, Joyce surveyed me across her desk. "Your hair was much longer then," she said, smiling at me.

"I remember how sick I got right after that," I answered, thinking back, "I never knew why. I didn't even recognize her . . . or you."

"Oh, but she recognized you," Joyce said, "I remember when you guys reunited after the 'accident,' she called me so excited that she had met up with you again. She told me she would never tell you about the first time you met. I was so wrapped up in my own life that I didn't even think twice about it. I had spent so many years taking care of her, and everything else, that when she got better all I wanted was to reclaim my life that I had put on hold for so long. It was selfish."

"And now?" I said.

"She relapsed, a couple months before you came here. She knew something was wrong. She called me one night to tell me she'd been to the doctor, and they had run some tests and they had come back positive. I sent for her to live with me again so that I could take care of her."

In descending dread, I suddenly realized the horrible mistake I had made.

"She wasn't pregnant?" I asked.

"No."

"I felt something growing inside her," I began to shake.

"It was the disease, Dani," she said with an expression of sympathy on her face.

The room seemed to spin around me. What had I done? Abel, I had been so mad at him, for no reason. I put my face in my hands trying to steady my thoughts. Never had I felt regret the way I did at this moment. The palm reader had said Abel's unborn child's life would depend on him being there for someone. She had implanted that thought in my head. Everything else she had predicted was right. Had I entrusted my life and the lives of others in myth?

"Oh my God," I whispered. I had never tried to justify what I had done to Abel, but this made it so much worse.

"Danielle, are you okay?" Joyce asked.

"No, I don't feel so good."

"Danielle, I know this is immense, but I need your help today. We're running out of time."

"What do you mean?"

"Peyton is running out of time. They gave her three weeks .. . that was five weeks ago."

"What am I supposed to do?" I asked.

"Save her." Two simple words loaded with significance.

"I can't . . ." I argued.

"Yes, you can."

"No, I've tried, remember we've been through this."

"You can," she asserted. She removed the wrap that was around her arm to reveal the skin into which she had plunged the knife.

There was nothing.

"You can," she repeated.

"How is that possible?" I asked, "Why couldn't I do it before?"

"I've studied your case very closely, I've listened to what you've said, and I've done my research. The reason you cannot access any of your abilities is because of the medicine. When I first started seeing you, I replaced your medication with placebos to get all of it out of your system. That's why your pills looked different, that's why it seemed they weren't working. That's why I made you get rid of that sedative."

"But why would that make a difference?" I asked.

"Your ability seems to be a manifestation of your emotions. The medications we give you inhibit extreme emotions, whether that be anger or happiness, you can produce some, but no extreme form of one or the other. That's why you feel you are a danger to people when you don't take them, because . . . you are. I need you to access the deepest emotions you have."

"Even if I could help, I could never get to her, wherever she is."

"That doesn't matter, you won't be here much longer."

"What do you mean?"

"I'm removing you from this place . . . tonight," she said, "With all the 'issues' you and I have had as of late, you wouldn't believe how hard it was to get approval from the top authority for your release."

"My . . . release?" I repeated, overwhelmed. I couldn't even begin to imagine this day, those words. Now, the thought of going out into the world with no preparation was nothing short of terrifying. Joyce recognized the distress on my face.

"Dani, calm down, once you leave here I can't give you anything to ease the anxiety, I need you fully aware, fully alert," she said.

I shook my head, unable to grasp fully the implication of her words.

"It has to be tonight."

"What's the plan?"

Chapter Sixteen:
The One that Won't Let Go

Joyce had obviously been working on this plan since day one. She had approved a scheme for me to be removed from the institution under the care of a guardian. Since the last thing she wanted was to involve my family, she paid some guy to impersonate my father, arranging for him to 'take me home.' He would then deliver me to her, and she would take me to Peyton.

All I could think about was actually being able to see Peyton again. What if I couldn't help her? What if I couldn't leave? What if they suspected something? What would she look like? Would I be able to recognize her? I thought about what Joyce's plans were for me after I had achieved what she wanted, or if I couldn't accomplish what she wanted.

When they collected me from my room to leave, I was sitting at the end of my bed. I had all my things packed up in a small bag ready to go. It amazed me, how I had got along with so little to entertain or distract me over the years. I had never planned for this day to come. I wondered what life outside this place would be like. It was a scary thought.

The door opened. "Danielle, your fathers' here," someone said.

I looked up, astonished. Then, remembered it was only someone pretending to be him. Not actually him. I wondered if I would ever find my family once I was out of here, what would I say to them? How would I explain . . . anything?

I rose to my feet and walked out of the door. Was I leaving this room behind forever?

"It's normal to be nervous," one of the people accompanying me said.

"I don't even know why anyone would think letting her out of here is a good idea," the other scoffed.

"Shut up!" the first person said, "Ignore him."

I did. In fact, nothing either of them was saying registered.

"Danielle," a man waved, this must be him.

I walked up to him. He was tall, like my dad with light skin, more facial hair than my father, but they had their similarities. I don't know what it was about him, but when I saw him, I hugged him as if he was my father. Thankfully, he hugged me back.

"Well, we're all set to go," he said.

We left the place, I climbed into his car, and he drove away. Anxiety began to build in me with every mile we covered. I now knew what Joyce had meant about getting Peyton back to a place where it was safe when she was ill. It meant a place where you could control what happened around you. Even driving in the car made me nervous. I had forgotten how fast they seem to go. I remembered driving to my brother's baseball game with Peyton, it eased my mind a little.

"You alright?" the man said, breaking the silence.

"Yeah."

"I normally don't do things like this, breaking the law, you know," he said nervously.

"What do you mean?" I asked.

"Well, I'm just saying, that I know what I'm doing isn't exactly legal, but I owed Joyce a favor," he laughed, nervously.

"A favor?" I asked.

"Yeah . . ." he said.

"Why?"

"My wife she um . . . we were very young when we got married. And in her early twenties, she developed a severe mental illness. I didn't have insurance or anything. Our lives were chaos for years and years. I tried to get her help, but it was just so expensive and the care that I could afford was terrible and didn't help her. A couple of years ago, we met Joyce, and she took an unusual interest in her case. She's worked very hard to help my wife. The improvements were unbelievable. Before she was in and out of institutions monthly. Now, it's been a year and four months since she's been in a hospital. She's not perfect, but she's the person I remember. The person I fell in love with," he said.

"Your wife . . . What did she have?"

"Joyce says it's a kind of schizophrenia," he replied.

"Oh, yeah?"

"Yeah, sometimes she would claim to see, hear, and experience the most out of this world things. Her descriptions were so vivid. To be honest, at times I actually believed her," he said with an embarrassed laugh.

"Interesting," I drifted away into my thoughts.

* * *

When we finally reached our destination, it turned out to be a hospital. He parked alongside another car and opened the door.

"I hope she finds what she's looking for," he said, giving me a broad smile as I alighted from the car.

"Thank you," I said, closing the door.

The car next to his was Joyce's, I assumed. It looked as if it cost tens of thousands of dollars. She lowered the window a little to let me know it was her. I rounded the car to the passenger side and got in beside her.

She sat quietly at first.

"This is it," she said, "She's in there. I'm counting on you, Dani."

"No pressure," I said.

"You can do this. Just as you did before," she said.

"And if I can't?" I held her gaze.

"That's not going to happen." She looked at me with an expression telling me it wasn't an option. This made me even more nervous, considering the last time I consciously used my gift, I had killed someone. Maybe that was all it was good for.

"Let's go," I said, wanting to get it done with.

As we entered the hospital, Joyce coached me with every step we took about what to say, how to act, who I was. I tried hard to pay attention, but could focus on nothing. My nerves were getting the best of me. I crossed my arms, so no one would notice how much I was shaking.

"Now, when you see her she'll be hooked up to a ventilator. She is heavily medicated, so she probably won't know that you're there," she said.

"Wait, what do you mean?" I asked.

"She's not coherent. She hasn't been responsive to anything or anyone in almost a week. It's like she's already gone," she said. She took my hand as if in an involuntary reflex. Without pausing to think, I returned her grip. I felt my hand shake in hers and began to sweat out of nervousness. She didn't seem to notice.

"Joyce, I didn't think you would make it in time, but I'm glad you did. Who's this?" a nurse asked assessing suspiciously.

"This is her cousin on her father's side, they were very close," she explained.

"We prefer to only have immediate family at this time," she pointed out.

"She's going to die, either way, people need to say goodbye," Joyce said fiercely.

The nurse just nodded and walked away.

"Ready?" she asked, facing a room that I assumed was Peyton's.

I wasn't sure if I gave any affirmative response, but I entered the room. Joyce followed me.

As I did so, I felt my legs get weak beneath me. It was her. When I saw her I was reminded more of our forgotten meeting, more than any other time. She looked so fragile, nearly lifeless. She was nothing but bones. All her features were hollow, her eyes closed. Her head was wrapped. I imagined this was to cover her lack of hair or sores. She looked like a completely different person.

As I approached her, I clutched the side of the bed to steady myself.

"It's a difficult sight, I know," Joyce said from behind me.

"I should never have left her," I said, fighting back the first tears of pain I had felt in years, "This would have never happened."

"Get it all out this time, Danielle, I don't ever want this disease to come back."

"I'm scared," I said.

"Don't worry. I know you, you won't hurt her. This is your job," she said.

I nodded and returned my gaze to Peyton.

I reached down slowly and grasped Peyton's hand. It was so small, so cold. I pulled my hand back and looked at Joyce. What did she expect from me?

She walked over to the sliding door of the room and closed it.

"I've done some terrible things since you've been gone Peyton," I said, touching her face softly, "I'm not sure I'm the person you think I am."

I put my hand on her arm and felt something begin to awaken inside of me. I felt part of me leave my body. It was my shadow. It walked away from me around to the other side of her hospital bed. All I had ever noticed before about my shadow was how dark and dangerous it was. Now all I could see was sadness and deep concern. It stared at me as if asking what to do. My shadow placed its hand on Peyton's other arm, and I felt a small shock reverberate through my hand and pulled back. My shadow watched me. My right hand began to emit a blue light.

"Take off the ventilator, the IV, everything," I said.

Joyce had her hand up to her mouth biting her nails, and her other arm wrapped around her waist. She looked at me confused.

"What? Are you sure?" she said.

"You'd better have faith that this will work," I said.

"Faith in what?" she asked.

"Something bigger than us," I said, removing her IV. Joyce began to help me. As we removed other items, machines started buzzing and beeping, but no one came rushing in.

"Why aren't they trying to help?" I asked.

"She signed a DNR," she said, "and I told them not to disturb us when the time comes."

"Start praying," I said, returning to her bed.

My shadow had been in the background observing, knowing what was about to be asked of it.

I laid my left hand on Peyton's right hand and extended my other hand above her chest. As I did so, the blue light began to emit around me. My shadow put its right hand on Peyton's left hand and it's left hand over mine, and a red light began to swirl around it. I experienced a twinge of worry, but dismissed it, I needed its strength.

The machines beeped loudly, it was hard to focus. I saw her chest moving slower and slower as her life attempted to escape her.

"Do something, Danielle," Joyce beseeched, pacing the room nervously.

"Come on, Peyton . . . come back to me," I urged her.

"Access your emotions, Danielle," Joyce said.

As she spoke, memories flashed before my eyes of me opening my front door and seeing Peyton there, when we went to the park in the pouring rain, the first time I had my arms around her, when she grabbed my hand at my brother's baseball game, at Christian's when she ran her fingers through my hair, at Abel's when she kissed me. I suddenly felt all the love I had ever felt for her, and all the pain I had ever caused everyone who loved me.

The blue light and red light collided, and a blinding purple light engulfed the room, emanating from between my shadow and myself. It was the perfect balance between love and hate, the rawest emotion. It was so strong it pushed back on me, but I held onto my shadow's hand tight, as it looked at me uneasily, and I knew I must be showing it the same expression. The energy overwhelmed the room. Joyce collapsed to the floor. As I held onto Peyton, I felt the poisonous disease pulsing through her veins. I felt my soul slowly attempting to eradicate it one cell at a time. I tried to contain myself, but I knew I would have to lose that control and let it take over.

The memory of the day of the accident returned to me. The expression in her eyes as if she knew that second would be the last second of her life, and instead of closing her eyes in fear she had looked at me. Her green eyes locked onto mine, mine locked onto hers. I knew in that instant I had to save her. There was no other option.

I felt everything become deranged. The poison began rushing out of her, and into me. It was like razor blades being dragged over every inch of my skin, and battery acid being poured on top of that.

The orb solidified, sucking all the light, life, sound, and time in the room into it. Time froze for a moment.

It drove itself into Peyton's chest. And the purple light exploded throughout the room creating a shock wave that shook the walls.

The force knocked me backward, and I collapsed to the floor. My shadow floated back into its proper home inside me.

From the floor, I attempted to catch my breath. I pulled myself up from the side of the bed as best I could, still feeling the poison linger like a cold sweat.

I wasn't sure if I had saved her, or given her the final push into the afterlife. I took hold of her hand and scrutinized her intently. The machines continued to beep out of control. I glanced back at Joyce, who had her hand to her chest still trying to pick herself up off the floor. I looked back at Peyton waiting for a sign.

Joyce made her way to the opposite end of Peyton's bed, taking her other hand.

"Peyton," she said, touching her daughter's face tenderly.

The color began to return to her face, black rings around her eyes faded, and her skin was glowing as if she'd spent a day in the sun.

Peyton turned her head slightly toward her mother's voice with her eyes still closed.

I was so surprised I stumbled back into the chair behind me. Joyce looked up at me with a mildly irritated expression as if I were disrupting the moment.

"Mom," I heard her voice say.

"That's right," Joyce said, wiping her eyes as tears escaped to run down her cheeks. "I'm here."

I was shocked, it worked. I wanted to jump up and down in consummate excitement.

"Who else is here," she asked in a groggy voice.

Joyce looked up at me. This was my chance to make things right, to tell her I was sorry, to . . . my thought froze all of a sudden. Show her what? That I'm still the same person as when she last saw me? The person who hurt her the most, abandoned her, and left her to die.

I put my hand up and shook my head so that Joyce would not acknowledge my presence. She was clearly perplexed.

"No one, sweetie . . . it's just me," she said.

She was so close to me, just feet away. I could talk to her. I could tell her I missed her, and she would welcome me with open arms, but I just couldn't.

I took a step back, and another step. Then, quietly exited the room.

I made my way outside to Joyce's car in the parking lot. After almost an hour, she appeared.

"I was wondering where you went," she said with obvious concern, taking a seat on the curb next to me, "She's asleep now."

"Good . . . that's good," I said.

"Are you going to see her?" she asked, waiting for an explanation.

"No . . . I have to leave."

"Dani, she'll want to see you, she misses you. She never forgot about you."

"I know, but I can't do that to her," I responded.

"Do what?"

"I can't keep doing this. I know that she would want me back in her life, and accept my flaws, and accept the pain I carry with me, and help me with that burden as long as I didn't leave her, but I don't deserve to be in her life. Not now at least. I'm nothing but toxic. She will always be the world to me, a memory I never want to live without, but there is something missing in me, and I intend to find it. I want to be better, I want to be whole . . . I want to be that person that she thinks I'm capable of being, that person she always claimed to see in me. Until then, I can't stay. I've done all I can for now."

"What are you going to do?"

"You know, I have no idea . . . but I think I know where to start. I'll need a place to stay for the night and a favor. Do you think you can help me?"

"Of course, anything."

We got into her car to search for a nearby hotel where I could stay.

"You should be self-sufficient for a while. I covered most things such as identification, you had a trust account from your great-grandmother that matured on your twenty-first birthday with a sufficient amount of money to support you comfortably for at least a couple years. You'll probably need to work on getting your driver's license. Oh, and I have your social security card, birth certificate, and . . . death certificate as well."

I laughed to myself at her last comment.

After a short drive, we arrived at a generic hotel with plenty of vacancies.

She went into the reception to make a reservation and escorted me to the room. It was a standard hotel where you entered the rooms from the outside balcony. We went inside and there was the typical queen size bed, nightstand, TV, and mirror. There was a faint scent of bleach from the sheets that caught my attention. The blankets that adorned the bed were a dark maroon color with gold trim. I laid my bag on the bed and sat down.

"This hotel is awful," she said, standing with her arms crossed, appearing to avoid coming into contact with anything in the room, "We can go to another one."

"It's fine."

"I'll probably just head back to the hospital tonight once you're all settled in here, and just sleep there. Are you okay with staying here alone? I can come check on you in the morning," she said, hopefully.

"That won't be necessary," I said.

"Here," she reached into her oversized purse, "I'm sure you want this back."

She handed me my journal, in all its tattered glory. I smiled.

"Thank you."

"So, what was the favor you wanted?" she asked, returning to our prior conversation.

"Oh, yeah . . ." I said with a twinge of hesitation, "Do you have any . . . medication?"

"I don't have any of your medication, but if you need something to take the edge off," she said fumbling through her purse, "I have my Clonazepam, it's anti-anxiety, it should calm your nerves."

"How many do you have?" I asked.

"Oh, plenty. I just filled my prescription. How many do you want, one or two?"

"I want all of them," I said.

"Well, I can give you a few for the next couple days, and write you a prescription so you can get it filled, that way you're taking something that is legally prescribed to you. Yes, I think it would fit in well with your prescription regimen."

"No, I want them all tonight," I said, my face expressionless.

Joyce grew silent.

"Why?" she asked.

"You know why," I replied.

"I can't do that."

"Yes, you can, just leave them on the dresser when you leave. I'll do it when you're gone." I said.

"Why do you have to do this now?" she said with frustration.

"Because — "I started.

"Danielle, you could die! Then what?"

"You know that's not going to happen," I replied, as reassuringly as possible.

"Danielle," Joyce said sitting down on the bed, "I want you to know you are not a terrible person, you have the ability in you to do so much good in this world. You've just been cast with this dark shadow around you. The things you have endured would haunt anyone. You will find what you are looking for, I know it. You just need to start by forgiving yourself for the things you did and not accepting blame for the things that you can't. Danielle . . . what happened to your mom . . . that wasn't your fault."

Her words brought a lump to my throat. She leaned forward, kissed me on the forehead, and got up from the bed. She crossed to the dresser and placed the bottle of pills on it. She then walked to the door and opened it.

"Find your way back," she said without turning around and left closing the door behind her.

When she left the room, I stood up from the bed and removed the blanket so that all that remained were the white sheets and pillows.

"Well, we're halfway there."

I tossed my journal and the bottle of pills onto the bed. I went into the bathroom and filled one of the plastic cups provided for guests with water.

I returned to the room and set the water on the night stand, then picked up the bottle and popped the top off, pouring the pills out onto the bed. I counted them one by one. . . . twenty-eight. I sat back against the headboard and selected one pill, picked up the water, took a sip, and tossed the pill back with it.

I opened up my journal and flipped through it as I continued to take the pills one by one with the water, then two by three.

After several minutes, the words began to blur slightly. I reached for the last pill and swallowed it. I flipped the pages slowly through the journal from start to finish. The words became a whimsical dancing of pages as each page flipped by, and my consciousness slipped away. I reached the back cover and it read:

Happy 13th Birthday to my favorite niece—Love Christian

Then everything slipped away.

I awoke in the place I hadn't been in a very long time. Pure white. My peaceful place. I rolled over in the soft sheets and sat up, running my hands through my hair.

"Good to see you again, Dani," came the familiar voice of Anarah.

I looked to my right, and she was sitting at the end of the bed.

"Yeah," was all I could say in response.

"You have a lot of healing to do," she said.

"Well, let's get started," I said.

"We can't yet," she said sadly.

"Why is that?" I asked.

"I think you know the answer," she said, looking to the left side of the bed. There, just as I had left her, sat Peyton.

247

"She's still here," I said.

"She is, and the healing process can't start until she leaves, she's blocking that process. Dani, it's critical— " she began, but I cut her off.

"I understand," I said, watching Peyton, who regarded me with a smile.

As this transpired, I noticed there was an orb of light that wandered about. It changed from blue to red to green, and purple and floated throughout the room aimlessly.

"What is that?"

"It's what still remains here of you. It's the part of you that you left behind. It's been waiting patiently for your return so that it can reunite with its owner."

I looked over at Peyton.

"You told me a long time ago that if other people come here, once they leave . . . the mind loses them," I said.

"You invited her false essence into here, in order to remove it, you have to extract everything that reminds you of her true being," she said, "You won't remember her, she will only exist in your memories as a blur of an acquaintance. Someone you might have seen in passing, if at all."

I dropped my head and rubbed my hand against my forehead.

"But how could I forget her? She's everything."

"Your mind will erase her . . . it will detour and distract should she come into your mind, it will rearrange your memories to devalue her presence."

"She always made me second guess the belief that I was a terrible person. If she never came into my life . . . how would I ever believe otherwise?"

Anarah sat quietly without response.

"Will she remember me?" I asked.

"Her memories will not fade immediately . . . but over time," she said.

"Peyton," I said, addressing her and getting up from the bed.

"Dani!" she responded as if realizing I was there for the first time.

She stood up and hugged me. I kept my arms around her for a long time. I didn't want to let go. Almost everything about her was just like Peyton. Her eyes, her skin, the smell of her hair. Almost everything. I stepped back.

"What is it?" she asked.

I looked into her eyes for the last time, hoping if I studied them long enough I might never forget them.

"I need you to leave," I said, and even though it wasn't really her, the words hurt. My voice shook with every syllable.

"But I don't want to leave you, Dani."

As she said this, I knew the only time Peyton had addressed me as Dani was the day of the funeral.

"But you have to. You're not real . . ."

"You don't really want me to leave, do you?" she asked, frustrated. I began to separate from our embrace, but she continued to reach for me.

"Don't do this, Dani, you know what happens," she said as tears began to escape her eyes, "What are you going to be without me?"

"I don't know."

"Danielle, please don't do this to me! I need you, please don't leave me again!" she sobbed through tears, "Please, I am begging you. Don't you let me go. Give me another chance! I'll do anything. Please, please, Danielle."

"I can't, I'm sorry," I said as tears streamed from my eyes too.

"Fine, Danielle, run. Run away like you always do. You ran away from your family, your mom, you left me to die!"

Every word she spoke broke my heart into more and more pieces. This pain, this unimaginable pain that had become so foreign to me. I hadn't seen her for years, but the pain of letting her go was as fresh as alcohol on a first-degree burn. All I wanted to do was say I'm sorry and stay there with her forever. Would that be such a bad life? She was the one I loved, she will always be the only one I love.

But, this was not her.

"You need to leave," I said one more time, and turned my back on her.

I stood there for a second, wishing it would be over quickly.

"She's gone," Anarah's voice said.

I crawled into the bed and let the tears stream down my cheeks. I tried to contain my emotion. It was an all-consuming pain. Pieces of who I was suddenly vanished. I thought I'd never be whole again. I didn't have Peyton, I didn't have my mother, I hadn't seen my family in years. I had nothing. Where did I go from here? Peyton's allusion was right, who would I be without her, as if I'd never met her? Anarah lay down next to me and wrapped her arms around me and began to run her fingers through my hair. I pretended she was my mother trying to soothe me as she had done so many years ago. My body trembled against her as the pain tried to escape, but she held me tight. I rested my head against her and began to let everything go.

"Rest now," she said, "Soon it won't hurt anymore."

The orb of light flew closer to me, and little flakes of that light detached and flowed into my body, each hitting like a large droplet of water and becoming absorbed into my being. Each drop that hit calmed my mind more and comforted my soul.

My mind started to drift off slowly, and the healing began.

* * *

I awoke slowly from my slumber, my face buried in the sheets of the bed, no blanket. My senses returned to me as I could smell the bleach on the sheets once more and the forgotten smell of stale cigarettes. Through an overcast sky, the light came into the room through a large window with only a thin curtain attempting to keep it at bay. I slowly sat up on the side of the bed trying to retrace my thoughts. It was similar to being excessively drunk the night before and knowing there are gaps in your memory.

I took a deep breath and inhaled the stale air of the room, and as I breathed in, I felt different. Though the air was stagnant and stuffy, my body took in the air with desperation. It devoured it like a breath of life. Every air particle absorbed into my bloodstream like a desert in drought.

I quickly got up and went to the bathroom to peer in the mirror. Physically, you might say nothing in my appearance had changed from the previous day, but I was finally able to see myself. There was a light in my eyes, dim, but there. I reached out to the glass and admired my reflection. I touched my face and felt the comforting warmth of my skin and the warm blood flowing through it and beneath it, traveling throughout my body. I put my hand on my chest where my heart rested.

Thump, thump, thump, thump . . .

My heart beat strong, steady, and alive. A smile overtook me as a tear ran down the side of my face. Comfort surrounded my being.

I was whole again.

I kept my hand on my chest for a long time soaking in that feeling. It was mine. It was not staggered nor weak, it did not pump ice through my veins; it was not a black hole.

While looking at myself I saw my imperfections, I saw the pain, the struggle, the hurt, the weakness, the fear, I saw the lost soul. I was not good, I was not bad, but I was fully alive, no longer a ghost among the living. Was the darkness still there? Yes, and I knew it always would be. It was a part of me, my shadow. Everyone has a shadow they cannot evade. It is their burden, their heartache, their darkness, their secrets, their reminder of their struggle, and a reminder of the struggles they have overcome.

Everything had a new significance. I took my time packing up my things, enjoying every aspect of the hotel room, as my excitement grew for the even more beautiful world outside. When I finished I gathered up my things in my backpack and picked up the key to head to the lobby. I stepped outside and saw the sky had darkened and it began to drizzle.

I stood on the balcony outside my room and observed the rain. It smelled of fresh earth, and mud. I listened to the sound of the drops as each one fell to its resting place and gathered in puddles in various crevices. I reached my arm out to let the drops fall on my hand and arm. The temperature of the rain was slightly cooler than the air it fell through.

I walked across the parking lot to the lobby, and the door opened automatically letting me in. I proceeded to the clerk at the front. The lobby was lit with incandescent lamps throughout that reflected beauty of the stained wood that encompassed it. I walked across large squares of tan, marble tiles and made sure to place each foot in a full square. As I reached the desk, I put my bag down and placed my journal and keys on the desk.

The clerk who had been focused on his newspaper, quickly set it down and greeted me.

"Good morning," he said with a smile and a slight African accent. He had dark skin and short dark hair. He seemed slightly older than me with a smile that revealed perfect teeth.

"Hi, um, I'm checking out, I guess," I said, uncertain of the appropriate procedure for leaving a hotel.

"Oh yes, of course," the clerk reached for the keys, "I apologize for not acknowledging your presence sooner. I was just reading an article. It's nice to have some good news every once in a while."

"Oh, no problem, I agree," I said, glancing over at the paper, attempting to decipher it upside down. The headline read: Bross University Student's Miraculous Recovery from Death Bed.

The article showed two pictures, one, a girl in a hospital bed looking very ill, the other a school photo of a beautiful girl with long flowing hair and an attractive smile.

"She just got better," he said with astonishment in his voice, shaking his head as he typed into the computer.

"Hey, I think I recognize her, I think we went to school together," I said.

"At the University?"

"No . . . high school," I said, thinking of the unlikelihood that I had gone to school with Joyce's daughter.

"Where was that?"'

"In Crosswood."

"Crosswood?"

"Yes . . ." I responded.

"Of course, you're Danielle. Sorry, the room name was under Joyce. Here," he said putting a large manila envelope on the desk with a ticket on top of it, "Miss Joyce said you would pick this up when you departed the hotel."

"What is this?" I said, looking at the ticket and picking up the envelope to peek inside.

"I don't know what's in the envelope, but that is your bus ticket," he said.

"Bus ticket to where?" I asked, confused.

"To Crosswood."

I peered inside the envelope. It had all the documents Joyce had said she had gathered for me: identification, a smaller envelope, and some cash.

"Thank you," I said, attempting to gather all my things at once.

"No problem and the room has already been paid for, so we're all good here. Anything else I can help you with?"

"Um yes," I said, stuffing some things into my bag, "Where is the bus station?"

"Oh yes, if you exit the front door to the right, it's about three blocks down, on your right. It's small, but you can't miss it. Looks like your bus should be leaving in about two hours."

"Okay, great. Thanks for your help," I said, turning to head out the door.

"You might want to wait a while before leaving, and take cover from the rain," he suggested.

"I think I'll be alright," I said, looking back, "It's just water."

Chapter Seventeen:
Whole Again

I made my way to the bus station. It was a small building the size of a large gas station with a large semi-circle drive in for the buses. I didn't bother going into the station and just sat outside on a bench under the roof cover. I looked through the envelope Joyce had left for me to confirm all its contents. I pulled out the smaller envelope and opened it. Inside was a letter from Joyce.

Danielle,

I can never thank you enough for what you have done. Although I was not always the best doctor, nor were you the best patient, I learned more from you than any other person I have treated or known. I know you struggle with the darkness inside you, among the chaos in your mind. But I also know you struggle with it because you are fighting for the light, and that is admirable. I know you have spent so much time trying to kill this thing inside of you that you hate, but I'm not so sure that is wise. I know it seems like a monster lives in you, but it's more like a stray dog that needs compassion and affection, and love to show its strength and loyalty. It has a primal sense to protect the ones it loves and destroy anything that threatens them. Danielle, I encourage you to tame that beast. What I saw last night from it, was not hatred, nor anger. What I saw last night took all of you, not just the parts of you that you want the world to see. If you could accomplish that with only part of your soul imagine the possibilities. If you want a full life, you must mature the other side of your soul. I know it has a lot of catching up to do, and perhaps these words won't make sense today or tomorrow. However, I believe with all of my heart that you have a purpose in this world, and though your past and this perceived affliction might haunt you daily, I urge you to be stronger than the darkness. I caution you, however, that in order to tame the darkness, first, you must delve deep into it. I pray that you do not lose your way, but once again find the light, and come out the other side complete.

Dr. Joy

I finished reading Dr. Joy's note, folded it back up, and placed it into the envelope. She was right in that much of what she was saying I did not understand, but I trusted her that in time I might. I let the words resonate for almost an hour, but found no further meaning. I realized some things you are not meant to understand till a certain point. I made a mental note to hold onto the letter.

As I sat under the roof, the rain began to pour down harder. A crowd of people began to take cover in the area I was as our bus approached for boarding. It pulled around and stopped several feet ahead of us. People began to organize their things for the rainy trek to the bus. After about fifteen minutes they began loading passenger's luggage into the side compartment, and the people began to climb inside.

Before the line began to grow, I made my way toward the bus entrance. A few people were in front of me displaying their tickets. I fumbled with the stuff in my hands to reach for my ticket in the pocket of my backpack. Just as I had grasped it, a man behind me stumbled, cannoning into me. As he did, my journal came loose from under my arm and fell to the curbside into the stream of flowing water. I immediately reached for it with my free hand. When I pulled it from the water, it was soaking wet.

"Oh my gosh, I'm so sorry," the man said as he attempted to help me gather my things, "Please tell me that wasn't important."

"It was everything I needed to know about my past up until this point . . ." I said with despair, more to myself than the man.

Another older gentleman, who had apparently heard my comment, spoke up from behind him.

"Perhaps it's a sign to let go of the things in your past, and not let them define you," he said with a smile.

I returned his smile.

"Perhaps you're right."

I shook my journal off so that it would not drip, and the man who had knocked it out of my hands gave me a plastic bag to keep it in as it dried out. I climbed onto the bus and presented my ticket and made my way to the back to take a seat.

I shoved my bag under the seat in front of me, not wanting it too far from reach and glanced out the window as others piled into the bus.

I rested my head against the window as the rain pattered against it, watching the droplets run down the glass, as the bus engine hummed, waiting to leave.

As I watched the droplets, I began to drift off. As my dream materialized, the droplets began to dry and suddenly the sun shined through the bus. It could have been a summer afternoon. I looked up to realize the bus had changed. No longer were there many passengers awaiting their destination, it was just me. The bus was no longer a passenger bus, but a school bus.

I heard the noise of tires screeching and woke from my dream with a jump. The passenger next to me glanced at me briefly. She was a woman in her early forties with pale white skin, red lipstick, and dark red hair. She was quite beautiful, yet motherly in appearance.

"Nightmare?" she asked.

"Something like that," I said, letting my heart settle.

The dream quickly faded in my mind, though I attempted to hold on to it. There was something in that dream, something I wanted, but the thought slipped tantalizingly away.

"I don't know how people can sleep on the bus," the lady said.

"Yeah . . . I don't know. It's unusual, I've never been able to sleep while driving," I said.

"Well, lucky for you, you missed most of the trip. We're about ten minutes out."

"I was asleep for four hours?" I asked in disbelief.

"Oh yes, quite peacefully for the most part."

"Weird," I said, drifting into my thoughts.

"Are you visiting family?" the woman asked.

"I guess you could say that," I replied, "How about you?"

"Returning home actually, from a business trip in Dallas. This is the third bus I've been on, and the trip was nearly eight hours. I should've just flown, but my flight was canceled and I didn't want to wait until tomorrow to see my husband and son."

"You're from Crosswood?" I asked.

"Not originally. I moved there about a year ago from Florida. Are you from Crosswood?"

"Yeah, I grew up here."

"You seem so young to say that in past tense. How long has it been since you've been home?"

"Three years."

"That's quite some time. Are you staying very long?"

"No, I just have some unfinished business," I replied, "Then I'll be leaving."

"Where to after that?"

"No idea," I said with a forced laugh.

"Well, that's okay. You can only live in the moment if your next step isn't yet planned."

"I agree," I said, as the bus came to a stop. I grabbed my bag in preparation to exit.

As we filed off the bus, the woman turned around, "Well, it was very nice talking to you. Oh, so sorry," she said extending a hand, "My name is Olivia."

I reached for her hand cautiously.

"Danielle," I replied, "Nice meeting you as well."

As I exited the bus, I made an immediate left and walked across the street away from the bus and the crowd awaiting it. Here in Crosswood, it wasn't raining. The sky had many clouds, but the sun still shone through them. It was breezy outside and rather cool. I'd assume it to be February. I was instantly familiar with the area though it had changed. It looked a little less small town, and a little more commercial with more fast-food chains, and a modernized landscape.

I knew where I was heading wasn't far from the bus station. Perhaps this is why Joyce suggested I take the bus. Maybe she knew where I intended to go. I made my way up and down the roads, trying not to draw too much attention to myself. I knew it was possible for someone to recognize me, not to mention, I probably looked like a homeless person.

I stopped for a second and realized technically I was a homeless person. I laughed how, apparently, my mind was quick to judge the very situation I was in.

After about twenty minutes of walking, I arrived at my destination.

I looked up at the entrance gate that stood open. Beautiful iron bars were mounted in a black arches and rolled down into white brick, and then more, tall, black, iron bars created a fence around the enclosure. I read the sign inscribed on the bricks as I proceeded inside: Crosswood Cemetery

I walked down the dirt paths crisscrossing the cemetery. The grounds were well kept and the grass was green, but I wasn't sure where she had been laid to rest. I wandered for a very long time, reading multiple headstones. While making my way toward one of the trees, I found her.

Bridget Blake 1965—2003

I dropped my bag where I stood, and approached her headstone, avoiding others in my path. I felt my legs grow weaker with every step I took. A metal ball seemed to expand in my throat and made the mere act of breathing a painful endeavor. My vision began to blur as tears filled my eyes and caught the sun. I attempted to not resist the emotions, but the instinct to suppress them came more natural.

As I arrived at the foot of her grave, I collapsed to my knees facing her headstone. I laid my face against the grass, and I felt a tear escape me.

"I'm sorry," I whispered.

As the sun began to set, I slowly sat up wiping the tears from my face and sat cross legged next to my mother's grave. I plucked at the grass as I gathered my thoughts. I pondered all the things I now wished to say to her. At the foot of the headstone was a small bundle of dead flowers that you could tell was once quite beautiful.

"I know . . . it's weird that I'm here. I've been gone so long. Even before I was sent away I was already gone. It's so strange; I feel like I'm saying goodbye to you for the first time. Like it happened yesterday. I don't blame you for what happened to Nathan. It's not your fault, what happened to him, and it's not your fault what happened to you. Slowly I'm beginning to see that what happened wasn't my fault either. At least not everything. I wish you didn't feel like you had no way out, I wish I hadn't judged you, and I had just been there for you," I said as a few more tears ran down my face, "I'm sure you know my secret by now, be sure to thank Grandma Elizabeth for me. I'm still trying to figure it all out . . . I feel as if I have no answers, no place to start from. I've been running from my past for a long time, and I don't think I'm done running yet. I won't be back to visit for a very long time. I think my future lies away from this place. I just want you to know that I will never forget you, and I do love you, and I forgive you . . . And I hope you'll forgive me, too, for what I'm going to do."

The wind rustled a little in the trees as the sky began to light up orange and red behind the earth. I reached my hand to the flowers and touched them. They glowed slightly as the life returned to them. They became saturated in purples, reds, and yellow, and the petals began to stretch to the sky as they bloomed once more.

I arose from my position knowing there was one more thing I had to do before my departure. I made my way back across the cemetery grounds toward the entrance.

"Danielle?" came a voice from behind me.

I stopped in my tracks. Without turning around I attempted to place the voice as well as contemplated proceeding to leave without acknowledging it.

"Mom, I'm hungry," came the unexpected sound of a toddler's voice behind me.

I turned around to confront my curiosity.

"It's really you," said Trish.

"Trish?" I said in disbelief.

"Dani, wow I haven't seen you in forever, not since . . . that day." She seemed to be recalling our last encounter and trailed off.

"Yeah."

"I heard the craziest stories about you. People were saying that you died, or that you were arrested, and that you were crazy. All I know is one day you just disappeared. Where have you been?" she asked bluntly. She never did have a knack for subtlety.

261

"Mental institution."

"Oh, I'm so sorry. I didn't mean to bring it up."

"It's fine," I said, watching the little boy with sandy blonde hair, combed to the side in a gentlemanly fashion, tugging at her pant side. She picked him up and slung him around her waist.

"We'll go eat in just a minute, sweetie," she said.

"Who's that?" he said, pointing at me.

"That's mommy's friend, Dani."

"He's yours?" I asked, beginning to understand how much time had passed since I had last been in this town.

"He is," she said.

"Forgive me, I know I have been gone a while, but is he. . . . Cain's?"

"No," she said sadly, but with a forgiving tone at my assumption.

"Oh, I'm sorry. I just thought maybe –"

"We're actually visiting his father." She glanced at the gravestone they were next to.

Abel Stevens 1985-2003

My stomach sank, and heat pulsed up my spine like boiling water. My hair stood on end, and I felt as if I might be sick. I tried to maintain my composure as I took a step back.

"Abel's . . ."

"It was right before Cain and I got together. I didn't find out I was pregnant till after he passed, and I just couldn't bring myself to not go through with it. Cain treats him like his own, he spoils him like crazy. In a way, it seemed to make it easier for Cain to deal with Abel's death, like he still has some part of his brother to hold on to."

"I see," I said, at a loss for words.

"Are you okay, Dani? You don't look so good," she said, putting her hand on my arm.

"Yeah, I'm fine. I just have to be going."

"I'm sorry. I didn't mean to upset you by bringing it up. I know you tried to take responsibility for Abel's death, to protect Cain. I was there. I know what really happened. It was just a freak accident. Speaking of Cain, I'm sure he'd like to see you. He always liked you, but I guess we all knew you had your sights set on someone else," she said with a smile.

"Someone else? What do you mean?"

"Oh, of course, you two were always so secretive and in your own world. When you disappeared I just figured you two ran off together."

"I'm sorry. I've been gone a while, I guess I just don't remember a lot from high school. I'd like to see Cain, but I'm actually just about to leave town."

"Already? Oh, did you already visit your family? I still see your dad and brother a lot. They come into the store where I work, but they didn't mention you being in town."

"No, I haven't visited them. I was just visiting my mother," I said.

"Well, you should go see them. I imagine they miss you."

"Yeah, I'll think about it, but can you do me a favor?"

"Of course."

"Please don't tell anyone you saw me here or saw me at all. Not anyone . . . please?"

"Okay, Dani . . . I can do that."

"Thank you."

"Well, at least give me hug goodbye," she said reaching out her free hand toward me.

I hugged her back, and she smiled at me.

"And be sure to come find me if you're ever in town again."

"I will."

"Promise?" she said, pointing a finger me.

"Yes, ma'am," I replied with a laugh.

"Good. Take care of yourself, Dani."

"I'm going to try."

She walked away and waved back as she left. There was something comforting about her presence, her optimism and personality. I knew we had very little in common, but I liked her and appreciated who she was.

As the sun set and shadows gave me cover from being noticed, I became less concerned about my presence in my home town. After walking the streets for hours and passing hundreds of strangers, I became more surprised that I had happened to run into Trish.

I hesitated as I reached my destination. I closed my eyes and let the air pass through me as fantasies reeled through my mind in an attempt to convince me to continue. Something devious in me pushed forward. I ran my hand across the brick of the mailbox, as I made my way up the walkway to the house and stood at the door, feeling the anxiety and sick excitement rise in me every moment I stood there. I enjoyed the adrenaline rush so much I desired to live in that moment a while longer, but instead raised my hand and gave three hard knocks on the door.

I waited for several moments with no response. A sense of disappointment began to wash over me, but I stood there determined. After a few more moments, I heard someone approaching the door. The doorknob rotated, and the door flung open. The initial expression of joy and anticipation immediately transformed into anxiety and terror. Just the reaction I was hoping for. This brought a devious grin to my face.

"Dani?"

"The fear on your face is well placed. Nothing gives me more joy than to be the person who invokes such a response, Christian."

Thank you for taking the time to read Manifesting Shadow. If you enjoyed it, please consider telling your friends or posting a short review. Word of mouth is an author's best friend and much appreciated. Thank you again, Church Calvert.

Made in the USA
Coppell, TX
18 December 2021

69290571R00163